PAX BRITANNIA

E V O L U T I O N
EXPECTS

JONATHAN GREEN

Abaddon
Books

WWW.ABADDONBOOKS.COM

For Jonathan Oliver, who shared a vision.
And for Mark Harrison, who helped bring that
vision to life.

PAX BRITANNIA

EVOLUTION EXPECTS

It came out of the Smog like some nightmare of fire and fury made horribly real. With blazing eyes it scoured the narrow street, catching first the crumbling brickwork of the warehouse, then the heels of the fleeing Chinese and the beaming face of Dr Feelgood, as he promoted his patent panacea, until finally its baleful gaze fell on Credence Jones. Twice as tall as a man, and as broad as it was tall, the steaming colossus lumbered out of the Smog. It opened its fiery maw and the same incandescent light of its eyes shone from deep within its throat, the smiling face of Dr Feelgood caught in the shimmering heat-haze.

The alleyway was almost too narrow to contain it.

For a moment, the monster turned to study the cowering thief. Its face was an impassive, stony mask, and yet its eyes blazed with unadulterated rage while its gaping maw revealed the fiery rage at its heart. For a split second, Credence began to believe, with self-deceiving hope, that perhaps the creature had come to his rescue, that it had witnessed his predicament and seen fit to intervene on his behalf.

And then the behemoth reached for him with one massive hand, its heavy, clay-like fingers still trailing greasy strands of persistent Smog. As Credence feebly tried to kick himself clear of the hulking demon, its hand closed around his head, cracking his skull like an egg.

WWW.ABADDONBOOKS.COM

An Abaddon Books™ Publication
www.abaddonbooks.com
abaddon@rebellion.co.uk

First published in 2009 by Abaddon Books™, Rebellion Intellectual
Property Limited, Riverside House, Osney Mead, Oxford, OX2 0ES, UK.

10 9 8 7 6 5 4 3 2 1

Editor: Jonathan Oliver
Cover: Mark Harrison
Design: Simon Parr & Luke Preece
Marketing and PR: Keith Richardson
Creative Director and CEO: Jason Kingsley
Chief Technical Officer: Chris Kingsley
Pax Britannia™ created by Jonathan Green

ISBN: 978-1-906735-05-0

Printed in Denmark by Norhaven A/S

Man with all his noble qualities... still bears in his bodily frame the indelible stamp of his lowly origin.

(Charles Darwin, *The Descent of Man*)

PROLOGUE

The House that Jack Built

Taking a deep breath to steady his nerves, feeling like he could vomit at any moment and his heart pounding nervously within his chest, wiping the sweat from his hand, Thomas Sanctuary put his palm to the brass plaque beside the front door. There came a harsh buzzing from somewhere behind it and Thomas's heart sank. The biometric reader hadn't recognised him.

His anxious mind was suddenly filled with possible reasons for the mechanism's failure to identify him. Had his palm-print been removed from the lock's memory core? Or had he changed so much in the last ten years that his palm-print was no longer recognised by the device? Or was it simply that the device was faulty? Thomas put a hand to the solid iron door-knocker and then paused.

Focusing on his breathing to calm himself, he wiped the sweat from his hand on the coarse fabric of his old tweed jacket and put his palm flat against the plaque once more. This time, after a second of whirring machine-cogitation, there was a faint click and the door swung open of its own accord – another of his father's inventions.

Thomas Sanctuary's pulse quickened once again. He hadn't felt this nervous since his first day spent at Her Majesty's pleasure. Ten years had passed since then, and now here he was, back at his father's door as if he had never been away. Taking another deep breath, he stepped over the threshold and into the house.

Although he hadn't set foot inside the house in over a decade, to him it seemed as if little had changed. In fact, the place had the rarefied air of a museum; the portraits hung on the walls of the circular atrium in which he now stood, the porcelain vase on the table beside the door and the display of stuffed and mounted hummingbird species imprisoned for all time inside the large glass cabinet at the bottom of the stairs.

No, not a museum, Thomas thought as he stared up into the steely eyes of his father, the inventor and recluse James Sanctuary, *a mausoleum.*

That was precisely what Sanctuary House had become, since his father's passing, he could feel it in the cold, still air of the hall; a shrine to the man who had ruled this place with a rod of iron.

The grand portrait of his father dominated the atrium, reminding all who entered who was master of this house, even now, five years after his death. It depicted James Sanctuary standing proudly beside his drawing board, the pen and ink outlines of his latest invention set out upon it. Whenever he had set eyes upon the painting in the past, Thomas Sanctuary had only ever seen his father, aloof and domineering, and hadn't really taken in the background. Now that he looked more closely, he could see what appeared to be a sinister skeletal structure, metal rods and hinges replacing the bones and joints. Even the head of whatever it was looked not unlike a grinning skull with great empty eye sockets. Undoubtedly some hare-brained scheme of his father's, another of his failures in the making.

Bitterness suddenly welled up inside of Thomas. Nothing he had done had ever been good enough for his father. Not that his father had ever been a great success. His inventions, those that had worked, had never taken off. The palm-reader worked perfectly, of course, but his father stubbornly refused to share that particular idea with anyone else.

The family fortune had already been there, and was not the result of James Sanctuary's inventions or financial acumen. As a result, he had never been satisfied with his achievements. Every one of them had been a letdown, even those that made it past the planning to actual construction.

James Sanctuary had beavered away in his study-cum-workroom at the top of the house, night and day when he was engaged on a new project. He filled the conservatory space there with all manner of apparatus along with his discarded creations, never once stopping to enjoy the unprecedented views the sun-room afforded of Hampstead Heath, Highgate Cemetery and the city beyond, while Thomas had tinkered with his father's abandoned creations himself.

There had been a time when Thomas and his father, who had always been distant and aloof, had come as close as they ever would to connecting over their mutual tinkering with a clockwork toy that Thomas was adapting or a wind-up automobile that his father had let him play with. But as he got older, and his tinkering had become something more focused and purposeful, his father had lost interest in Thomas's little projects, to the point of being openly disdainful about them, as if trying to put him off.

Now that Thomas found himself reappraising his relationship with his father, he began to wonder if it had been jealousy that had fuelled the rift between them – a father's envy of what his own child appeared able to do and which he could not.

Thomas was roused from his musings by the tapping of footfalls on the cold tiles of the atrium floor.

Out of breath and obviously caught off-guard by his unexpected arrival, Mrs May, his father's portly housekeeper, bustled into the hall, no doubt roused from her abode on the ground floor. If Sanctuary House was a museum of antiquities then Mrs May was its curator.

"Why, Master Thomas, I wasn't expecting you to... today," the housekeeper blustered. Thomas knew that when the palm-reader admitted him to Sanctuary House that it would have sent a signal to the housekeeper's room, setting the appropriate bell jangling, alerting her to his arrival. "It's been... Why, it must have been..." She faltered, her cheeks flushed red, her chest heaving beneath her uncomfortably tight black housekeeper's dress and white pinafore.

"Ten years, Mrs May. It's been ten years. It's good to see you again."

"And it's good to see you, Master Thomas," the housekeeper puffed, the rumour of a smile brightening her plump features. "You're looking... well."

"Am I?" Thomas regarded himself sidelong in the mirror that formed part of a coat and hat rack, the moth-eaten elephant's foot still beneath it, he noticed. The walking stick propped within it was instantly recognisable as his father's.

The same could not be said of the not so young man staring back at Thomas from the looking glass. His hair was flecked with grey and sparser than it had been, his cheeks more hollow, his eyes more sunken, his lips drawn thinner, his jaw less clean-shaven.

"And you, Mrs May, are you well?"

"Quite well, thank you."

"You didn't need to have stayed, you know," Thomas said, fixing her with the same steely gaze as his father. "After he died, I mean."

The housekeeper flinched at Thomas's choice of words and screwed up the hem of her apron in her hands in discomfort.

"It was what your father wished, Master Thomas."

"So I understand."

"It was his dy... last wish that Sanctuary House be kept as it was."

"As a memorial to his genius, I suppose."

"For you, Master Thomas. He wanted it kept ready for you."

For a moment neither of them said anything more, the housekeeper and the heir to James Sanctuary's legacy watching one another across the hollow space of the hall. An uncomfortable silence filled the void in the conversation between them, heavy with all those things that were best left unsaid, for the time being. It soon proved too much for Mrs May and she quickly broke the silence, least Thomas say something neither of them really wanted to hear.

"I was just making myself a pot of tea, otherwise I would have been quicker coming to the door, but, like I said, I wasn't expecting... you. Would you like a cup?"

"To come back, you mean?"

"I beg your pardon, sir."

"You weren't expecting me to come back."

"I... I didn't know, Master Thomas. The last time you were here... You did not leave on the best of terms."

The argument, Thomas thought, *never to be forgotten.*

"You did not send word that you were coming."

"A cup of tea would be lovely," Thomas said, his face set in a mournful grimace. He turned towards the stairs that curved around the inside wall of the circular void three-storeys high.

"Very good, sir."

"I'll be in my father's study. Bring it to me there, would you?"

"You wouldn't like to wash and change first?"

"Bring it to me there, if you would be so kind," he replied dismissively.

"Very good, sir."

Thomas put his hand to the polished brass doorknob and opened the door to his father's inner sanctum. As he stepped over the threshold into the room, he felt the same excited tingle of reverential awe he had on those rare occasions when he had been allowed to enter the place where his father's mad ideas fought their way out of his head and onto paper, before manifesting as incredible contraptions of iron, brass and wood. Even though he understood his father all the better now – his faults and failings laid painfully bare – he still felt like an excited child again, for the moment at least, the memories of those wonderful visits to this veritable Aladdin's Cave of invention blurring into one blissful kick of nostalgia.

First there was his father's desk, covered in tiny working models of larger inventions that themselves delighted both the eye and the mind. Then there was the billiards table. Thomas had never known his father partake in a game, or even so much as pick up a cue, but the table had always been here, and stacked neatly upon the green baize were his father's fastidious journals and the meticulously annotated plans for scores of wizardly contraptions; the record of a life of invention.

There were work tables too, laden with half-finished and half-forgotten pieces – an iron-gauntlet with what looked like a wrist-mounted catapult attached, a miniaturised explosive shell of some kind, and a steam-powered grappling gun. Larger pieces stood where they had been abandoned before completion, smothered by heavy dust sheets now, his father having given up and moved on to work on another idea that intrigued him. Other contraptions were suspended from the ceiling.

He passed row after row of bookshelves – James Sanctuary's personal library, containing everything from the histories of the Roman writers to more obscure texts on early Islamic scientific scriptures – built into gothic-arched alcoves in the walls. The library shelves gave way to the steel and glass construction of the conservatory, and Thomas threw a glance at the leafless trees of the apple orchard below the house, before turning his attention to the view of Highgate Cemetery and the Smog-laden city beyond. But it did not distract him for long; he was too intrigued at the potential his father's workroom had to offer him.

He felt like a boy who had been given the keys to the sweet shop. Rarely allowed in here as a child and never, since he left to pursue his own studies at University, suddenly all this was his, to do with as he pleased; the representative of Mephisto, Fanshaw and Screwtape had declared it so, as sole beneficiary of his father's estate, other than for a small annual stipend for Mrs May.

And Thomas was sure that somewhere within this room there lay the means to achieve recompense for what had been done to him a decade ago – the tools with which he could exact his revenge.

Smiling properly for the first time in a long time, Thomas took in all that the study had to offer, passing the grandfather clock that stood to the right of his father's desk, and which appeared to be stuck at twelve o'clock, even though it was now past three, and completed his circuit of his father's sanctuary from the world.

He stopped beside the desk and glanced down at the journal that lay open upon it. He read the date and then, feeling a flush of nervous excitement that he might be found prying into his father's personal thoughts, read the entry beneath.

Thomas, my son.

Thomas felt a cold rush of blood as he read his name.

All this is now yours. Sanctuary House, my unfinished projects, but most of all the suit. This is my legacy to you. See if you can succeed where I could not.

It was as if his father was speaking to him from out of the past, but it wasn't the man he had known. Here, within the pages of his journal, James Sanctuary was a man who not only knew his failings, but openly admitted to his own short-comings, and who recognised in Thomas, someone who could finish what he had started.

Thomas only noticed the tears when they obscured his vision and he had to wipe them away to keep reading the journal entry. Salt water splashed onto the page, smudging his father's careful copper-plate words.

Tempus fugit, my boy.

Make me proud.

JS

Thomas looked from the running ink of his father's final words to him – those which he had never been able to pass on in person

– to the grandfather clock again, stuck as it was at twelve.

Time flies. Why of all the things his father could have written for him to read in his journal had he written that?

Putting the book down, Thomas moved back to the clock. His father had been meticulous about time-keeping, even if he had been dire at it himself. He would miss whole mealtimes and even whole days in pursuit of his latest project, battling with whatever baffling puzzle it had thrown up for him, but he had always insisted on the clocks in the house being set to the right time – all the time. In fact, Thomas could remember the gentle ticking of the grandfather clock underscoring his visits to his father's study.

Checking the time again on his own battered fob watch, one of the few items he had managed to hold on to whilst incarcerated, Thomas opened the glass panel in front of the clock face, reading the words '*Tempus Fugit*' engraved there too. The key to wind the mechanism was in its hole.

It had become such a part of Mrs May's daily routine, to check the clocks at his father's behest, that Thomas found it hard to believe that she should have given up the practise when she had obviously been at pains to keep everything else just as it was when his father died.

He turned the key; once, twice... At the third turn there was a click and the front of the clock-case opened. Thomas looked down in surprise and felt an adrenalin rush of excitement course through his weary body. It was no wonder the clock wasn't working; it was missing its pendulum. In place of the pendulum, inside the clock, was a brass plaque palm-reader, like the one he had used to open the front door of the house.

Without hesitation, Thomas reached inside the clock and pressed his hand firmly against the metal plate. There was a moment of mechanical cogitation from some hidden Babbage unit, and then a louder grinding of gears.

Thomas took a step back as the section of wall against which the clock stood, between the towering bookcases, began to revolve, revealing what had previously been hidden within an alcove behind the wall.

Thomas stared in awe at his father's legacy to him, at the very thing that would become the instrument of his vengeance against those who had seen him put away for ten long years for a crime he didn't commit, while his father became a recluse, festering away within this very house until he died of shame.

And the red-glazed eyes of the skeletal thing from the drawing board in his father's portrait stared back at him.

ACT ONE

Spring-Heeled Jack
and the Limehouse Golem

January 1998

In the first hour, Adam's dust was gathered; in the second, it was kneaded into a shapeless mass. In the third, his limbs were shaped; in the fourth, a soul was infused into him; in the fifth, he arose and stood on his feet.

(*The Talmud*, Tractate Sanhedrin 38b)

CHAPTER ONE

Made of Clay

London fog, as thick and as yellow as custard, oozed along the rat-runs and alleyways of Limehouse, like some predatory beast. It probed at doorways and drains with its jaundiced tentacles, leaving a cloying reminder of its greasy touch on everything it came into contact with. The Smog caught in the throat, clogging the lungs of those who inhaled it, taking the young, the old and the infirm, and the asthmatic. It reduced visibility, causing problems for river traffic as well as that on the busy streets of the capital, and it proved to be the perfect accomplice for those who did not want their business becoming public knowledge. It was a trusted ally of London's criminal fraternity in particular.

This late January night the Smog had sunk low over the oily river, following the course of the sluggish waterway from the industrial complexes of Battersea, through the beating heart of the capital past the Houses of Parliament, Blackfriars Bridge and the Tower, to the dilapidated docks and overcrowded slums of Limehouse. What little moonlight that penetrated the grubby shroud smothering the city, combined with the yellow glow of gas-lamps and the few electric lights that festooned the streets in this part of town, to give the mist an otherworldly glow. The searching tendrils looked like the ectoplasm certain members of the Spiritualist Church claimed to be able to manifest from their own bodies during a séance.

The Smog was always bad around this time of year. There had been a time in the past when the Thames would freeze, the ice so thick it could support the wagons, stalls, people and even cook-fires of the Frost Fairs. But now it never got cold enough in the capital. The unsleeping factories saw to that. The pollutants and effluent that made up the Thames by the time it had finishing passing the capital, made it even less likely that the river would ever be able to freeze.

Of course, the Smog was a problem all year round and every year it only got worse. Ever-increasing industrialisation was the key: and it wasn't only the dirigible factories on the Isle of Dogs or the cavorite works across the river at Greenwich, that relied on the burning of fossil fuel on an unprecedented scale. Everything from the sleepless railways to the lunar transport vessels that took off from Heathrow and Gatwick on a weekly basis all took their toll and contributed to the ever-present pollution. It was just that during the winter months the Smog took more lives than it did during the other three seasons put together.

The Smog smothered everything in its anesthetising shroud, including almost all sound. The only ones abroad in the oily darkness at this time of night, were the occasional robo-Bobbie and those members of London's criminal fraternity out about their clandestine business.

Credence Jones was just such a man.

He crept through the streets, force of habit meaning that he kept close to the walls, skulking in doorways every so often to check that he wasn't being followed, when the jaundiced fog itself would have been enough to keep him hidden. But you never could be too sure. Since the disappearance of the Oriental criminal mastermind known to all as the Black Mamba and following the fallout from the Wormwood Affair, in the wake of what were supposed to have been Her Majesty's 160th jubilee celebrations, Limehouse was disputed territory. You couldn't be certain who had staked a claim, and for a lone operator like Credence – a cat-burglar of the old school – you had no-one to watch your back.

The burglar stopped at a street corner and peered into the murk clogging the alleyway ahead of him. Brick-built warehouses, turned black by time and pollution, rose up above him like a man-made canyon, the shadowy spider's web of the Overground network just visible above the corrugated iron roofs of the barn-sized warehouses.

Credence had a love-hate relationship with the Smog. When it came to his line of work, he wouldn't be without it. There were many times when a good, honest London pea souper had concealed him from the prying eyes of the Metropolitan Police, or helped him evade an unusually brave have-a-go copper. But it was a fickle mistress; it could just as easily hide those creeping up on a man about his business. And then there was little Maggie. Her condition was worsening by the day as the consumption ate her up from the inside, and the unclean air only served to help the tuberculosis tighten its hold on her.

As he thought of his youngest, a smile formed on Credence's face beneath the kerchief mask he wore, tied tight across his nose and mouth to filter out the worst of the Smog. The contents of the sack slung over his shoulder would fetch a pretty penny, once it had been passed through Arbuckle's Pawnshop, and would provide him with enough to be able to take her to a proper doctor – like that Dr Cleary he had heard about, down in Canning Town – rather than one of the local quacks or backstreet abortionists they usually had to rely on round these parts. Perhaps it would even leave him with enough to buy some medicine too and save him the trouble of having to nick it, although he wasn't entirely averse to that idea; it was just that the sort of places where he would have to go to get hold of it had better security than a man like him liked to deal with.

He was right in the heart of Limehouse now. He only had to make it to the river and from there he could make his way back upriver to Wapping and the slum he and his family called home. And he knew these streets like the back of his hand – better, in fact. He knew of a hundred ways through the warehouses and around the wharfs.

It was an area the Peelers preferred not to have to enter unless it was *en masse*, and then they could practically guarantee that they would find the place deserted. No, the Police and the criminal gangs had an undeclared understanding; Limehouse was left to the Irish, and their illegal stills, the Chinese and their opium dens, and the Jews. It might be the case that the disappearance of the Black Mamba and the destruction of the Darwinian Dawn's operation in the area had left a power vacuum, but it would not last for long. Soon there would be another top dog in charge, who would effectively police the area for them, to a degree, but until that time, the Police preferred to let the rival gangs get on with it, and not get involved in their turf wars themselves, only stepping in when trouble spilled out into the City, beyond the rat-runs of Limehouse itself.

Credence Jones set off again through the viscous fog. Through the obscuring cloud he could just make out the posters and music-hall bills that plastered the walls of the alley-way and which in some places, he could quite easily have believed, were the only things holding the rotting brickwork of the slums together – posters promoting the latest Chinese Magic Show at the Palace Theatre and yet more advertisements promoting Dr Feelgood's Tonic Stout as a patent panacea for all ills, capable of treating everything from constipation to rheumatism.

Senses heightened, his outwardly calm manner giving no clue as to the adrenalin surge flooding his system, through the muffling mist – which filtered out the distant rattle and chuffing of Overground trains and blaring horns within the streets of the capital – his ears picked out another sound, a footstep out of time with his own.

He barely faltered for a second but kept going. If he was being followed the element of surprise could work as well for him as for his pursuer. To stop now would be to lose that advantage and force whoever it was that was at his heels to play their hand. If he kept moving he might yet lose them in the Smog.

A figure, dropped onto the cobbles in front of him, as if it had stepped through a portal from another world right before Credence's eyes. The figure was athletic of build, male, bound from head-to-toe in black, and was possessed of the lithe agility of a cat. He landed in a crouch, with one leg extended and a bamboo pole coming to rest across his shoulders. The black-clad Oriental made barely a sound, his arrival leaving curling eddies in the Smog.

Credence froze, knowing that he must be surrounded. He had met their kind before. The Yellow Peril, the popular press called them. Untrustworthy, slanty-eyed gits the lot of them, as far as Credence was concerned. The Chinese infested Limehouse like a plague of rats. Here, at the heart of the capital of the British Empire, this place belonged to the Chinese as much as it belonged to the Irishman or the Jews. It certainly wasn't British in anything other than name.

His heart beating faster now, he began to weigh up the few options open to him. A flood of excuses came to mind, the decision to fight or flee uppermost, but both pointless considering his current circumstances. He was a middle-aged crook, with a fondness for pies, pints and baccy, and he was alone. His enemy were trained warriors who could kill with one strike from their bare hands, trained by rigorous near-religious discipline. He turned his head, scanning the street behind and in front of him. And there were at least a dozen of them.

Credence opened his mouth to speak and then let out his breath in a defeated sigh. There was no point him saying anything. It was clear from the narrowed eyes behind the slit of the villain's mask that nothing he said would alter the judgement that had already been passed before the tong had even revealed itself.

He slipped a calloused hand into a pocket and felt the reassuring shape of the cosh beneath his fingertips. Chances were that he would soon be given no choice but to fight, and, if that were the case, this old school burglar would give these Chinese a demonstration of British fighting spirit.

The figure in front of Credence rose from his crouch and took a darting step forward. He never once took his eyes off the small-time crook and, as he stepped closer, the suffused light permeating the Smog reflecting from the glistening surface of his staring eyes, Credence felt another instinct take hold and scuttle up his spine on spidery legs – the unconscious unease felt in the presence of something not altogether natural. There was something not right about the Chinaman's eyes – even for an Oriental – and, now that he saw it, Credence realised that there was something wrong with the shape of the face behind the black face-cloth.

Credence registered the sound of colossal footfalls behind him a split second before he saw the change in the Chinaman's eyes, and felt the juddering impact-tremors a moment before that.

Then there was no mistaking the cobble-cracking impacts of something immensely heavy on the street behind him, the echoes of the thundering footfalls thrown back from the canyon walls of the street accompanied by a bellowing roar, like the super-heated roar of a furnace, as something came at them out of the night.

Instinctively Credence threw himself sideways. Where moments before the Chinese had been cool, calm and collected, focused in the face of an unwitting invasion of the streets they now claimed as their own, now they were a disorganized, panicking rabble, fleeing in terror before the monster that was bearing down on them out of the Smog and the night.

Credence hit the side of the street and stumbled to his knees in the dirty puddles collected in the lee of a rotting warehouse, throwing his arms over his head and screwing his eyes shut tight in fear. But fear of what he might see come roaring out of the fog soon became the lesser of two evils compared to not knowing what it was that had suddenly appeared, as the limp body of a Chinaman dropped to the ground beside him and the scream of another was cut short, the sharp wet crack that came after it, all the more terrible for it.

Credence Jones opened his eyes.

His would-be attackers were in disarray. From where he lay, huddled on the numbing ground, Credence could see one of the tongs cowering before the might of whatever it was that was emerging from the Smog behind him. He could not see it, but he could hear it – great thudding footsteps and throaty, furnace-fury bellows – and he could see the effect it was having on the Chinese.

Some of the bolder members of the gang were shuffling away from whatever it was, a few yards at a time, not ready to flee from it completely yet, nor daring to turn their backs on it. A sense of ancient warrior honour refused to let them run, but common sense and a shared dread prevented them from fighting back.

Others, less convinced by their shared warrior's code, turned tail and ran screaming into the night as another body came bowling out of the mist.

Screaming an incomprehensible, yet obvious, battle-cry, the leader of the Tong found his courage again and bounded back along the alley to challenge the unknown aggressor.

Credence heard something like the thwack of bamboo making contact with something solid and inflexible, quickly followed by a horrible crunching sound which was joined by a cry of pain so intense as to render its owner insensible.

The body of the wretch flew out of the mist over Credence's head. The Chinaman's limp form hit the wall of the warehouse on the opposite side of the street and fell, headfirst, onto the cobbles in a broken heap.

Credence started to panic as more of the Chinamen lost their resolve and ran screaming back into the fog. He had to know what it was that had unwittingly saved him from a surely certain and painful death at the hands of the territory-hungry gang.

Pushing himself up into a crouch, he turned to see what it was that he could already feel stomping towards him, closer and closer every second. The blood instantly drained from his cheeks, his skin became clammy – he was sure his heart even missed a beat – and cold slivers of icy fear surged through his veins.

It came out of the Smog like some nightmare of fire and fury made horribly real. With blazing eyes it scoured the narrow street, catching first the crumbling brickwork of the warehouse, then the heels of the fleeing Chinese and the beaming face of

Dr Feelgood, as he promoted his patent panacea, until finally its baleful gaze fell on Credence Jones. Twice as tall as a man, and as broad as it was tall, the steaming colossus lumbered out of the Smog. It opened its fiery maw and the same incandescent light of its eyes shone from deep within its throat, the smiling face of Dr Feelgood caught in the shimmering heat-haze.

The alleyway was almost too narrow to contain it.

For a moment, the monster turned to study the cowering thief. Its face was an impassive, stony mask, and yet its eyes blazed with unadulterated rage while its gaping maw revealed the fiery rage at its heart. For a split second, Credence began to believe, with self-deceiving hope, that perhaps the creature had come to his rescue, that it had witnessed his predicament and seen fit to intervene on his behalf.

And then the behemoth reached for him with one massive hand, its heavy, clay-like fingers still trailing greasy strands of persistent Smog. As Credence feebly tried to kick himself clear of the hulking demon, its hand closed around his head, cracking his skull like an egg.

The demon opened its crushing hand again, heedless of the brain matter dripping from its massive fingers, and stomped off along the alleyway, shoulders scraping the walls on both sides of the narrow street as the juggernaut continued on its way, after the Chinamen.

An instant later it was swallowed by the fickle Smog, leaving nothing behind it but the carcasses of the fallen, including the headless corpse of Credence Jones.

CHAPTER TWO

A Pest Problem

The waiting room smelt strongly of jasmine, artificially so, Ulysses Quicksilver thought. Nonetheless, the fragrant scent of flowers helped put him at his ease. However much he might not like to admit it, he *did* feel nervous. Despite all that he had faced in his life, and overcome – from the snowbeast of Shangri-la to the Kraken and, most recently, the Umbridge-Chimera – the thought of this visit to the Daedalus Clinic, and his consultation with a certain Doctor Pandora Doppelganger, did not fill him with confidence.

But then Ulysses had quickly developed a not altogether irrational fear of doctors, since the last time he had gone under the knife, the knife in question had been in the hands of the deranged surgeon Seziermesser. The trauma he had suffered at the hands of the German vivisectionist was one of the reasons why he had left it until now, the end of January – a good two months after all that had transpired, following his investigation into the theft of the Whitby Mermaid from the Holbrook Museum, here in London.

But he was here now.

He suddenly realised that he was rubbing at the shoulder joint of his left arm and stopped just as abruptly.

He looked around the waiting room, black gloved fingers drumming uneasily on his knees. It had the air of a hotel, or an exclusive set of offices, or a gentlemen's club. Everything was just so, from the spray of flowers in the crystal vase over a mantelpiece to the brilliant white stucco plasterwork of the ceiling. It was certainly a million miles away from the struggling charitable hospices that the poor had to rely on, and certainly nothing like the sinister sanatorium of the Royal Bethlehem Hospital, better known to those incarcerated within and to the world at large as Bedlam. But that didn't stop him from feeling uneasy as he sat there waiting to be seen.

The receptionist was appropriately – in descending order of priority – pretty, young and efficient, her long blonde hair coiled in a tight bun on top of her head and her bright red lipstick, along with her tailored cream suit and low cut blouse turning her into every hot-blooded male's archetypal fantasy secretary figure; demure and subservient whilst having the appearance and poise of a dominatrix.

She looked up from the ghostly glow of her green-lit Babbage engine's cathode ray display unit and smiled coyly at Ulysses. The smile appeared genuine, but there was something just too well-practised about it at the same time.

He smiled back nervously, the tense grimace he had been unwittingly maintaining softening for a moment, having temporarily mislaid the old Quicksilver charm for the time being, and glanced from the girl to the white-painted door bearing the name plaque 'Dr P. Doppelganger' once more.

He felt his body tensing involuntarily, his breathing quickening, becoming shallow, as visions of scalpel blades, red with droplets of his own blood, and blinding arc-lights sprang uninvited into his mind. For a moment he even thought about getting up and walking out, forgetting about his appointment altogether.

"Doctor Doppelganger will be with you shortly," the receptionist suddenly piped up, as if reading his mind and wanting to put him at his ease again.

Ulysses smiled again, sinking back into the chair. "Don't worry," he said, with forced bravado. "There's no hurry."

Ulysses took a deep breath to calm himself, inhaling the heady aroma of the jasmine, letting the memory of the scent of it take him back over two years to one particular valley, hidden deep within the Himalayas and the monastery of Shangri-la.

I'm just being ridiculous, he thought. He had braved much worse than this in his life – a fully-grown stampeding Megasaur, the Megalodons of the Marianas depths and the Barghest of Ghestdale – it was just that the short time he had spent under Doktor Seziermesser had left scars that ran much deeper than those that had formed where his severed left arm had been replaced with... well, whatever had come to hand, as if happened.

Not doing a very good job of distracting yourself are you, old boy? He thought and turned his attention to the low table covered with carefully arrayed periodicals, from the *London Illustrated News* to the most recent instalment of the latest penny dreadful by Stefan Konig.

Amongst them was a neatly folded copy of the day's *Times*. Ulysses eagerly picked it up and read the front page banner headline in full.

JUPITER STATION LAUNCH ON SCHEDULE, SAYS PM

The papers were full of it at the moment; Prime Minister Devlin Valentine's golden goose, or so the new PM no doubt hoped. It was claimed that with the *Jupiter Station* in place in the skies over London, the Weather Machine could set to work dealing with Londinium Maximum's worsening air pollution, improving the quality of life for the many millions living under the ever-present shadow of the Smog, the legacy of a century and a half of relentless industrialization. There had to be a price to pay for being the original Workshop of the World and then the Gateway to the Stars.

But the Wormwood Affair, and the terror attacks perpetrated under the name of the Darwinian Dawn, had proved that there was another price to pay for being the foremost polluter in the world; the planet's environment was changing beyond all recognition. Greater extremes of weather were being experienced all over the planet, from longer and colder winters in the heart of Europe and Russia to the increased desertification in Africa.

But Devlin Valentine was a man with an eye to the future, although whether it was with an eye to his own future or genuinely that of the planet's, Ulysses wouldn't yet like to say. He was certainly keen to improve the image of Magna Britannia across the globe, from its put-upon colonies in Africa and Asia to how it was perceived by emerging nations such as the United Soviet States of America to Britain's long-held rivalry with China. And having been given a brutal wake-up call in the aftermath of Queen Victoria's 160th jubilee celebrations, Valentine was keen that Magna Britannia was seen to be doing something about the problems that it had been mindfully ignoring for so many decades.

Valentine was a much younger man than his predecessor, ready to lead the greatest Empire on Earth, and indeed the Solar System, into the twenty-first century, or so his campaign slogan had declared. But whatever else he might be, there was no doubt that Devlin Valentine was a man with a plan.

The *Jupiter Station* was simply the first stage in a much larger plan. But for the time being, that plan seemed to involve distancing himself as much as possible from Valentine's predecessor, making sure that he was seen to be as completely different from Uriah Wormwood as possible.

His first months in office had seen the collapse of the Carcharadon Shipping Line, in the wake of the *Neptune* Disaster, and the death of renowned industrialist Josiah Umbridge. Companies now fought like animals to fill the economic void as others circled the dying corpse of Umbridge Industries, waiting for it to breathe its last so that they might garner rich pickings from the crumbling business empire.

"Mr Quicksilver?"

The receptionist's voice roused Ulysses from his perusal of the paper and his considerations on what to make of the new PM – he had as healthy a disregard for politicians, particularly Prime Ministers, as he did a newly-developed distrust of doctors.

"Sorry," he said, recovering himself. "I was miles away."

"Doctor Doppelganger will see you now."

The white-painted door opened and two nurses emerged. Ulysses was momentarily taken aback. They were identical in every way, from their starched white uniforms – the hems of their belted dresses ending daringly above the knee – to their long black hair, and the way they wore it, to their high-sculpted cheekbones, eerily piercing green eyes and rouged rosebud lips.

It was one of those rare occasions when Ulysses didn't know what to say as he looked the pair up and down. Images of the 'perfect' secretary were sent away to do the filing while fantasies of an altogether different nature filled his head.

"This way please, Mr Quicksilver," the pair said in unison.

Ulysses went to reply when he realised that his mouth was already agape and so shut it instead. Tossing the newspaper back onto the table, he got to his feet – rather too eagerly, considering how he had been feeling about his appointment with Doctor Doppelganger up to that point.

The carbon copy nurses stepped aside and ushered Ulysses into the doctor's consulting room, the same smiling expression on their identically alluring faces and he felt a shiver of unease pass through his body.

"Good morning, Mr Quicksilver," an older woman's voice came from within and Ulysses immediately turned his attention to Doctor Doppelganger, feeling himself physically recoil on hearing her German accent. The last time he had encountered a doctor with a German accent the madman had proceeded to remove his left arm below the shoulder so that he might stitch it onto the nightmarish vivisect body he had prepared for his insane employer.

"Doctor," he replied curtly.

"Please, Mr Quicksilver, take a seat."

One of the pair who had welcomed him pulled out an

upholstered chair that he might sit down. He did so, never once taking his eyes from the woman behind the large mahogany desk in front of him. She was as striking as her assistants, although a generation older, at least. Her hair was streaked with grey highlights and where other women her age might have tried to hide such an obvious sign of aging, she wore hers proudly, like a badge of her experience and expertise. She sat stiffly upright in her padded leather chair, her hair in a tight bun on the back of her head, a pair of pince nez glasses perched on the end of her nose. She looked over them now as she regarded Ulysses as she might a naughty schoolboy and he realised she had the same striking green eyes and high cheekbones as her assistants. He glanced back to the two now standing either side of him, just to be sure.

"Ah, yes, you are most observant, Mr Quicksilver," Doctor Doppelganger said at his so obvious reaction, "these are indeed my daughters, Mercy and Clemency. They are assisting me today. Now, what can I do for you?"

There were a few things the twins could help him with, Ulysses thought, but that would have to wait for another time.

"Well, it's rather..." Ulysses began, struggling to find the words suddenly, now that he was in the presence of the formidable Doctor Doppelganger. "It's like this," he tried again and then faltered once more. "Well. It's rather embarrassing, to be honest."

"Mr Quicksilver," Doppelganger said in a tone that was half sympathetic and half impatiently chiding. "I am a doctor. There is nothing that I haven't seen before."

"I wouldn't be so sure about that," Ulysses muttered under his breath.

"We of the medical profession deal with what you might consider embarrassing conditions all the time. You have nothing to be ashamed of. Perhaps it would be easier if you just showed me. Would that be easier for you?"

"Yes," said Ulysses, releasing the pent-up tension in his body with his exhalation of the word. "Perhaps it would."

He stood again and, having taken off his jacket, unbuttoned

his waistcoat and then set about undoing the buttons of his Egyptian cotton shirt. Dr Doppelganger and her disconcertingly identical daughters watched him with measured interest. As he pulled off the shirt he became painfully aware of the scars of old wounds that criss-crossed his body and, now that his injuries were brought under such close scrutiny, making him feel self-conscious all over again, he exposed his left shoulder and left arm last of all.

To her credit she barely even raised an eyebrow in surprise. "I see," was all she said as she got up from behind the desk, moving over to where Ulysses stood, to examine the arm more closely.

Adjusting her glasses she peered at the marks left by Seziermesser's sloppy needlecraft and, taking a fountain pen from the desk, began poking at the leathery grey flesh of what was now Ulysses' left arm.

"Does this hurt?" she asked as she continued to prod at the limb where the ape's arm had been attached to his shoulder.

"No."

"And can you feel this?"

Ulysses nodded. "As if the arm were my own."

"So, no noticeable nerve damage then?"

"Not so far as I can tell."

"And this happened to you when?"

"November."

"Last year?"

"Indeed."

"Incredible." It was the most emotion Doppelganger had shown since the consultation had begun.

She began squeezing the long grey chimpanzee's fingers, moving the arm into various different positions, flexing the simian musculature, as her daughters looked on, intense hawk-like fascination on the faces of both of them.

"Aren't you at all curious?" Ulysses asked at last, feeling that someone had to acknowledge the strangeness of the situation they all now found themselves in.

"As to why you appear to have a chimpanzee's arm attached to your body in place of your own, you mean?" Doppelganger peered down her nose at Ulysses, looking like a disappointed headmistress about to admonish an errant schoolchild. "I believe in client confidentiality. *Total* confidentiality. You will be paying me enough so that I do not feel the need to ask. You can put your shirt back on now."

She returned to her seat behind the desk. Taking out a fresh patient report form she took the lid off the fountain pen and began to write. Ulysses craned his neck forward, as he began to get dressed again, trying to read what she was writing. It was a typical Doctor's scrawl; the only words he could make out with any certainty was his name at the top of the page, in the box labelled 'Patient'.

After the break in conversation passed the point of comfort, and Ulysses had started drumming his fingers on his knees again, Doctor Doppelganger finally spoke.

"Doctor Gallowglass recommended me to you, did he not?"

"That's right. Victor's an old school friend, from my Eton days."

"Quite so. Well, Mr Quicksilver, you will be pleased to hear that I *can* help you."

Ulysses relaxed a little, feeling a portion of the weight, that felt like it had been laid across his shoulders, lift from him. "That's good to hear. But I'm intrigued, doctor. How precisely can you help me?"

"Doctor Gallowglass did not tell you what it is we do here?"

"No. Only that you could help me."

"Well, to put it quite simply, we will help you by growing you a new arm."

Ulysses stared at her in disbelief. He had tried to visualise all sorts of solutions to the problem of his inhuman arm but had failed to come up with that one. He had got to the point where he would have been happy to settle for Doctor Doppelganger shaving the coarse black hair from the arm and applying some kind of bleaching treatment to the leathery grey skin. He had certainly not expected this.

"You'll grow me a new arm?"

"Quite so. I have perfected a procedure that will allow me to replicate a new arm for you, a thing of flesh and blood and bone, grown from a sample of your own flesh, which I can take from what is left of your upper arm."

"Will it... hurt?"

"A little," Doppelganger admitted, "but judging by the scars on your body, it won't be anything you won't be able to handle."

Ulysses had to agree with that assessment. "And will it take long? Can you do it now?"

"It will take some time to grow you an entirely new arm," the doctor said in that condescending tone of hers. Did people expect superior smugness when they visited a private Harley Street clinic, Ulysses wondered. "Several weeks, in fact. But we can take the tissue sample now; it will only take a few minutes. We can begin right away, if you are happy to proceed."

"Well," Ulysses sighed with relief, the stress lifting from him almost entirely now. The thought that all he needed to endure was something akin to a blood test was much more appealing than the thought of having the offending limb removed again. "As they say, there's no time like the present."

"There is the small matter of my fee," Doctor Doppelganger raised the issue as if that was a greater source of awkwardness than any embarrassing condition of the flesh.

Now it was Ulysses' turn to adopt a condescending tone. "Doctor, if I had any doubts as to whether I would be able to afford you services, I wouldn't have come here in the first place."

"Then let us begin," Doctor Pandora Doppelganger announced with a smile. "Mercy? Clemency? If you would show Mr Quicksilver through to the other room I will be with you shortly."

As the twin nurses stepped forward to flank Ulysses and follow their mother's instructions, in the lull that followed, he felt a faint, yet familiar sensation at the base of his skull.

The scream cut through the walls to the ears of all inside Doctor Doppelganger's consulting room. In Ulysses' experience, a sound like that could only be described as a death-scream.

Ulysses burst from the consulting room, Mercy and Clemency trotting anxiously after him. He passed straight through the waiting room, ignoring the appalled look on the receptionist's face, and raced on up the corridor in the direction of the other consulting rooms of the practice, following the blood-curdling scream to its source.

Moments later, he was throwing open a door, eyes locking onto the body lying on the floor, half hidden behind a desk. Only the corpse – with its smart Savile Row suit and a stethoscope still around the dead doctor's neck – wasn't of as much interest to Ulysses as what appeared to be a giant cockroach crouched on top of it.

The undoubtedly dead doctor's clothes were saturated with blood, his torso a ruddy ruin where the cockroach had cut open his ribcage to get at the juicy organs within. As Ulysses entered the room, the vile insect raised its malformed head, its gore-stained mandibles clacking spasmodically. His legs almost gave way as he confronted the horrendous truth with which he was now faced.

A face that had once, unmistakeably, been human, but which was now hideously malformed – jaws distended by the mandibles that they had been forced to accommodate – stared back at him. Tears ran freely from eyes that were becoming compound orbs even as he watched, and the lips moved, attempting to form words despite the encumbrance of the raw-fleshed mandibles – that Ulysses could now see had been created when the wretch's lower jaw split down the middle, the two halves stretching out to the sides – and in a voice thick with blood and saliva pleaded: "Help me!"

As Ulysses stared in frozen horror at the creature – its insectoid limbs still forming from what had been the victim's own arms and legs, now reshaped into new bone-twisting alignments, the middle pair of its three leg-sets forming from the wretch's ribs – it scuttled away from the partially devoured doctor and up the wall, never once taking its swelling and darkening eyes from Ulysses.

"Help me!" the wretch managed again before his words became incomprehensible insect noise.

The scratching at the back of Ulysses' skull intensified suddenly and then, a split second later, the giant cockroach leapt for the doorway and freedom. Forewarned, the dandy was ready for it. As 180 pounds of mutating cockroach flew through the air towards him, Ulysses lashed out with his simian arm.

The punch connected with what Ulysses supposed had once been the man's solar plexus – which was now hardening chitin – with a sharp crack, as Ulysses put all his weight behind it.

The cockroach tumbled back into the room, landing on its back, legs clawing the air helplessly, and Ulysses did not hesitate in pulling the door shut again.

"What's going on?" came the clipped Teutonic consonants of the startled Doctor Doppelganger.

"Well, Doctor," Ulysses said, turning to face her, but keeping a firm grip on the handle of the consulting room door, "it would appear that the Daedalus Clinic has a something of a pest problem."

CHAPTER THREE

Test Flight

Thomas Sanctuary stood on the parapet, at the very edge of the ostentatious crenulations of Sanctuary House, and gazed towards the teeming metropolis, feeling like a man reborn.

His heart was pounding in excited anticipation. He flexed his shoulders, adjusting the weight of the jetpack on his back, pulling on the straps of its harness to ensure that it was securely attached. Four weeks ago, when he had first set eyes on the suit and tried it on, he had barely been able to stand; ten years enforced lassitude and a prison diet having taken its toll on what had once been the half-decent physique of an ex-University rower. And there has been little point in making an effort to improve his physique when there had been nothing to look forward to when he eventually got out again either.

But now that his life had purpose – a burning need to put right the injustices of the past – he had started upon a gruelling physical regimen, making himself take time out each day from working on his father's final and greatest creation, and had begun to put right the damage that ten years' incarceration had done to his body. The suit, particularly the jetpack, weighed more than his withered frame had at first been able to support; with it on he had hardly been able to move.

Now, thanks to Mrs May's nutritious home-cooking, and lots of it, married to his new exercise regime, through which he pushed his body to the limits of endurance, he came close to regaining the level of physical fitness he had enjoyed as a younger man, and the mental focus to match. Only now that focus was centred wholly on completing the challenge his father had set him from the beyond the grave.

Make me proud, James Sanctuary had written, and Thomas was determined that he do just that, by seeing those who had ruined his family name pay for their crimes.

Thomas pulled the mask of the suit down over his face and gazed out at the city through the red lenses of its goggles. From the towers and spires of the Upper City and the multi-levelled tracks of the Overground, to the Smog-shrouded streets and public parks, to the festering slums, suddenly the dark palette of dusk took on an altogether different hue. From the intense white of a super-heated steam gouting factory chimney to the deep scarlet of the trees on the heath and the even deeper maroon of the cobbled streets, everything appeared in shades of red, as if the city were bathed in blood.

He stretched out his arms, checking the cape would still unfold properly to form the gliding wing he would need to help control his descent, making sure that is wasn't hooked onto the jetpack. His father appeared to have been inspired by the structure of a bat's wing, replacing the flying mammal's long, thin finger bones with light-weight metal rods and the webs of skin between with a strong, but lightweight fabric. With Thomas's arms relaxed at his sides, it hung behind him, a plain black cloak. But as soon as he flung out his arms, a spring-loaded mechanism forced the steel frame to extend, turning the loose folds of the cloth into a taut membrane, that would allow him to ride the thermals created by the firing jetpack.

His father had come so close. He had designed the suit, the

gliding cape, and the amazing infra-red, night-vision goggles, as well as the chemical propellants that would react to release enough energy to allow a man to fly. His only stumbling block had been a problem with over-heating, which meant that the jetpack had never worked properly and, without the jetpack, the suit was nothing more than a cumbersome get-up.

All that Thomas had had to do was incorporate a cooling system and make a few adjustments, so that the suit fitted him like a glove. Not that the suit needed much adjusting – it was almost as if it had been made for him. But Thomas still found it hard to entertain that idea that that had been his father's intention all along, contrary to the message James Sanctuary had left him, and the existence of the suit itself. However, they had gone a long way to improving his image of his father, to the point where, during moments of exhausted guilt and self-pity, he wished that they had been given the time to re-build their relationship.

And now, here he was, strapped into the hard leather of the figure-hugging suit, potentially a bomb on his back, just waiting to explode, teetering on the brink of the battlements, three storeys up, a cold wind whipping the cape behind him.

There was nothing more to be done now other than to take the jetpack out for its first proper test flight, throwing himself into the void in the name of invention and revenge.

He checked the harness one more time – not wanting the jetpack to take off without him, or worse still, to fall out of it mid-flight – the buckles of his boots and the belt that held everything together. He made sure his thick leather gloves were on securely and buckled tight, took a deep breath and thumbed the ignition switch he had fed through the suit, from the control, to his hand.

There was a faint click, the crackle of a spark, followed by the hiss of the pilot light igniting and then, with a whooshing roar, the jets fired as the pack's chemical propellants were fed through the complicated arrangements of pipes and combined within the internal workings of the jetpack.

As Thomas tensed his legs in preparation for the imminent

launch, he gave thanks for his father's foresight in giving the seat of his rubberised leather trousers an extra layer of fire-retardant padding.

Bending his knees ready to make the ultimate leap into the unknown, Thomas adjusted the throttle via the control held in his right hand. The roar of the jets increased and, feeling the pack tug on the harness, pulling him upwards, he leapt into the air, his heart in his mouth, and thumbed the throttle to what he judged to be launch velocity.

Thomas rocketed skyward, the sudden G-forces pushing his head back so that he found himself staring up at the rapidly approaching soot-stained clouds. His body, straight as a torpedo, went into a slow spin as he hurtled heavenwards.

He felt exhilarated, amazed and terrified, all at the same time. But still a small, focused part of his brain addressed the matter of his whirling trajectory. One of the jets must not be firing properly, he thought, which could be down to the feed not coming through evenly.

His body pummelled by the wind and rippling G-forces, Thomas slowly reduced the throttle, decreasing the jetpack's velocity. The jets spluttered for a moment, and he felt his stomach lurch as his upward momentum suddenly ceased. His pulse raced and then the feed lines cleared and both jets fired again, hurtling freefall becoming a smoother horizontal descent.

All this had only taken a matter of seconds, but Thomas was already high over the city, having crossed Highgate Cemetery, and having left Sanctuary House far behind. It was only then, hearing the whip-crack of the toughened fabric billowing behind him in the slipstream created by jetpack, that he remembered the flight-cape.

Throwing his arms out in front of him, fists balled, the metal framework sprang open and the cloak immediately snapped into shape.

Thomas went from being a human rocket, barely able to control his own trajectory, to soaring over the city, skimming the low cloud smothering London in a miasma of hydro-carbon pollution.

Stretching out his legs behind him, streamlining his body, he felt his speed increase still further, as he made himself more aerodynamic, and the jetpack ran more efficiently as a result.

Thomas immersed himself in the moment, every nerve and fibre of his being revelling in his night-flight. It was an incredible feeling of freedom and exhilaration. For a moment he even forgot the end to which he had laboured so hard and so long to complete what his father had started.

He was also starting to adjust to his new, ruddy view of the world, the night's sky appearing as dark as a gleaming pool of blood.

Countless people had enjoyed this view of the city before, as the great passenger dirigibles came in to land over Hyde Park, but surely no-one had ever experienced it as he was experiencing it now. He was closing with one of those airships now, its elongated gas bag drifting like some huge whale through the sea of toxic Smog, the cause of the pollution also clearly visible to Thomas from up here, the chimneys of scores of factories and hundreds of homes spouting smoke and vapours into the miasmic air.

And then the dirigible was behind him, the Tower of London emerging from breaks in the Smog ahead of him, the capital's maximum security prison instantly recognisable, even though the building work to repair the bomb-damaged structure had not yet been completed, White Tower itself was picked out in shades of pink and red, but clearly visible, despite the fact that night was falling fast across the city.

He was starting to feel cold. For prolonged flights at these altitudes the suit needed better insulation. He would add that to the list of things that needed changing before he took the suit out for its second flight.

He was glad of the mask, for this very reason, even though it smelt strongly of rubber. Without it, or his gloves, the cold night air would have stung at his hands and face and he would have been practically blinded.

He looked down at his battered fob watch, which he had had the foresight to attach to the straps of the jetpack harness. By his reckoning, the jetpack carried enough fuel for thirty minutes of burn time, or enough to carry him right across London and back again, if he so wished.

Using his whole body to direct his flight, cape taut behind him, he made a swooping turn, banking over the Tower, then turning back towards the river, Tower Bridge coming into view ahead of him. It was too much of a temptation to resist. Thomas has tested the jetpack and glider wing within a horizontal plane, but he still needed to master changing altitude at the same time.

Tensing his stomach muscles, he pulled his legs up while at the same time angling his head and outstretched arms so that they were now directing him downwards. He felt the effort of his exertions taking their toll on his aching muscles as his flight subjected him to all manner of unaccustomed forces.

He immediately began to descend, the jetpack secured across his back adjusting to the change in direction as Thomas angled his body. The looming towers of the bridge soared away above him. He was coming in too fast. Suddenly, there was the cantilevering platform of the bridge directly ahead of him, only it wasn't opening.

If he remained on his current course, in a matter of seconds he would slam into the stonework with enough force to break every bone in his body and ram his skull down into his spine. To pull up now would leave him rising and out of control; chances were he would still hit the balustrade of the bridge. Thomas had only a split second in which to make his decision and act upon it.

Angling himself down further he shot under the span of the bridge, closing at speed with the oily sludge and scattered detritus suspended on the surface of Old Father Thames. And then, every muscle in his back and shoulders straining, he pulled up sharply.

He felt the toes of his boots momentarily touch the surface of the river, throwing up a spray of oily water in his wake, and then he was rising, his sudden, rapid climb becoming steeper with every passing second. The turrets of Tower Bridge dwindling beneath him, Thomas found himself giving voice to a great whoop of joy, exhilarated by the thrill of being able to fly.

The night was dark around him now, but he could still see just as clearly as before, the cityscape beneath him painted in varying degrees of red, pink and white. He saw the white-hot smokestack of an Overground train as it chugged north on the Northern Line. The surface of the Thames appeared as a cold near-black burgundy, while people, setting out for the evening or returning home after an honest day's labour, appeared as warm magenta blobs beneath their buttoned-up coats.

Revelling in his bird's eyes view of the city, Thomas banked again, turning back over the sky-scraping towers of the city.

He would have to think of a name for himself, he pondered as he flew, an alter-ego in which guise he could set about his mission to exact revenge. He soared over the city, wings outstretched, like some strange amalgam of man and bat. *Man and bat, bat and man*, Thomas thought.

And then it came to him, the perfect secret identity – the Vespertilian.

He passed through a cloud of churning pollutants, leaving curling eddies in the smoke-stream behind him, glad again for the mask, but feeling that his breathing could be even better aided if he added some form of filter.

It took him a moment to realise that the cloud was in fact smoke rising from the crowded buildings below, rather than from some chimney stack or other.

The column of smoke was already billowing high into the sky, merging with the cloudy barrier of the Smog.

Scanning the maze of streets directly beneath him, Thomas tried to judge as best he could where he was. He saw the loop in the river, the rectangular lozenge-shaped basins of the docks, their fetid standing water glittering darkly in the reflected lights of the city and decided that he must be over the East End of London, somewhere over Wapping, or Limehouse perhaps.

Checking his watch again, Thomas saw that he still had approximately twenty minutes of burn time, during which he would have to cross the capital again. One thing that worked in the jetpack's favour, however, was that it allowed Thomas to travel as the crow flew, avoiding the warren of streets that riddled the capital. There was time enough, he decided, to take a closer look at what appeared to be a tenement fire.

Already having a better understanding of how the jetpack would adjust to his altered body shape, Thomas pointed himself towards the source of the billowing column of smoke. This time he descended at a more even pace, maintaining greater control over his descent. Keeping his body angled into the turn, decreasing spirals brought him closer to the source of the smoke, and the fire he could now see raging within the boxy building stood at a street corner amidst the twisting thoroughfares of Limehouse, archways, the Overground and tenement-supporting bridges rising over one another, creating a treacherous aerial labyrinth for Thomas to negotiate as he came down.

Now that he was approaching street level, Thomas was suddenly reminded of how fast he was travelling, the sensation of a sedate pace created by distance taken from him in an instant.

Suddenly he was hurtling towards the street, the burning structure directly ahead of him, hungry flames licking at a sign attached to the side of the building, the words 'Palace Theatre' flickering in the incandescent flames between billows of black smoke.

The end of the street lay before him, looming tenements rising up on every side now and, suddenly, he had no choice but to attempt to land. But there was too much to think about, too many variables to consider. He had planned to return to Sanctuary House and come down somewhere within the apple orchard, or on the heath – somewhere open at least – not in a narrow rat-run of an East End street.

As the cobbles rose up to meet him, the polished stones glowing a ruddy orange, writhing with liquid fire, he tried to manoeuvre himself into an upright position, desperately hoping to somehow turn the momentum of his hurtling, rocket-propelled flight into a decelerating run. Arms flailing in sudden uncontrolled panic, his glider wing folded up, and he lost what little control he had left.

At the last second he cut the fuel feed to the jetpack and felt its weight slam down on top of him. He lurched forward, completely unbalanced now, and landed heavily on his front, skidding to a stop in an agonised heap, thankful for the thick leather of his suit.

Thomas lay in front of the blazing Palace Theatre, images of the Chinese magician Lao Shen crinkling and blackening in the heat, windows cracking and exploding. His body was a knot of pain, muscles burning from the strain they had been put under during the test flight. His knees and elbows had been rubbed raw with friction burns through the fabric of his suit.

He turned towards the crackling flames, feeling their heat through the leather of his suit, supernovae bursting across the glaring white and red world he saw through the tinted-goggles of the mask, his head reeling. He felt like he was still hurtling through the air and waited for the world to stop spinning around him.

And then he saw it.

It emerged from the intense white heart of the fire, fighting its way clear of the burning building, demolishing what was left of the entrance doors as it did so. In his red-tinged world, the hulking shape – like some living mountain of clay, moving like an animated brick outhouse – glowed almost as hot as the raging conflagration, and yet appeared insensible to the scalding temperatures and not at all perturbed by the fact that the lobby of the theatre was collapsing in flames around it.

With relentless, purposeful steps, the behemoth shook itself free of the last shattered door frame and paused. Thomas felt its eyes upon him and knew that the true moment of testing had come. His knees and elbows screaming in agony, his struggled to his feet, pulling himself up tall before the advancing hulk.

And then the monster turned and set off, trudging away along the streets, away from the fire and the smoke, into the cooling darkness.

Thomas set off after the retreating hulk at a limping run, soon catching up with the lumbering brute. Up close it was huge, at least eight feet tall and just as broad, its hide cracked like old glaze, its body *plinking* as it cooled.

"Stop!" Thomas shouted, not knowing what else to say, his voice strangely altered by the mask.

To his surprise the monster stopped.

It turned slowly, its baleful gaze sweeping over Thomas and he suddenly felt very small and vulnerable. He was already backing away as the colossal arm swung at him. It caught him across the chest, knocking the wind from his body as surely as if he had run into a steel girder. And then he was flying again, backwards through the air, his limp body describing an arc before he crashed down only a few feet from a pile of burning rubble.

As he lay there, curled in a ball of agony, listening to the roar of the burning theatre merging in some unholy symphony with the distant wailing of sirens and the half-heard cries of helpless onlookers, the fire dwindled before his eyes as the shadows swarmed forward to claim him.

CHAPTER FOUR

The Queen of Hearts

The Mark IV Rolls Royce Silver Phantom, rolled to a halt outside the shuttered Belgravia townhouse. Passers-by, keen not to be seen themselves gave it furtive glances as they quickened their step and hurried on their way. The passenger door opened and the renowned dandy, *bon viveur*, and Hero of the Empire, Ulysses Quicksilver stepped out. He looked up at the unassuming building, taking a moment to make sure that his top hat was on just so and to straighten his plum frock coat.

"Thank you, Nimrod," he said, "that will be all."

"Do you want me to wait, sir?" the Ulysses' aging manservant asked, everything about his manner, from the tension in his body language to the look on his face as he peered up at the facade of the townhouse, making it patently clear what he thought of Ulysses visiting such an establishment.

"No thank you. This isn't the lair of some lunatic megalomaniac monster. I think I'll be able to handle myself in there."

"I don't think *you'll* have to worry about handling yourself," his manservant muttered.

"That will be all," his employer repeated reproachfully, and shut the door of the automobile.

The note of its engine a near-silent, pleasing purr, the Silver Phantom pulled away from the kerb and drove off into the encroaching night.

Nothing about the exterior of the building gave any impression as to what it was, much like the Inferno Club that Ulysses had occasionally frequented in the past. But, much like the Inferno Club, it didn't need to advertise what it was, as everybody who was anybody already knew.

Ulysses adjusted his emerald green silk cravat, re-securing the diamond pin and then, cane in hand, he strode up to the door. He rapped on the portal three times with the bloodstone tip of his cane.

Some moments passed before the door was opened by a burly bald ogre, who looked like he had a brick outhouse somewhere in his ancestry. He was dressed in a penguin suit that was straining to contain his barrel chest and bulging arms, and he had disconcertingly pink eyes. The albino stared down at Ulysses, a gormless idiot expression on his face.

"Ah, Mr White, how've you be keeping?"

The giant albino stared at him dumbly.

"It's Quicksilver, old boy. Ulysses Quicksilver. Run along and tell..." – he suddenly faltered, faced with the silent giant's lack of a response – "or whatever it is you do... Anyway, let the Queenpin know that I'm here, will you?"

The giant stepped back from where he had been effectively barricading the door with his bulk, admitting Ulysses to the small lobby, closing the front door after him before stepping through another door, leaving Ulysses alone in the gloomy vestibule. He had been gone for less than a minute when he returned and allowed Ulysses to pass into the house itself, without ever speaking a word.

Ulysses was immediately greeted by a sight that he hadn't enjoyed in a long time, since before he ever set off across Asia in pursuit of the kingpin of the Opium trade in London, the villain known as the Black Mamba – the Queen of Hearts' own Temple of Venus

He had entered an opulently dressed reception room – its walls papered with coral and cerise flocked wallpaper, bearing a grandly ornamented design – complete with Corinthian columns draped with extravagant velvet drapes.

It looked like a high-class tart's boudoir, which was fitting, seeing as the place was home to the Queenpin of prostitution herself. And if a visitor to this House of Sin had any lingering doubts as to the nature of the business that took place at this exclusive address, the presence of the two scantily clad young women, banished them immediately.

Ulysses felt a stirring in his loins that he had not enjoyed for a long time.

Each of the girls was young and lithe, their physiques tending towards voluptuous, with wide hips, narrow waists and swellingsbosoms, all barely held in place by tightly-knotted corsets. They were heavily made-up, especially their lips and around the eyes, and the addition of stockings and suspender-belts only served to make them appear all the more appealing. Nothing, about their apparel, or lack of it, had been left to chance.

The only differences between the two, was that one was blonde and blue-eyed, the crimson of her underwear contrasting strongly with her natural colouring, and the other brunette, the electric blue of her own outfit a perfect contrast to the colour of her eyes, which were as rich and dark as chocolate. One was petite, the other long-limbed, one milky skinned, the other's skin as warm and as dark as Jamaican Rum.

Almost all tastes were catered for within the Temple of Venus, although there were aspects of the world's oldest profession that the Queenpin would not even countenance and which she punished with the lethal ferocity of a mother wronged.

"Good evening, sir," the blonde girl said. "And what can we do for you?" She sidled up to him, making the most of all that Mother Nature had given her.

"I'm here to see Her Majesty," Ulysses said, hardly looking her in the eye as he stared at her corset-enhanced cleavage.

"Her majesty?" the black girl echoed. "She doesn't see just anyone, you know? She's very particular. Has her 'special' clients," she laid a hand on his shoulder as she pressed her body up against him.

"You're new here, aren't you?" Ulysses said, never once dropping his guard, keeping his hand firmly on his cane.

"Not that new," the young temptress replied.

"Maybe not, but new enough."

"If you're looking for something sweet," the buxom blonde said, sliding an arm around Ulysses waist, "I'm as sweet as sugar. All you need is one taste of these cherry lips."

"Or would you prefer a little spice?" the other asked, drawing herself closer still.

In one fluid motion, she slid her hand from his shoulder, down his chest to the front of his tightening trousers.

"Oh, sir!" she suddenly gasped. "I do declare that you do. Or have you just slipped that stiff, hard cane of yours into your pocket?"

He took a moment to enjoy the sight of her taut body and high breasts.

"Maybe another time, eh, ladies? But, like I said, I'm here to see the boss."

"Suit yourself," the blonde said, turning and walking away, apparently losing interest in him, just like that.

"Her Maj is very particular about who she sees," his dark-skinned temptress said, making no effort to hide her disgruntlement at being rebuffed.

Relaxing his body again, letting out his breath in a loud sigh of easing tension, Ulysses reached into a jacket pocket and pulled out a leather card holder. He took out a calling card and handed it to the disgruntled whore.

"She'll see me."

Eliza looked down at the card disparagingly, attempting to feign disinterest. Then she looked back at Ulysses, giving him a sour smile. "Wait here. Mr White, keep an eye on this one."

The two girls left the reception room, disappearing into the depths of the house, leaving Ulysses alone with the hulking albino. He threw the giant an uncomfortable grin but Mr White simply stared back at him with imbecilic disinterest.

He could hear music coming from somewhere within the house, the occasional chink of wineglasses, laughter and the high-pitched, affected laughter of girls. There was also the occasional masculine belly laugh as well as the barely audible grunts and screams of sexual abandon.

Some minutes later, the time delay suggesting that she hadn't hurried back, the spurned Eliza returned.

"Follow me," was all she would say. She fixed him with her deep-brown eyes, but there was no desire there now, only annoyance.

Eliza led Ulysses along various corridors as they made their way through the house, up three flights of stairs, and across landings hung with portraits of the great mistresses – Lady Hamilton, Nell Gwynne, Madame de Pompadour and the like. They passed through rooms painted with eighteenth century pastoral scenes of shepherds and shepherdesses at play, and even one dressed to look like a Roman brothel, with erotic Pompeian frescoes on the faux-cracked plaster and containing semi-naked girls attending to a party of toga-clad, middle-aged men.

Finally they reached a set of cedar wood doors, the entrance to the inner sanctum of the mistress of the house.

The room was lit like much of the rest of the house, subtly, by latticed rosewood lanterns and yellow-flamed gas lamps. The Queen of Hearts was reclined on a chaise longe covered in cushions, when Ulysses was at last admitted to the room, as if she had been lying there posing for a portrait artist, appearing to be everything a prostitute was supposed to be.

She appeared demure, whilst at the same time dominating. She knew the Kama Sutra inside out and yet she could come across as coy as a sexually precocious sweet sixteen year-old.

She wore the scarlet dress as if it was an extension of her own body, another skin that she wore. It fitted her so well, making the most of the fine, carefully sculpted physique beneath, its bodice keeping her breasts high and firmly together, tapering at the waist, only to flare again from the hips.

She lounged there with a deceptive, languid ease, carrying an air about her of a woman who was mistress of all she surveyed. Yes, she could afford to be choosy now; she was the Madame of this establishment, High Priestess of the Temple of Venus, but she also liked to keep her hand in. After all, she enjoyed her work.

She moved and part of the dress fell away, a long slash in the fabric revealing a supple, shapely leg up to the thigh. Ulysses felt his heart skip a beat.

Ulysses didn't know if she was older or younger than him. She didn't look any different from the last time he had set eyes on her over two years ago now. He certainly couldn't tell by going on appearances and he thought it impolite to ask.

He gazed again upon her luxuriant dark hair – dark to the point of being almost black – which was swept back from her high cheekbones and arranged so that a few carefully placed tresses fell across her swan's neck and teased at the mound of her breasts, which were also draped with a fine pearl necklace. And then there were those languid green eyes of her, locked behind long, alluring lashes. It was easy to see why so many men who spent a night in her company fell hopelessly in love with her and were never the same again.

She kept her seemingly half-closed, cat-like eyes on him for the whole time it took him to walk from the doorway into the middle of the room, barely blinking once. She had a relaxed air of expectation about her, as if she knew how she liked things to be done when a gentleman sought an audience with her. Ulysses noticed that she was toying with his calling card in her mesh-mittened hands. He paused, hat in his hands and bowed his head slightly.

"Ulysses Quicksilver, where have you been, my dear? I was worried some nubile well-heeled heiress had finally forced you into becoming respectable and that you'd gone and got married."

"I was away for a while."

"I heard," she said, in a playfully chiding tone. But of course, she had. "But you've been back some months now and you haven't been to see my girls once. I was beginning to worry that some frightful female had got you in the family way."

"You know me better than that."

The woman inclined her head, continuing to regard him with those penetrating emerald-green eyes. "Once I thought I did. Now I'm not so sure. How are you keeping?"

"Well," Ulysses answered, almost too quickly.

"So why the appointment at the Daedalus Clinic?"

Ulysses almost blurted out "How do you know about that?" but answered his own question before vocalising it. Of course she knew. She made it her business to know. It was why he was here.

"It's nothing... serious. Really. I'm quite well, thank you."

The Queen of Hearts looked like she was about to cast scorn on his claims of good health but then also thought better of it, "I am pleased to hear it. And your visit here tonight? Wanting to give yourself a proper workout, are you? Put that legendary stamina of yours to the test?"

"No. Not tonight."

"I suspected not," the madam said, almost sounding disappointed. "So to business then. What really brings you here for the first time in nearly two years?"

"To business indeed. Actually, it's funny that you should mention the clinic."

"Funny? How?"

"Funny as in while I was there a man transformed into a giant cockroach. The police turned up – or at least they looked like Scotland Yard's finest, only they were far too competent – and the poor bastard was carted away in an unmarked van. And I want to know where he was taken."

The woman's impassive expression didn't even waver as Ulysses related his unbelievable tale, but then his line of work was not unknown to her.

"So you came to call on my services or, rather, my other service."

"Where else *would* I come, but here?"

"You could have asked your bosses in Whitehall," the Queen said, smiling cheekily back at him. "How's your new boss settling in by the way?"

"Friend of yours is he?"

"Come now," she said coyly, "what would little old me mean to a man of Lord De Wynter's stature?"

"You're Queenpin of London's prostitutes and, as a result, you are mistress of the largest unofficial spy network in the city. You're no doubt privy to changes in government policy before they've even been acted upon," Ulysses growled. "Don't give me all that *His Coy Mistress* claptrap," his expression suddenly serious. "Have you heard anything?"

"About giant human-cockroaches?" she said with weary disinterest, although Ulysses knew that her mind would now be working like a Babbage Engine on overdrive, trying to recall any snippets of information that she was privy to, that might throw up links to something larger involving the Daedalus Clinic. "No, nothing. Why are you so interested?" she asked, trying not to sound too interested herself.

"Oh, you know, loose ends. Possibly some unfinished business," he answered, making his own vague attempt at subterfuge. It was always the way with her; bluff and counter-bluff, always so guarded, especially when it came to anything about herself that lay beneath the public face she presented to London's underworld, the city and its men of power.

Always playing her cards close to her chest; and she was good at it too. For a woman who daily and willingly, exposed everything to any number of men – and, rumour had it, women – very little was known about her. Ulysses didn't even know her name, beyond her self-styled title of Queen of Hearts.

"I'll look into it for you. Next time I'm enjoying a little pillow talk I'll see what... comes up."

"Thank you. That would be much appreciated."

"And settlement of the bill?"

"I will make the usual arrangements."

"Very good, very good." She stretched languidly, looking even more cat-like as she did so. "I do so enjoy the little gifts you send me." She said, sensuously fingering the pearls at her neck. "I was thinking of getting something else pierced, or perhaps a jewel for my navel, what do you think?" She suddenly pulled her dress up over her stomach, revealing the taut olive-skin of her flat tummy.

"Y-Yes." Ulysses blushed, despite himself. "Why not? I'll speak to my jewellers."

"You're sure I can't persuade you to while away an hour or so in my company, now that you're here?"

Ulysses paused before answering. "No, but thank you. Not tonight." He was suddenly very aware of the ape arm hidden within the sleeve of his jacket, and even fancied he could feel his shoulder aching numbly.

"Very well then," the Queen of Hearts sighed. "But come and see me and my girls again soon, won't you?" she said, lifting a small brass bell from a table beside the chaise long and ringing it.

The door opened and the dark-skinned beauty Ulysses had met downstairs threw Ulysses an unimpressed look.

"Eliza will see you out. And don't leave it so long between visits next time."

"Ah, sir, you're back," Nimrod said, stating the obvious but sounding happily surprised, as he answered the door to his master. The rumour of a smile creased his face as he peered over Ulysses' shoulder at the steam-carriage chugging away along the Mayfair streets, back into the night.

"Not disappointed are you, Nimrod?" Ulysses said, grinning at his manservant.

"No, sir. Not at all. I mean, it is not for me to have an opinion on the matter," the butler replied, having deftly regained his perfected attitude of haughty indifference.

"Good. Then pour me a cognac, would you? Courvoisier, if there still is some in the drinks cabinet."

"Of course, sir." Nimrod turned to go about fulfilling his

master's wishes, but as he did so he stretched out a hand, a crisp vellum envelope held between white-gloved thumb and forefinger. "This came for you while you were out."

"Post!" Ulysses declared, taking the letter.

All that had been written on the front was one word: *Quicksilver*. Turning it over he saw that it had been sealed with a stamp of red wax, bearing the unmistakable – and some might say overly theatrical – impression of a capital letter Q with a question mark inside it. If felt surprisingly heavy. There was something chunky contained inside.

He hastily broke the seal, catching the heavy iron key that fell into his hand, and then proceeded to unfold the letter, reading it quickly, an expression of delighted curiosity on his face.

"Nimrod, better take a rain check on the brandy, I think. We're going out again."

"Very good, sir. I'll warm up the Rolls."

CHAPTER FIVE

Department Q

Leaving Mayfair, Nimrod turned the Silver Phantom onto Park Lane and then along Constitution Hill, proceeding past both Green Park, to the left, and Buckingham Palace, to the right, before finally turning onto the Mall.

Ulysses stared out of the window, lost in his own thoughts; thoughts concerning the enigmatic Queen of Hearts, the metamorphosed wretch from the clinic, not to mention the doctor dead at the freak's hands – or rather, at his mandibles – Doctor Doppelganger and recollections of the other de-evolved creatures he had encountered not eight months ago, particularly the lizard-cum-fishman he had fought beneath Waterloo station.

St James's Palace lay to their left, St James's Park to their right, shrouded in darkness now. The street lamps cast their stuttering yellow light across his thoughtful features.

The car passed beneath the Admiralty Arch, and the bronze of Her Majesty, commissioned by Queen Victoria along with the building to celebrate her 90th birthday, the statue showing her, as she had been, in her prime, before the creation of the esoteric life-support system that sustained her – or the Throne as it was more commonly known.

Nimrod turned the car into Trafalgar Square, the spot where Ulysses had first encountered the rogue Megasaur released from London Zoo in the aftermath of the Darwinian Dawn's attack on the Overground Line. Trains *click-clacked* on their way along the aerial Bakerloo Line, Nelson's column dwarfed by the railway's supporting pillars. From there they moved onto the street of Whitehall itself. The last time Ulysses had taken this particular route through town, it had been on the back of a raging dinosaur.

But Nimrod did not stop the car there. He didn't slow down at all. The Rolls purring along the street, past smoke-spouting omnibuses and horse-drawn carriages, past the entrance to Downing Street, official residence of new PM Devlin Valentine, on into Parliament Square – where Ulysses had finally brought the Megasaur's frenzied charge to an end – and on past the Palace of Westminster and the gothic tower of Big Ben. They continued on over Westminster Bridge, the effluent stream of the Thames sliding sluggishly between the spans beneath.

The Silver Phantom pulled up, at last, on the opposite bank of the river, in a pool of darkness between streetlights. Ulysses got out without a word, quickly crossed the pavement and, in three strides, was hurrying down the broad steps that led down to the Thames path and the County Hall building. But when he was only halfway down the steps he dodged sideways, and into the shadows surrounding the heavy door set back into the stonework of the bridge itself.

Ulysses slipped the iron key from his pocket and into the lock. It turned more readily than the solid metalwork might have suggested.

Ulysses opened the door, slipped through and shut it quickly behind him.

"Good evening, sah!" came a croaky voice from the darkness.

Ulysses jumped despite himself. He blinked, his eyes slowly becoming accustomed to the barely-lit gloom. A hunched shape detached itself from the darkness and took a step towards him.

The wizened creature peered up at him, bent almost double as she was by her dowager's stoop. As a representative of the female of the species, she was a far cry from the sort of women Ulysses usually liked to spend time with – such as the Queen of Hearts or those girls in her employ. She was stooped, toothless and, to complete the fairytale crone look, her nose was covered with hairy warts. She had to be seventy if she was a day. She wore layer upon layer of clothes – moth-eaten cardigans, old coats and a shawl – and her legs were hidden beneath crumpled grey surgical stockings. On her feet were a well-worn pair of sturdy hobnail boots. And she was carrying a large carpet bag.

"Ah, good evening, Penny, and how are you?" Ulysses breathed in relief. "You surprised me there for a moment."

"Oh, you know 'ow it is, Mr Quicksilver, sah. Can't complain, can't complain. The arthritis is playing me up again and I haven't passed a solid stool in days – it's all watery stuff – and me pins ache something rotten, but I can't complain."

Her breath came at him in noxious waves. In the close confines of the space behind the door, it was impossible to escape her peculiar aroma; a sickly mix of lavender water and stale body odour. Ulysses suspected that the old woman didn't so much wash as douse herself in lavender water every now and again in an attempt to hide the layers of stench.

"Right, okay. Right you are, Penny," Ulysses said with forced joviality, feeling that she had shared more with him than he really needed to know.

"But enough of the pleasantries. If you'd like to follow me, sah." The old woman set off at a hobble along a grilled walkway and down an iron staircase. He let her get a few steps ahead of him before following. "Me piles have been playin' up an' all."

The aging crone led him down turn after turn into the musty darkness beneath Westminster Bridge. Penny – or, to give her her full title, Penny Dreadful – wasn't her real name of course, but it was the one she went by now. Ulysses certainly didn't know of any other.

By the time they reached the bottom of the iron steps, Ulysses judged that they were now at a level well beneath the riverbed. Penny led the way onward, from the fetid stairwell, into a brick-walled tunnel that smelt of mildew. The old woman's shuffling footsteps, and his firmer stride, were accompanied by the background *drip-drip-drip* of moisture leaking through the brick-arched ceiling of the tunnel.

Every now and again a droplet would land on one of the caged electric lamps strung along the apex of the tunnel, causing it to fizzle and spit. Ulysses kept shooting anxious glances at the roof, remembering the last time he had found himself in tunnels beneath the city, hoping that this one wasn't about to flood like those of London's once feted Underground system.

As he trudged along the passageway, he ducked every now and again, so as not to brain himself on the suspended lights. He did his best to ignore Penny's continued complaints about all her various ailments – dropping the occasional "Ah", "Oh" and "I see" into breaks in the old woman's monologue – and distracted himself by considering what he already knew about the man who had summoned him. His new 'employer' Lord Octavius De Wynter.

He knew that De Wynter was one of the Establishment, the old guard, but that he was also a new broom, brought in to sweep the department clean of any of Wormwood's lackeys. His remit appeared to have been to shake things up a little, and shake things up he had.

There were rumours of certain high-ranking officials, who had achieved promotion during Uriah Wormwood's tenure, begin demoted, or forced to take retirement, or even carted off to prison following an internal investigation carried out by De Wynter himself. There was even talk of mind-wiping technology being employed, with variable results. Apparently the lucky ones died. The unlucky ones had to be lobotomised and were sent to live out the rest of their days at a nice, quiet, maximum security sanatorium in the country.

And according to Nimrod, Ulysses' father Hercules Quicksilver had had something to do with De Wynter in the dim and distant past, but his faithful manservant couldn't be sure how well they had known each other, or what circumstances had brought them together.

So all he really had to go on so far was what he could deduce from De Wynter's actions. He did not even know whether he was a supporter of the Whigs or the Tories, only that he was a die-hard dyed in the wool monarchist of the old school.

But this was different for a start; his former ministry acquaintance, Uriah Wormwood, had always preferred to meet at the Inferno Club, the favoured place for spies and agents of the throne to liase with their governmental contacts. Not that Wormwood had ever really liked having to get his hands dirty, meeting with Ulysses. But then, look what had happened to him.

And now here was De Wynter summoning him to the heart of the department's operations under Whitehall.

Having traversed their way back across the river, beneath the Thames, Penny opened an iron pressure door and invited Ulysses through, before pushing it shut again, its rusting hinges complaining – the old woman's strength never ceased to amaze him – and locking it again with a turn of a heavy wheel.

Ulysses had expected to find himself in some underground office complex, but instead he was surprised to find himself standing on a station platform – an Underground station platform. The Underground network was clearly not as flooded nor as inaccessible as the populace had been led to believe.

As if on cue, with a *whoo-whoo*, gouts of smoke and sooty steam filled the tunnel, heralding the arrival of a locomotive.

Ulysses marvelled at the train.

It wasn't particularly long – it was only an engine pulling two carriages – but it had been painted with the red, white and blue livery of the British crown, and very impressive it looked too.

With a loud hiss of steam the train screeched to a halt alongside the platform.

"Grand, isn't it?" the old woman said, looking up at Ulysses with a twinkle in her eye.

"What was that?" Ulysses turned to the old woman, realising that he was gawping at the train like an idiot, as if he'd never seen such a thing before, and quickly shut his mouth.

"All aboard!" Penny said, opening the door of the first carriage and, still stupefied, Ulysses obediently climbed inside.

The interior of the carriage was a far cry from the passenger trains of the Overground network, not that Ulysses ever travelled by public transport if he could help it, although he remembered how excited he had been to ride on the Piccadilly Line with Nanny McKenzie when he was still in short trousers. It was like they were travelling first class – the seats upholstered in the finest damask, the Royal crest worked into every gold-plated fixture and fitting, or so it seemed.

It made the presence of Penny Dreadful appear all the more incongruous, although she seemed quite comfortable seated next to him, legs swinging, her feet not quite touching the floor, an inane, toothless grin on her face.

The train set off into the darkness. Ulysses tried to peer through the tinted glass in the front of the carriage, intrigued to know who was driving, but couldn't see anything.

"Automated, you know. The whole thing," Penny explained, guessing what was on his mind. "It's like this train's one big automaton."

"So, where are we going, Penny?"

"To the Department, sah," the old woman chuckled to herself.

They trundled on through utter blackness, picking up speed. Every now and then Ulysses felt the rocking motion of the train shift as it took a bend in the tunnel, both descending and ascending as if it was one of those seaside peer rides that the lower orders seemed to enjoy so much.

The overall effect of this swaying journey was that by the time the train stopped again, probably only a matter of minutes later, Ulysses had no idea where they were beneath the capital. They could have been right back under Whitehall or under the British Museum for all he knew.

"This is our stop," the old woman said, as the train screeched to a halt in a cloud of steam beside another unremarkable platform. She opened the carriage door and Ulysses followed, fascinated to know how this journey would end.

"This way please, sah."

Another pressure door led into another brick-lined tunnel and, from here, Ulysses and Penny entered the sub-basement he had been expecting to find under Westminster Bridge.

"Welcome to Department Q," the old woman coughed.

It looked like the Department had taken over the sub-basement of a larger building. Large iron pipes ran the length of the roof. Sturdy doors led off from the broad corridor and everything was lit by the dull glow of wall-mounted electric lights, that bathed the gloomy corridor in a hellish half-light.

A constant cacophony of background noise filled the place, echoing from the walls and ceiling; the clanking of machinery, a high-pitched drilling, the occasional *crack* of a pistol being fired somewhere nearby, and what sounded like distant animal cries. Ulysses noticed that as well as red-brick, part of the structure of the basement was made up of older building foundations – large blocks of rough-cut stone and what looked like walls of Roman construction. How far down were they? And what lay above them?

A little further on the corridor opened out into a large cellar-like space with two further wings of brick tunnels, medieval cellars and Roman ruins extending to both left and right. Ulysses caught glimpses of lab-coated figures and what appeared, at first glance, to be homeless vagabonds moving about in the shadows, going about their business in conspiratorial huddles armed with clipboards and other curious pieces of apparatus.

Penny Dreadful ignored all of this activity and, instead, headed straight for a grand-looking walnut-panelled door set into the wall opposite the corridor from which they had just emerged.

Glancing back the way they had just come, Ulysses saw a painted wooden sign hanging above the arch of the tunnel that led back to the platform bearing the name 'Department Q' painted inside the symbol of the now abandoned Underground system.

Penny rapped on the door.

After what felt like a painfully long pause, a buzzer sounded and a red light mounted above the door, that Ulysses had barely noticed before, turned green. Penny pushed open the door and ushered Ulysses into the chamber beyond.

From the shape of it, it looked like the office had been built into the void of a railway arch, or something like it. Glass-fronted bookcases and display cabinets lined the walls, filled with all manner of intriguing items – from big cat skulls to a model of the starship *Regina* – but the room was dominated by the large mahogany desk that stood at its centre, beneath an extravagant crystal chandelier.

Squeezed into the leather-upholstered swivel chair behind the desk was a huge man. Everything about him was big. He was thickset, with a rugged, darkly handsome face that looked like it had been hewn from marble. Despite having obviously entered middle-age some years ago, the man still had a luxuriant head of nut-brown hair, which was swept back from a high forehead. Only his elongated sideburns showed any obvious signs of aging. He looked like he would be more at home on a country estate, with a hunting dog at his side and a shotgun broken over his arm. But here he was ensconced within the Department, at the heart of this operation, with the air of a man around whom everything else circled, like the planets around the Sun.

This was Lord Octavius De Wynter.

On the wall behind him were a host of clocks, each set to a different time, matching time zones around the world, and beyond. As well as London, Paris and St Petersburg, there were also such far flung places as New York, Hong Kong, Atlantic City, Pacifica, Tranquillity and New Sidonia.

As well as the obligatory Babbage unit, the desk also had a number of interesting objects lined up on top of it, from a Decade Diary, to models of Martian war machines that could only be described as six-legged tanks.

As Ulysses and Penny entered his office, the man looked up, fixing Ulysses with sparkling eyes, regarding him from beneath bushy eyebrows.

"Ah, Quicksilver, there you are," De Wynter said in his booming rich baritone.

"Hello, sir."

"Right, now listen up. I want you to get yourself over to the East End. To Limehouse."

"Limehouse?" Ulysses said, startled, at both the brusque way in which De Wynter had dispensed with all social pleasantries and then at his mention of that particular district of London. The last time he had been in that part of town, he had battled a host of automata drudges in the employ of former PM Uriah Wormwood and the Darwinian Dawn. Ulysses had seen an entire wharf and warehouse complex razed to the ground.

"So that's where the wretch was taken. But why?"

"Where who was taken? What are you talking about, man?" De Wynter blustered, looking annoyed. He was obviously a man not known for his placid temperament.

"The cockroach, sir. From the Daedalus Clinic."

"Oh that. Forget about that," De Wynter said, sternly. "This is a more pressing matter altogether. I want you to go to Limehouse to look into a series of attacks that have been taking place there recently. The ones perpetrated by this so-called Limehouse Golem, as the press have christened it. The latest attack was on the Palace Theatre, where that Chinese cove Lao Shen had his Oriental magic show. Place burnt to the ground before the fire could be brought under control."

"I've not heard about that," Ulysses said, feeling suddenly out of the loop.

"No, you won't read about it in the papers until tomorrow either. Which is why I want you there now, sorting it out. Do whatever it is you do and get me some answers. Ideally find this Golem and put an end to it, by whatever means necessary."

Ulysses' mind was reeling. He had come here, thinking that he would be given another angle on the incident at the Clinic. But this was something else entirely.

"So what did happen to the cockroach?" he asked, unable to completely let go of the mystery he had been set on solving. "Why not send Penny? Sounds like just the sort of place she could get some answers, Limehouse."

"Look, forgot about the damned cockroach, that's not why you're here."

"So the Department did have something to do with its disappearance?"

"You don't need to worry about that. You have your orders, now go."

"What? You mean that information's on a need to know basis?"

"And you don't need to know. You've hit the nail on the head. Culpable deniability. Let the matter rest, and get yourself over to the East End, there's a good man. *Tempus fugit*, and all that."

And with that, almost as soon as it had begun, his audience with the Department chief was over.

Ulysses found himself gawping dumbly, opening and closing his mouth like some brain-addled goldfish, speechless in the face of De Wynter's approach to man-management.

"This way, sah, if you would be so kind," Penny said, opening the door and ushering him back out of the office.

"Quicksilver," De Wynter suddenly called after him with a bellow like a foghorn.

"Yes, sir?" Ulysses paused at the threshold.

"Get me a good result on this one. The *Jupiter* launches in a matter of days and I don't want anything buggering it up like that shambles at the jubilee. Shut the door on your way out, will you?"

And with that, Ulysses was dismissed.

"Righty-ho," he said, giving Penny Dreadful, a forced smile. He felt strangely belittled after his brief encounter with Octavius De Wynter. "Best get going. After all, the game is afoot."

CHAPTER SIX

Spring Heeled Jack

Wincing in pain, Thomas Sanctuary pulled on the suit once again. His body was a mass of pulled muscles and skinned joints, the green and purple bruises and abrasions covering it a map of the trials he had endured when he had taken his father's final creation out on its test-flight. The injuries were also an annotated document of the trauma he had suffered during his encounter with what the press were calling the Limehouse Golem.

That had been the reason for the first improvement he had made. The body armour rig he was now pulling on over the leather and rubber bodyglove of the original suit.

He had constructed it from what he had to hand in his father's workroom. It inevitably added weight to the suit, and was bound to restrict his movement to some extent, but on his first outing, he hadn't proved to be the most agile creature in the air anyway. And besides, he didn't really see the encumbrance making much difference, except in helping to protect his already battered body.

The armour in place, he secured it to the suit beneath via a series of hastily added buckles. It covered his shoulders, chest and back, with curved plates coming down over his upper arms. Once he came to put on his newly improved gloves – now transformed into gauntlets by the addition of more metal – practically the entirety of his arms would be covered, only the less easily reached underarms still vulnerable to attack.

Next, Thomas pulled on the sturdy leather boots. There hadn't been much he could do with these yet, or else he wouldn't have been able to walk when he was grounded, but at least they already had steel toe caps. He had thought about adding some sort of toe weapon, but that would have to wait until he had more time to make further improvements. With the Limehouse Golem still out there, events were in danger of spiralling out of his control, and he had had quite enough of external events and other people dictating how his life should be run. It inevitably ended in misery and suffering.

He had been able to beef-up his leg protection, however, mainly to the knees and the front of his thighs. He had a feeling that he could expect a few more ungainly landings before he mastered the jetpack completely, and he didn't want to be crippled by them thanks to having taken all the skin off his knees, again.

Buckles and straps secure, he turned to the frame from which hung the jetpack. The flaring around the jets themselves were already showing signs of wear and tear, the metal scorched black and brown. Perhaps there was a more suitable material from which they could be made – an alloy of some kind? That was something else that he would have to look into another time. Since his initial flight, he had managed to carry out a little fine-tuning, mainly regarding the palm-held throttle control. It should now allow for greater variation in changes in velocity and, hopefully, mean that he could hover upright, if he proved adroit enough.

He had refuelled the pack's tanks from his father's supply of reactants and his shoulders ached as they took the weight of the pack again so soon after sustaining his injuries in the tussle with the golem. But once the harness was secured over the plates of armour, the pressure eased a little, and it had already started to feel like an almost reassuring encumbrance.

Open to its full extent, on another frame, was the cape-cum-glider wing. Thomas crouched awkwardly in the armoured suit, ducked beneath the outstretched wings and then rose to standing again with the cape now in place, securing it around his chest and shoulders, and connecting it to the jetpack harness, making sure that he was securely locked within it.

Turning to one of the work benches dotted around the room, he picked up the utility belt he had made for himself, designed to carry all those little items he had a feeling might come in useful during whatever escapades awaited him in his new role as a masked avenger. For the time being all that it held was a skeleton key and, most importantly, the micro-transmitter he had created – cannibalising parts of another of his father's discarded contraptions to do so – specifically for the operation he was about to embark upon.

Returning to the desk, looking for his gloves, his eye fell on the paper that lay there.

The front page, and most of those that followed it, were taken up with the Prime Minister's very public attack on China, regarding the Eastern Empire's lack of a stance on climate change, along with ongoing developments surrounding the launch of the *Jupiter Station*, now only a matter of weeks away. But in spite of all this media coverage of what was already being hailed, by some, as Devlin Valentine's day, Thomas had still managed to make page seven. He read the headline again, with an almost guilty feeling of self-satisfaction.

MAYHEM AND MURDER STALK THE EAST END

A warm glowed filled his aching body as he savoured the article. He felt... flattered. That was it. It felt good to be noticed, and he took pleasure from being the centre of attention, although, of course, he had not been portrayed as the hero of the piece. In fact, he had been vilified as much as anything else, practically tarred with the same brush as the Golem, whatever *that* really was. But then he hadn't made the most auspicious of starts in his battle with the beast. In fact, he had given a good example of what it meant to take a pasting. No, he had to admit that he had his work cut out for him, if he wanted to improve his image in the eyes of the public. But then, he had to admit, part of him also took a vicarious thrill from being feared by the general masses.

Distracted, skim-reading the article he had perused half a dozen times already, ignoring the bit at the start about the fire that had consumed the Palace Theatre and unreliable eye-witness reports stating that a terracotta giant had started the blaze, he paused at one particular passage.

Eye-witnesses reported that the creature attempted to strike back against the seemingly unstoppable juggernaut, but to no avail. But what was it?

Witnesses describe it as having the semblance of a man-sized bat, breathing fulminous smoke and with terrible burning eyes, 'like looking into the hellish pit of Hades itself,' as a Mrs Doris Channing of Limehouse, put it.

Another eye-witness, chimney sweep Sidney Proudfoot, told our reporter that it, 'just looked like some bloke in a Hallowe'en costume.'

But The Times *can reveal, after exhaustive research, that this is Spring-Heeled Jack, back to terrorise the city after 160 years.*

After his assault on the monster that attacked the Palace Theatre in Limehouse last night, some claim that he is a hero, here to help our beleaguered capital in these dire times we now find ourselves living in.

Vigilante or villain? What is the true identity of this Spring-Heeled Jack? This is the question Londoners are asking themselves now. Who is this strange caped figure, and does he fight for good or for ill?

Spring-Heeled Jack. The press had branded him with an alternative identity before he had properly created an alias for himself, through which to go about exacting his revenge on those who had engineered matters so that he was put away for a crime he didn't commit. And it was an identity that would strike fear into the hearts of his enemies. The greatest fear of all, the fear of the unknown.

Beneath the rather sensationalist piece of writing, there was a plea published on behalf of the Metropolitan Police, who were now dealing with the related case of recent attacks perpetrated in the Limehouse area, against both the Chinese and Jewish communities, some experts fearing a new era of gang warfare was about to consume the area.

The Police are offering a reward for any information regarding this masked mystery man – if he is a man – that will help lead to an arrest. A spokesman for Scotland Yard asked anyone who might know the man to come forward and even urged the rogue to give himself up and hand himself over to the Police at the earliest opportunity.

There was a genteel knock, followed by a polite cough, and Mrs May appeared at the study door.

"Your whiskey, sir."

She didn't bat an eyelid, seeing him got up like he was, but then she had been the one to find him when he had arrived back at Sanctuary House, the night before, his head still reeling, as he crashed back through the door of the rooftop conservatory, cutting the power just before he rocketed into the far wall, and it was there that Mrs May found him, battered and bruised and blacked out.

"Shall I prepare a light supper for when you return?"

"Err, let's see how it goes, shall we?"

"It's only that I was about to retire for the night," she explained, but without any hint of a complaint, despite the fact that she had been deprived of sleep, either tending to Thomas's injuries or helping him with the re-invention of his suit.

"Oh, of course. Sorry, how selfish of me."

"I'll leave some bread and dripping out for you then, in the kitchen, shall I?"

"Yes. Please. That would be ideal. Thank you," he answered

stiltedly, embarrassed. He had been so focused on his mission he hadn't given the needs of anyone beyond himself a moment's thought.

Suddenly, remembering why she had climbed all the way to the top of the house in the first place, Thomas took the glass of whiskey and knocked it back in one go. The alcoholic warmth eased the nervous knot in his stomach, helping to banish his doubts about the forthcoming venture, and helping him to take that crucial, final step.

He picked up the suit's headpiece and, having slicked back his unruly mop of hair, pulled it on over the top of his head. As the mask came down, he saw the world again through the bloody tinge of its night-vision goggles and was immediately transported back to the events of two nights before.

"So you're going out again."

"Yes, Mrs May." His voice sounded strangely altered by the mask.

"Does it really have to be so soon?"

He dropped the paper, with its artist's impression of a giant blood-sucking horned bat-monster, onto the silver tray on which she had carried his pick-me-up.

"Yes, Mrs May."

Opening the conservatory doors – the broken panes replaced now with sheets of ply board – the transformed Thomas stepped out onto the battlements of Sanctuary House.

The jetpack roared into life as he thumbed the ignition switch.

Shouting to be heard over the rising roar of the jets, he turned back to the open doors of the conservatory, regarding the slouched form of his exhausted housekeeper and unlikely confidante, he added, "Sleep well."

And with that he opened the throttle and took off into the encroaching night, rocketing up into the heavens.

CHAPTER SEVEN

The Rabbi

The air within the synagogue was redolent with the smell of dust and beeswax. Clouds of sickly-sweet amber incense clogged the vaulted ceiling space of the old building like the nicotine yellow Smog that clogged the streets beyond the holy sanctuary.

The glass of the high, narrow windows shone blackly in the reflected candle light. The Rabbi walked the length of the synagogue lighting the last of the candelabras.

Beyond the walls of the synagogue, crammed in as it was between the looming warehouse and teetering tenements, all was hustle and bustle. The constant background hubbub coming from the docks, the river, cars clogging the city's exhaust-choked streets even at this time of night, the clatter and bangs of ships being loaded and unloaded, and the shouts of stevedores from inside the synagogue sounded like the city's own song, sung over and over, just as King David had sung psalms of praise to God.

Inside the temple, all was still. The only sound was the tapping of the Rabbi's heels on the tiled floor and his own monotone humming as he subconsciously chanted from the scriptures of the Song of Songs to himself.

He passed beneath the lamp of the Eternal Light and approached the Holy of Holies, intending to take out the Torah scrolls and seek guidance from their chapters and verses.

Last Sabbath Day had seen a marked increase in attendance by God's children. Reports had it that the attack on the Palace Theatre had been carried out by a Golem. Rabbi Moses Babad felt a thrill of nervous excitement at the thought – had some student of Rabbinic lore really managed to create life from the clay of the Earth, as God had done on the sixth day, to be a vessel of His vengeance?

Although people had lost their lives, Jews as well as Irish and Chinese, some good had come out of it, although he could not condone it, of course. But then could he wholly condemn what had happened when it had brought so many of his stray flock back to the temple?

The downside was, of course, that he had taken to locking the door of the synagogue when it wasn't in use, for fear of reprisals against his community, and himself in particular.

The door! Rabbi Babad suddenly remembered. *It was still unlocked!*

The Rabbi spun on his heel, as quickly as his arthritic joints would allow, and set off at a trot towards the back of the building.

The sudden bang on the door startled him.

A man stood within the entrance porch of the synagogue, letting the noise and dust of the street into the sacred place for a moment before the door swung closed, shutting out the world once more.

The Rabbi could immediately tell that he wasn't one of his usual congregation. In fact, Rabbi Babad sincerely doubted that he was of Jewish stock at all. He was tall, with a slim to athletic build. His hair fell in a foppish sweep across his forehead and his eyes sparkled in the candle-lit gloom. Everything about him, from the clothes he wore – a crumpled linen suit with a rough silk waistcoat and mustard cravat, the whole ensemble finished off with a diamond tie-pin – to the extravagant bloodstone-tipped cane in his hand, to the way he carried himself, spoke of his obvious wealth and status. This gentleman belonged to the upper echelons of Magna Britannian society.

Catching the Rabbi's eye, the man strode boldly towards him, with a cheery, "Hello there!" completely failing to follow correct, and respectful, decorum upon entering this house of God. Rabbi Babad clicked his tongue in annoyance, a frown taking his features. He pointed to the small wicker basket on top of a bookcase just within the entrance.

A look of embarrassed surprise seized the man's face and with a hurried apology of, "Oh, sorry," he scurried back to the door and, taking one of the cloth skullcaps from the basket, placed it on his head. The kippah in place, he began to approach the Holy of Holies and the Rabbi.

"'Yes, my son?" the Rabbi intoned, in thickly accented English, the frown on his face becoming a placid expression of calm. "Can I help you?"

"I certainly hope so, Rabbi," Ulysses Quicksilver replied, feeling rather self-conscious having been reprimanded by the old priest before he had even been able to introduce himself. There was nothing like making a good first impression, and his had been *nothing* like a good first impression. He only hoped he claw something back from the gulf of his social *faux pas*.

"Then speak, and tell me what it is you seek to know, for we gain nothing through silence. It is not very often that we receive a visit from outside of the Jewish community. What brings you to Limehouse?"

Ulysses regarded the diminutive form of the rotund Rabbi, dressed in the traditional robes of an Orthodox Jewish teacher. He had a beard as thick and grey as wire wool, and his hair hung down around his ears in ringlets. He could be only a little over five feet in height, but that didn't change the fact that in the Rabbi's presence Ulysses felt like he was still in short trousers, back at preparatory school, facing the fearsome Biblical wrath of his Religious Studies teacher.

"I'm here investigating the recent attacks in the area. You heard about the fire at the Palace Theatre?"

"But of course," the Rabbi said, looking grave. "A terrible business."

"And I take it you've heard what people are saying was behind it?"

"It had nothing to do with me, if that's what you're implying."

"Then you know people say a Golem has done these things."

The other man tensed. "I have heard the rumours. But I promise you that no one from the Jewish community had anything to do with it."

"But the Golem is a creature from Jewish folklore, is it not?"

"I do not have to answer your questions," the Rabbi suddenly shouted, spittle flying from his lips. "There has already been enough anti-Semitic feeling stirred up by recent events. I do not need you coming here, harassing me in my own synagogue. What are you really doing here? Are you from the papers?" he said, suspicious.

"No, I can assure you that I am nothing to do with the press," Ulysses said calmly, reaching inside a jacket pocket and taking out a leather card holder, showing the distrustful Rabbi his credentials.

"Ah, I see," the Rabbi muttered, the fire within him suddenly doused.

"I am sure that reports of a Golem trashing the East End would indeed stir up plenty of anti-Jewish feeling. But can you be sure that that wouldn't lead to reprisals from your side, as it were?"

The Rabbi looked at the floor, saying nothing for a moment. "Would that I could. But as the Holy Torah teaches us, in the ninth commandment, I shall not lie."

"There you are then. Members of some local Chinese tong were attacked and killed recently, weren't they?"

"Yes. I heard about that. And I wish I could say that they were the only ones."

"But they weren't, were they?"

The Rabbi shook his head. "But if certain members of our community *had* taken matters into their own hands, say, it would only have been because they were provoked!" he said, the still-glowing coals of his anger being fanned by his discussion with this intruder into his world. He looked up again, fixing Ulysses with the sparkling black dots of his eyes, buried as they were amidst all the beard and hair. "But create a Golem? Do you really believe that such a thing is possible?"

"You mean, you don't?"

"I mean it hasn't been heard of in five hundred years!"

"You're talking about Rabbi Loew's golem, in Prague?"

"No! Rabbi Loew was one of the most outstanding Jewish scholars and would never have undertaken to create a golem. No, it is much more likely that if the Prague golem ever existed, it would have been the work of Rabbi Eliyahu of Chelm."

"I see," Ulysses said slowly, not wanting to enrage the Rabbi any further. He certainly had a temper, but was he the one behind the attacks, whatever it was that had actually performed them?

"But do you think it is possible to create life, in God's name?"

"As God created Adam from the dust of the earth? If one has faith, one can do anything. Certainly the Sefer Yezirah contains instructions on how to make one and the stories would have us believe that it is possible."

"And how is the creation of a golem achieved?"

"Some sources say that, having formed the golem's body from the soil, you must dance around it whilst speaking a combination of letters from the Hebrew alphabet and then use the secret name of God, ultimate creator of all things, to bring it to life. Others say that you write the Hebrew word for 'truth' upon its forehead, or that you write God's holy name on parchment and place it in its mouth, to animate it. But only one who strives to approach God, and so gain some of God's wisdom and power through that pursuit, could ever attempt to create one."

"So basically, what you're saying is, the only person who would be capable of such a thing would be you?"

"But I swear on the Torah scrolls that I have done nothing – nothing to be ashamed of."

"But have you considered that someone else might have set this Golem rampaging through Limehouse with the express intention of making others believe that you had?"

The Rabbi looked at him aghast. "Who would do such a thing?"

"That's what I'm here to find out," Ulysses said, giving the old man what he hoped was a reassuring smile. "And to answer your question, we first need to answer this one. Who would have something to gain from starting a turf war in the Limehouse distric – *Ahhh*!"

Ulysses' sixth sense flared a split second before the first resounding crash shook the building.

"What was that?" the Rabbi gasped.

It felt like an omnibus had driven into the side of the synagogue.

Ulysses tensed, ready to spring into action, the migraine pain in his head subsiding now that the danger had actually presented itself.

A second crash set the lights and the *ner tamid* swinging in front of the Ark, sends showers of ancient dust cascading from the rafters. From somewhere within the synagogue there came the sound of breaking glass.

"What is going on?" the Rabbi panicked, suddenly losing his cool. "Was this all a ploy? Were you merely a distraction?"

There was another crash that shook the building to its foundations.

"I promise you, I'm nothing to do with this," Ulysses shouted over the thunderous, wrecking ball impacts.

"Then what in God's name is it?"

Ulysses looked at him darkly. "I'll give you three guesses."

CHAPTER EIGHT

Jack be Nimble

"God in heaven!" the Rabbi exclaimed as yet another booming crash shook the synagogue, sending more dust falling in clouds around them and crazing the plaster on the north wall.

Ulysses leapt between the Rabbi and the shuddering wall, pushing the old man back out of what he hoped would be harm's way. Holding the shaft of his cane in his left hand, he grasped its bloodstone tip with his right.

"Stay back," he said firmly, his pulse quickening, that familiar itch at the back of his skull warning him of imminent danger.

His mind was awhirl. He didn't truly understand what it was that was on the other side of the wall. Although he believed the synagogue's unseen attacker was the golem, he didn't really know what the golem was. His automatic reaction had been to draw his sword-cane, but would that actually be of any use against whatever it was that was smashing its way through the temple wall? The only other weapon he had about his person was his pistol; would even that be an effective means of defence?

And then, with a great convulsive heave, the wall bulged inwards and came down.

From out of the cloud of plaster and brick-dust that came rolling towards them in the wake of the wall's collapse, something barrelled its way into the synagogue, splintered lathes and pieces of shattered rubble tumbling from its carapace. The scratching dust gusted into Ulysses' face, forcing him to close his eyes and throw an arm up to protect himself, but he was unable to prevent himself from inhaling a great lungful. His mouth filled with the taste of chalky plaster, his throat clotting with a sticky paste of saliva and powder.

Ulysses could hear the golem crashing towards them, sending pews flying left and right as it hurled the crushed furniture of the synagogue out of its way.

Ulysses staggered backwards and tried to see what it was that was ploughing its way towards him, its pile-driver footfalls shaking the floor beneath his feet.

Through the billowing clouds Ulysses saw a dreadful gaping maw, furnace heat distorting the air before it and eyes that blazed like headlamps piercing every corner of the gloomy building wherever they turned.

And then there was the noise, a grating, bellowing roar, like the ferocious roar of an engine-firebox and the grinding of heavy iron gears.

A fist like a wrecking ball spun out of the obscuring dust and, even as Ulysses threw himself out of its path, it connected with his body, the force of the blow whirling him round over the monster's head, sending him flying backwards through the air, to land a good twenty feet away in a pile of rubble, broken plaster and sundered lathes.

Ulysses lay there for a moment, his rapier blade still gripped tightly in his right hand, the scabbard of his cane still in his left, listening to the sounds of destruction sundering the stillness of this place of prayer, waiting for the pain to work its way from his back to his fingertips in the sting of pins and needles.

Slowly he pushed himself up into a sitting position, his head still spinning, a fine white shower of plaster dust falling from him with every movement he made.

He could see the golem more clearly now but he couldn't see the Rabbi.

The golem picked up a hymnal store in the massive fingers of one huge hand and hurled the bookcase across the synagogue, sending it whirling over Ulysses' head, missing him by mere inches.

The creature was colossal. It was at least eight feet tall, and just as broad across its armour-plated shoulders. Assuming the posture of a hunched prop forward – only one made from what looked like baked clay – it barrelled forwards with all the power of a battering ram.

The golem passed beneath the *ner tamid*, the hanging lantern scraping across the broad span of its shoulders. In the unsteady flicker of the flame, Ulysses saw now that it wasn't made of clay but that its carapace was in fact constructed from interlocking plates of ceramic. Through gaps in the behemoth's armoured shell Ulysses saw the heavy metal endo-skeleton of an automaton chassis.

The Limehouse Golem was a robot-drudge.

It looked like it had originally been commissioned to enter dangerous environments, such as burning buildings – some kind of search and rescue droid. Its huge hands were no doubt designed to move heavy objects such as fallen roof beams. Its eyes were blazing halogen lights, powerful penetrating beams to aid in its search and rescue work. But although it might be making a thorough search of the synagogue for survivors, rescue clearly wasn't what was on its mechanical mind.

As Ulysses scrambled to his feet, the golem-droid's head rotated upon its neck bearings, the powerful beams of its eyes blinding him as he struggled to clear his tear-obscured vision. With a grinding of internal gears it gave voice to a throaty roar and turned towards him again, stomping forwards on legs like reinforced steel foundation posts.

In an instant Ulysses was moving, scrabbling over chunks of wall and broken brick to put as much distance between him and the automaton as possible.

As he made his bounding run across the rubble-strewn floor, he sheathed his sword-cane; it wasn't going to do him any good here. He had battled fungoid replicants and artificially-engineered chimerae with it, but it wouldn't help him against this opponent. His initial doubts about the effectiveness of his gun were well-founded too now, so the pistol remained holstered in its harness under his arm.

If the Silver Phantom had still been parked outside, he was sure he could have found something he could have used against the droid in the boot of the car. There was still a pocket Gatling gun in there, under a tarpaulin. Even the grappling-gun he had last used in his pursuit of Uriah Wormwood's zeppelin the last time he had been in this part of town would have been better than nothing.

But given the current situation and his woeful lack of an appropriate weapon, what could he do? How could he fight the Limehouse Golem – a two-ton, eight-foot tall ceramic and steel monster – *mano a automatono*?

What *could* Ulysses do other than flee? Besides, somewhere amongst the piles of rubble and pulverised pews lay the Rabbi, and for all Ulysses knew he was still alive. The least he could do for the wretched old man was to lead the monster away from the synagogue to somewhere it couldn't do any more harm.

He darted and weaved as he ran through the building, scampering between rows of still standing pews, around in front of the Holy of Holies, hearing the guttural, furnace-roars of the droid bellowing behind him – almost believing that he could feel the scorching heat of its breath on his back – and the splintering of wood being destroyed as it came after him. In this way, he led the automaton back to the gaping hole in the wall through which it had entered the synagogue.

The chill night air blowing into the fusty sanctuary caught in his lungs, giving him another adrenalin kick as he emerged into the street, trailing plaster dust, and came face to face with the crowd of passers-by who had collected around the hole in the wall.

Ulysses stumbled to a halt, momentarily startled at encountering the curious denizens of Limehouse. In his hurry to get away from the golem-droid, he hadn't stopped to think that there might be others around who had witnessed its attack.

The crowd were just as surprised to see Ulysses. Several of them gasped and one woman couldn't stop herself from screaming as he leapt through the sundered wall, dusted as white as a ghost.

His spectral appearance did have an advantageous side-effect, however. The people parted before him, backing away from the insane and wailing apparition as Ulysses screamed at them to move – not for his own benefit, but so that they might save themselves from what he knew was coming after him.

With a roar, the golem emerged from the synagogue, bringing down another landslide of bricks and rubble.

Women screamed. Men swore. People ran.

"The Rabbi's still in there!' Ulysses shouted as he barged his way through the crowd. "Help him!"

And then he felt the tide of people move with him suddenly, rather than against him. Terrified screams filled his ears, reverberating from the close-packed tenements and shop-fronts as the crowd encountered the Limehouse Golem in all its awful majesty.

People fled before the relentless charge of the lumbering droid. Some fell, but there was nothing Ulysses could do to help them. The best he could do – the *only* thing he could do – was to lead the golem as far away from where it might hurt anybody else, and then try to think of a way of halting its juggernaut charge.

Part of him wondered if the golem-droid would simply give up and return to wherever it came from, allowing Ulysses to track it to its lair, its mission to destroy the synagogue – he assumed that's what its primary objective had been – complete, just as eye-witnesses reported it had done after the fire had taken hold at the Palace Theatre.

But for some reason, the Limehouse Golem had seemed focused on getting to Ulysses.

He could understand it if the robot had been programmed to protect itself, except that Ulysses hadn't done so much as lob half a brick at the shambling droid. So what had he done to earn its enmity? Was it simply because he had got up and fled from the synagogue? Had its instructions been to neutralise anyone it met within?

But it was pointless to consider might-have-beens now. The fact of the matter was that the droid was after him, and apparently would not rest now until Ulysses had been neutralised with lethal force.

Then the screaming crowds were gone and Ulysses was alone on the street as he ducked into a side-alley, skirting the edge of a barn-like structure, the cries of panic fading into the distance.

The street ahead of him was thick with Smog. He must be close to the river, he thought, faltering before the roiling bank of oozing mist.

Ulysses would have liked to think that entering the Smog would hide him from the pursuing automaton, but he doubted that very much. He was sure it would make no difference to its artificial vision systems, whereas he would find it even harder to see where he was going. But if he turned back now he would immediately put himself in harm's way, coming face to face with his pursuer, and still without any means of defending himself.

And then the decision was made for him as the golem turned into the alleyway after him, one hand clawing at the corner of the street, the brickwork crumbling at its touch.

Ulysses decided that he had been lucky to survive his initial encounter with the golem. One squeeze of just one of those huge, steel-claw hands would crush a man's skull as if it was nothing more than a pineapple. If the mechanical monster hadn't caught him a glancing blow, he was sure that his whole ribcage would have been crushed, his lungs punctured in a dozen places. Yes, Ulysses thought, he had been lucky. But was his luck about to change?

He ran on between the mouldering warehouses, feet splashing through rust-coloured pools of standing water, ripples appearing in the puddles ahead of him, the golem's crashing locomotive motion sending tremors through the packed earth.

Ulysses heard the clattering of an Overground train overhead, the sound of it muffled by the Smog. He heard the ringing of a ship's bell out on the river and the mournful cry of a foghorn. And then he heard the lapping of water, and the hollow splash of wavelets from the wake of a boat's passing. His own running footsteps changed in tone and timbre as packed earth gave way to wooden boards.

Ulysses stumbled to a halt, and looked down over the edge of the jetty at the hungry black waters of the Thames. In his desperate flight through the mist he had almost run straight into the river. He had enjoyed a dip in the Thames not so long ago, and he wasn't in any hurry to repeat the experience.

He stood there, toes at the very edge of the jetty, panting for breath.

A slow smile spread across his face. Here might just be a way to fight the golem-droid and win. Raising himself to his full height, Ulysses turned to face the advancing droid.

The giant automaton gave voice to another metallic howl and Ulysses saw the fog burn away before the red-heat of its gaping cavernous maw, its peg-teeth like the crenulations of a castle's battlements, the beams of its eyes piercing the jaundiced yellow mist.

"Come on then!" he shouted, suddenly feeling supremely calm and confident. "Come and get me!"

As if it had been summoned to battle by his challenge, the golem-droid emerged fully from the mist, the oozing Smog parting before it as it charged towards him, its steel jaws open wide, ready to bite his head clean from his shoulders in a moment.

It stopped abruptly, sending a few loose stones splashing into the water. And there it waited, staring blankly ahead of it, the beams of its lantern eyes remaining fixed on Ulysses, splayed metal toes crushing the bricks of the riverbank.

"Come on!" the desperate dandy shouted again. "Come and get me! I'm right here! Come and get me, you bastard!"

The golem's head swung from left to right, like a dog sniffing the air, as if scanning the waterfront for something. But it remained where it was.

Ulysses Quicksilver and the Limehouse Golem stared each other in the eye, neither one moving, until the waiting became an unbearable moment of tension. And then, just when Ulysses thought he couldn't bear it for another second, the droid simply turned, lifting a foot as it rotated about its waist, ready to scrape its way back along the alleyway.

With a roar like a thousand fireworks going off at once, a black blur rocketed out of the Smog behind the droid and slammed into it with incredible force. The giant robot wobbled for a moment, unbalanced and then put its foot down again, only this time behind it, stepping onto the boards of the jetty.

Ulysses heard a series of clangs as something rained down blow after blow against its hardened carapace.

The monster howled in protest and raised its colossal fists, ready to smash its attacker into the riverbank.

With another screaming rocket roar, the black blur hurtled up into the sky until only the spurting flames of its engines were visible. But in that split second, Ulysses thought he caught a glimpse of something like a man-shaped bat.

Accompanied by an ominous creaking sound, Ulysses felt the structure of the jetty waver and drop an inch, and his attention snapped back to the reeling droid. The golem was trying to recover its footing but every movement it made, the jetty sank another inch into the mud of the riverbed.

Hearing the rocket-scream above him, Ulysses leapt into action, away from the edge of the pier, back towards the teetering droid and the riverbank. The speeding black blur slammed into the golem-droid, hitting the hulking automaton squarely between the shoulders.

Ulysses dodged a flailing arm, as the robot made a grab for its assailant, the muscles of his legs on fire. He felt the jetty subside beneath him, what had been a relatively flat surface suddenly dropping away, but he kept up the pace and, with one last herculean effort, flung himself bodily forwards as, with a splintering groan, the jetty gave way completely.

Ulysses landed on his front, knocking the air from his lungs against the riverbank, and rolled onto his back in time to see the gigantic robot drop into the water.

The golem-droid's entry into the Thames threw up a great plume of sludgy black water, showering Ulysses' already ruined suit with effluent from the fetid river, and splattering his face and hair with its oily residue. But at least he had been saved from another dunking in the city's largest sewage channel.

Ulysses slowly sat up and immediately felt the wall of the riverbank crumble beneath him. He had landed at the exact same spot as where the golem-droid had halted, its great weight and crushing toes weakening the mouldering wall. Heels kicking against the crumbling black earth of the collapsing riverbank, Ulysses scrabbled for purchase. But despite his efforts he was only rewarded with handfuls of mud and stones. And then he was sliding over the edge and there was nothing he could do to save himself.

His fall was abruptly halted by a strong hand which grasped him by his left wrist and pulled. Ulysses winced as his shoulder flared in pain, but he held on and felt nothing but relief as the dark stranger hauled him back up onto the waterfront.

"You want to take better care of yourself," came a strangely distorted voice.

Ulysses rolled onto his knees, gasping for air, and then staggered clumsily to his feet.

"Thank you," he managed through teeth-gritting pain and breathlessness, craning his head to properly see what his bat-like saviour really looked like.

But there was no-one there.

Ulysses turned his gaze back to the black waters of the Thames, but there was no sign of the Limehouse Golem either. It had sunk to the bottom of the befouled river without leaving any trace other than the choppy vortex amidst the roiling waves where it had entered the water and, of course, the trail of destruction that wound back through Limehouse to the synagogue. The droid had been swallowed up by the darkness, along with Spring-Heeled Jack.

CHAPTER NINE

The Personal Touch

Ulysses climbed down from the cab that was now infused with the mingled aromas of Thames effluent, black mud and plaster dust, pausing to pay the driver double to make up for the state he had left the vehicle in. He stepped onto the pavement outside his Mayfair residence and was surprised to see a young woman standing halfway up the steps to the front door, her stance – and the way she had pulled her shawl tight about her shoulders – suggesting that she had been waiting some time.

"I'm sorry," he said as he approached her, "do I know you?"

"Not in the Biblical sense. Not yet at any rate, and you're not likely to smelling like that neither," she replied in a broad cockney accent.

"I know that voice," Ulysses said, peering up into the girl's face, hidden beneath the curled tresses of her long black hair and the shawl. On seeing the dark tone of her skin, as smooth and warm as ebony, and catching the reflection of the gas-lamps in her chocolate-coloured eyes, his suspicions were instantly confirmed.

"It's Eliza, isn't it? I didn't recognise you with your clothes on."

"Hark at him! Mr Lah-di-dah. And I didn't recognise you all covered in shit and stinking like an open sewer. What happened to you anyway? Go for a midnight swim in the Thames, did you?"

Before Ulysses could think of a suitable riposte, the door opened.

"Good evening, sir," Nimrod said, affecting his most aloof and condescending tone. "I was going to ask how the evening's endeavours panned out but I think that considering your condition and present company" – at this the manservant gave the young whore a withering gaze – "it might be *indiscreet*."

"Well, it's been eventful, I'll grant you that," Ulysses admitted, giving his put-upon butler a weak smile, "but nothing a glass of cognac and a hot bath can't put right."

"Very good, sir. I shall run one for you now." The butler took a step back to allow Ulysses into the house. As he did so, he made a point of not looking the young woman in the eye.

"All in good time, old boy," Ulysses said, his weariness making way for his indefatigable curiosity. "All in good time. We have a visitor."

"Yes," the manservant said, drawing out the single syllable, "I know."

"He's had me waiting out here half the night!"

"I did ask this young woman" – Nimrod emphasised the word 'woman' as if to suggest that he could have chosen something much more demeaning – "if she would mind coming round to the tradesmen entrance in the morning, but she was most adamant."

"Tradesmen's entrance? Will you listen to him? Do I look like a tradesman?"

"Well you have chosen to work in the world's oldest profession," Nimrod threw back.

"Yes, yes, alright. That's enough," Ulysses said making a placating motion with his hands. Nimrod and Eliza both took a breath as if they were about to speak. "*Both* of you," Ulysses added more firmly. "Now perhaps we could resolve this matter inside and not on the street, if that's alright with you?"

Nimrod maintained his air of aloof indifference while the young woman glared at him, pouting in annoyance as Ulysses ushered her inside.

"You should have called me, sir." Nimrod's tone was chiding.

"I would have done, old chap, but my personal communicator was damaged during an encounter with the Limehouse Golem. And I do believe I ran into that terror of the streets Spring-Heeled Jack. The rogue who's been terrorising the whole of London."

"All in the course of one evening, sir? It *has* been an eventful night." Nimrod's nose wrinkled in disgust at the distinctive aroma of blocked drains that Ulysses trailed after him into the house. "I'll see about that bath now, sir, if you don't mind."

Nimrod raised a last disapproving eyebrow in Eliza's direction and then turned on his heel and made for the stairs.

"Alone at last," Ulysses said, giving the young woman a broad grin. It was not reciprocated.

"If you say so," Eliza replied, still looking none too impressed and making a point of keeping her distance.

"Ah, come on. Give a man a break, can't you?" Ulysses sighed. "If you had any idea what I've been through this evening, I think you might make the effort to be a little more sympathetic."

"You want sympathy? Fine, but it'll cost you," the whore replied cocking her head on one side and giving him a coy look. For the first time since he had given her the brush off back at the Queen of Hearts House of Sin, something of the made-up, skimpily-dressed prostitute emerged from beneath the loose fitting white blouse and long ochre skirt.

"Now that's more like it," Ulysses said, the smile returning to his face. "So, much as I would like to believe that you couldn't leave things as they were between us back at Her Majesty's Temple of Venus, tell me, what is it that really brings you to my door at this time of night?"

"The Queen sent me."

"I see. Then you have a message for me?"

"I do. She told me to tell you that the bugger went to Bethlehem,"

Eliza repeated, enunciating each word separately, as if recalling an exact phrase she had been forced to memorise. "Her Maj said you'd know what that meant."

"Indeed," Ulysses confirmed, eyes twinkling.

He turned, as if he was about to make his way after his manservant and then turned back to the girl, patting the pockets of his jacket as if looking for something, sending a cloud of dried plaster dust and caked on mud into the air amidst the priceless ormolu antiques.

Finding what he was looking for at last, he took out his wallet and, rifling through it, pulled out several notes. "There you are, my dear. For your trouble."

The young woman whipped the money from Ulysses' fingers before he had time to change his mind and stuffed the folded bills down the front of her blouse.

"Thank you, sir," she said, giving him a curtsey.

"You don't mind seeing yourself out, do you?" Ulysses said, nodding towards the door, "only I think that I'm long overdue this bath."

"'Course not. It's been a pleasure doing business with you, sir," Eliza fixed him with a long languid look from those cocoa brown eyes, looking up at him demurely from beneath long black lashes.

"Likewise," Ulysses said, suddenly enraptured by her alluring gaze.

"Right you are then," she said, with a suggestive giggle. "I'll be seeing you, Mr Quicksilver." And with that she skipped back down the hallway in the direction of the door.

Ulysses lay in the bath, eyes closed, savouring the sensation of knotted muscles relaxing in the camomile and lavender-scented water, the many cuts and bruises he had sustained – more than he had been aware of at the time – stinging all over his body.

He tested his damaged shoulder. It had been a recurring problem ever since he had first injured it during his aerial battle with the dastardly Black Mamba over the Himalaya Mountains. Perhaps he should get Doctor Doppelganger to replace that for him too.

He eased himself back under the bubbles, so that his whole body was submerged. Subconsciously he stroked at the leathery flesh of his chimpanzee arm. The feel of it reminded him once again that it was an alien thing and should never have been a part of him. But then, given the circumstances, Nimrod had been given little choice other than to let the insane, yet undeniably talented, vivisectionist work on him again. Under careful supervision from Ulysses' loyal manservant, Doktor Seziermesser had to put right the terrible wrong he had done him. But it wouldn't be long now before he waved goodbye to his ape's arm for good.

Ulysses closed his eyes and his body tensed as the memory of that grim, formaldehyde-scented operating theatre beneath the Umbridge Estate came to mind, and was soon joined by bloody visions of scalpel blades and a huge fanged maw. Ulysses remembering gagging at the smell of death and the iron tang of old man Haniver's blood.

The visage of the snarling Barghest beast, like some manifestation of hell, morphed into the twisted face of Josiah Umbridge, waving serpent-like atop its transplanted neck, and this in turn became the pitiful face of the human-cockroach, staring down at him from the corner of the ceiling inside the dead doctor's office, begging him to help.

Ulysses' eyes snapped open. The Queen of Hearts had come good again. So the victim of this unexpected transformation had been carted off to the Royal Bethlem Hospital in Lambeth, or Bedlam, as it was more commonly known. It made sense, for how could anybody who had undergone such a metamorphosis remain sane? He thought of Umbridge the industrialist again. The terminally-ill Umbridge was a perfect example.

So he now knew where he would be heading, first thing in the morning – or rather, as soon as he had broken the night's fast with a slap-up Full English; Mrs Prufrock's signature dish.

There were still other questions to be resolved though. He and the publicity-shy vigilante Spring-Heeled Jack might have seen off the Limehouse Golem, but he had yet to determine who had been behind its attacks. And then, concerning the cockroach-wretch again, what was it that had triggered his terrible transformation so quickly?

Other grotesque images came unbidden into his mind then; the dissolving fishy-features of the doomed Professor Galapagos, and the howling faces of the de-evolved apemen. A terrible thought wormed its way inside Ulysses' brain. Could it really be happening all over again?

The click of the bathroom door opening roused him from the depths of his deliberations, although he kept his weary eyes closed. Despite the horrors that haunted his dreams, sleep would not be long in coming this night – at least for what was left of it.

"Ah, Nimrod. Is that my night cap? Thank you. If you'd be so kind as to leave it on my bedside table and then feel free to turn in for the night yourself."

The unexpected touch of the hands on his shoulders sent a jolt of shock through his body and he rose within the bath suddenly, sending a wave of soapy water cascading over the side of the large cast iron tub.

But then the hands began to caress his aching shoulders, smooth fingertips applying skilful pressure, massaging the night's stresses and strains from his tired muscles.

Ulysses relaxed, sinking back into the warm water and letting out a sensuous groan of pleasure.

Slowly the hands slipped down past his neck to his chest, the fingers teasing at the hair they found there.

The first touch of warm lips against his neck was another crackling thrill of stimulating excitement, putting him into a heightened state of arousal.

"If you charge for sympathy, I hate to think what this is going to cost me," he murmured.

The lips were there at his neck again, and then the tingling sensation of breath on his ear.

"This one's on the house," Eliza whispered, sending ripples across the surface of the bath as she slipped her hands beneath the water.

ACT TWO

Strange Brew

February 1998

There is no medicine like hope, no incentive so great, and no tonic so powerful as expectation of something better tomorrow.

(Orison Swett Marden)

CHAPTER TEN

The Weather Machine

As the Prime Minister took the stand, the chattering hubbub of the gathered reporters hushed and the press conference came to order. Devlin Valentine looked out across the sea of expectant faces.

"Ladies and gentlemen of the press," he began. "Welcome."

The crowd of journalists, photographers and cameramen were silent now. This was what they had been waiting for, to hear Prime Minister Valentine speak.

"Thank you for waiting so patiently. As you know, we are all gathered here, this afternoon, for one very exciting reason; to hear about the greatest advancement the empire of Magna Britannia has seen since the Moon landings. It gives me very great pleasure to reveal to you all, for the first time, the one thing that is going to make more of a difference to the lives of Londoners – those faithful servants of the throne who labour night and day within our glorious capital to make this magnificent city what it is – than anything else since the invention of the steam engine."

With a grand sweep of his hand, Devlin Valentine drew the journalists' attention towards the cloth-draped easel on the far side of the dais.

"I give you – the *Jupiter Station*!" he announced triumphantly.

On cue an aide pulled the drape from the easel, revealing the framed print beneath. Beneath the glass was a magnificently detailed technical drawing of something that looked not unlike the Heisenberg-Steinmeyer Orbital Station – that remained in geo-stationary orbit many miles above Greenwich, monitoring interplanetary traffic entering and leaving Earth's atmosphere – and was shown from almost every conceivable angle.

The press conference's attendees expressed all the various responses Valentine had been hoping for, from gasps of amazement to excited murmurings that filled the room with a heightened sense of anticipation.

He surveyed the room again, letting those present enjoy their moment of wonder and enthusiastic discussion and smiled to himself.

The day-to-day business of running an empire was a ceaseless and thankless task – there was the ongoing Chinese situation to manage, that had taken a turn for the worse following recent events in the Pacific, there were rumours concerning the Russian royal family, some of the ancient Romanian bloodlines being said to be gaining undue influence over those in power there, and talk that Germany was mobilising for war again – but this was his pet project, the means by which he would make his enduring stamp upon the face of Londinium Maximum.

The development of the *Jupiter Station* was the one thing of which he was most proud, the one thing that he wanted more than anything, with which he would make his mark on the world stage, while at the same time being seen to have learnt from his predecessors' mistakes.

He didn't want another Darwinian Dawn on his hands. Magna Britannia was not about to fall into chaos and ruin on *his* watch; he would not allow it!

He turned to study the plans again. He never tired in taking pleasure from seeing them.

From side on, the *Jupiter Station* looked like a ring of metal and glass, in aspect not unlike Joseph Paxton's famous glasshouse constructions that had so influenced architectural developments throughout the twentieth century, from the Undersea habitation domes of cities like Pacifica and Atlantis City, to the first structures put up on Mars – their modular design making them ideal for the rapid construction of buildings of almost any size.

Protruding above and below this outer service ring was the near-spherical polyhedral structure of the central Hub. This housed the station's control room and helm. Projecting above and below these were shown various transmitters and aerials as well as other devices, inscrutable to the untrained eye.

From above and below, it could be seen that the whole thing was circular in form – its diameter at least as wide as two rugby pitches placed end to end – made up of an outer ring connected to the central Hub via six tubular arms – three of which were access corridors, the other three mainly structural in purpose but also carrying other services throughout the station, making it look not unlike a spoked wheel.

The plans on display now even included a cross section of the outer ring – that was shaped like a huge torus – as well as a detailed artist's impression of the interior of the control room.

As the excitable clamour began to die down, Devlin Valentine took control again, addressing those assembled, his voice reverberating from the speakers placed around the room.

"That's right, ladies and gentlemen, the *Jupiter Station* – The world's first Atmosphere Regulation and Stimulation Engine, or, if you prefer and as you and your colleagues have already dubbed it, the world's first Weather Machine!"

Valentine held his dramatic pause until he knew that he had the whole crowd before him on tenterhooks. Then he continued.

"The launch of the *Jupiter Station* will herald a new age of improved living and working conditions for the people of this fair city. For Londinium Maximum *is* a fair city, and I want all the nations of the world to see that too, and they will when the Smog lifts!"

There were more gasps from the packed room.

"Yes, you heard me correctly, ladies and gentlemen. When the *Jupiter Station* is operational, the toxic Smog that had blighted our city for the last 150 years will be gone at last. And with the Smog gone, public health will improve, infant mortality will drop, living conditions will become better for all, life expectancy will rise and we will enter the next century with a new, healthy and prosperous future ahead of us all.

"Magna Britannia will no longer just be the Workshop of the World. Our empire will also be the leading power safeguarding the future of Planet Earth.

"But that is not all the *Jupiter Station* will bring to this proud nation. We can look forward to picnics in the park on a balmy summer's day, perfect growing seasons for our horticulturists, farmers and allotment owners, and even white Christmases again."

At this last comment a ripple of polite laughter passed through the crowd. Devlin Valentine had to admit that he was enjoying himself; the press conference was all he had hoped it would be, and it gave him the opportunity to shine, to present himself, once more, as the Saviour of the Magna Britannia.

"And who do we have to thank for this opportunity to heal the wounds of the past, to put right the damage our forebears unwittingly caused this nation, in forging it into the greatest empire history has ever known? Just one man, ladies and gentlemen, one man. And that man is industrialist and philanthropist, Halcyon Beaufort-Monsoon.

"And we are particularly fortunate today, ladies and gentlemen, for Mr Beaufort-Monsoon is here with us today."

Valentine gestured towards the side of the dais as, from behind a potted aspidistra, an old man in a wheelchair was rolled onto the stage by his nurse.

"Ladies and Gentlemen, it gives me great pleasure to present to you, Mr Halcyon Beaufort-Monsoon!"

Devlin Valentine brought something of the circus showman to the role of Prime Minister. He was the P. T. Barnum of the world political stage, and it was a persona that had proved successful so far. He was, after all, Magna Britannia's new great hope, younger than any of his recent predecessors, a man with passion and verve and energy.

Valentine started the applause himself, clapping enthusiastically, while the rest of the room politely, though less-enthusiastically, followed suit.

The old man was hunched within his chair, a rug pulled up over his legs, peering at the crowd myopically through thick, bottle-bottom lensed glasses, wearing a suit that seemed two sizes too big for him.

His nurse, on the other hand, was a striking woman, attractive in a slightly severe way, her appearance made all the more sinister by the fact that she wore a red eye patch over her left eye with a white cross upon it, scars like the points of a pentacle emanating from underneath. Her luxuriant long hair, artificially coloured a deep-red, was bound into a bun on the back of her head. Her tight-fitting dress, tailored to the knee, was reminiscent of a nurse's uniform, in that it was crisp and white, but the high collar and low-cut front, with the obligatory red cross across her ample bosom, were reminiscent of another style of dress altogether.

A nurse like that to attend to your every whim, twenty-four hours a day, would almost be worth getting old for, Valentine thought.

He realised that he was staring when the nurse glared at him with her one remaining, heavily mascaraed eye. He immediately felt uncomfortable and looked away, swallowing sharply and feeling his cheeks flush. He was suddenly reminded of the old adage: *be careful what you wish for.*

Flustered for a moment, the Prime Minister turned back to the press conference. "Halcyon Beaufort-Monsoon, ladies and gentlemen," he repeated, unnecessarily.

The applause continued for half a minute more, the old man smiling weakly at the crowd and waving one liver-spotted hand at the gathered journalists and interested others.

"As you can see, ladies and gentlemen, Mr Beaufort-Monsoon is a little infirm and has asked that I speak to you today on his behalf. He, like me, wants to give something back to the city and, by extension, the empire that has given him so much. And his gift to this nation is the *Jupiter Station*.

"I see this as the beginning of a new era for our magnificent empire, one in which we shall learn from the lessons of the past and work together in the present to change our ways and build a better and brighter future for Magna Britannia and the rest of the world."

Valentine paused again to let his words sink in, to savour the grandiose triumph of the speech.

"Thank you very much," he said at last. "I will now take a few questions from the floor."

Hindsight was a wonderful thing Devlin Valentine considered after the press conference had finished. In hindsight, things had been going swimmingly up until he asked for questions from the floor. With hindsight he should have ended things without giving the ladies and gentlemen of the press a chance to throw in their two pennies worth.

Some of the questions had been just the sort of thing he would have expected.

"Is it true that we can expect to see your name in the New Year honours list, Mr Beaufort-Monsoon?"

"This is undoubtedly a remarkable scientific and technological achievement, Prime Minister. How does it feel to be involved with such a momentous project?"

"After the *Jupiter* project, what's next on your agenda?"

But then, as the novelty of the *Jupiter Station's* official unveiling began to wear off, some of the reporters grew more confident and the questions became trickier.

"Is it only London that is going to enjoy these new health benefits you speak of when civic leaders up and down the country are crying out for the means to rid their cities of pollution that is also the consequence of decades of rapacious industrialisation?"

"Lucy Gudrun, *Oxford Echo*. You say the launch of the *Jupiter Station* will lead to a new era of prosperity and better living conditions, but aren't you just passing London's problems on to someone else?"

"Isn't this just dealing with the symptoms of pollution and not the cause? Do you know what effect changing the weather over London might have on the rest of the country's weather patterns or even in the wider world beyond?"

"Isn't this just another publicity stunt performed by a London-centric government, happy to let others do all the work and take all the suffering?"

This had prompted Valentine's own biting response.

"I am well aware of the fact that London is only one city but it is the *capital* city and the one which had been most blighted by the industrial boom and, more recently, the race for space."

He was suddenly aware of all the cameras trained on him, including those of the MBBC. This was his big moment, when he would address the nation. Later that day, the highlights of this press conference would be broadcast along with the rest of the day's news, although whatever that was destined to be would pale into insignificance compared to his moment of rhetorical triumph.

"In fact we are so confident of the success of the *Jupiter* Station that as soon as the final preparations have been completed at our hangar on Hampstead Heath, the construction of another three platforms will begin, these bound for Birmingham, Newcastle and Manchester. Now ladies and gentlemen, if you will excuse me?"

"Prime Minister!"

"No, no more questions now, thank you."

"But Prime Minister –"

"Thank you, but that will be all. You will appreciate that there is much still to be done and that our great nation does not run itself, so, if you will excuse me..."

And with that, Prime Minister Devlin Valentine left the stage, followed by a procession of aides and bodyguards, as well as the old man and his nurse.

"It's been a genuine pleasure, not to say an honour to meet you at last," Valentine said, taking the old man's hand and shaking it vigorously. "Really it is. And I cannot begin to tell you how grateful I am... that you have seen fit to donate this magnificent Weather Machine of yours to our cause. I can assure you that you will not be forgotten when it comes to drawing up the next honours list. How do you like the sound of Sir Halcyon Beaufort-Monsoon?"

"Enough of the histrionics, Valentine," the old man said sharply, cutting him off in mid-flow.

"Oh," the Prime Minister said, somewhat wrong-footed by the old man's response. "But I meant every word."

"Yes, I'm sure you did."

"I was only being sincere –"

"That was a bold move, wasn't it?"

"I beg your pardon?" Valentine said, suddenly unsure of himself.

"Saying that you'll be rolling out the *Jupiter Station* programme to those other cities."

"As I said in there, if the *Jupiter Station* proves to be a success –"

"Which it will."

" –then I fully intend that we go into production with another three."

"And who'll be paying for those?"

"The taxpayer, naturally. It shouldn't be a problem, should it? I would have thought that you would be glad of the investment in your company after making such a public gift."

"Like I said, a bold move. Some might go so far as to say... rash."

"But you're forgetting the old adage, 'fortune favours the bold'."

"And you're forgetting the saying 'act in haste and repent at your leisure.'"

"This is an issue that I am fully committed to," Valentine said earnestly. "I am determined to heal the ills of our society and I plan to start with London and then look to what needs to be done elsewhere."

"But some areas are beyond saving. Take Seven Dials for example," Beaufort-Monsoon said with a callous smile.

"Then we must choose our battles wisely."

"You are an ambitious man, Valentine. Let us hope that your ambition does not turn to hubris."

Devlin Valentine wasn't usually the kind of man to be lost for words, but at that moment he was. He didn't know how to respond to the old man's warning. Was Beaufort-Monsoon merely giving him the benefit of his wisdom, the accumulation of age, or had it been something altogether more sinister. Valentine couldn't shake the feeling that it had almost sounded like a threat.

Not knowing how to respond to the old man's words, he didn't.

"Just assure me that the *Jupiter Station* will be ready for Launch Day."

"Oh, do not worry, Prime Minister. You'll have your moment of glory. You will have your... ascension day."

And with that, the old man's nurse turned his chair and wheeled Halcyon Beaufort-Monsoon away, leaving Devlin Valentine feeling skin-crawlingly uncomfortable, wondering what manner of deal he had made.

CHAPTER ELEVEN

Bedlam

Lying in bed beside the girl, his dressing gown wrapped around him loosely, his chin resting on the black leather that hid his incongruous chimpanzee's hand, Ulysses Quicksilver stared at her, a relaxed smile on his face. He had been awake for a good ten minutes and had spent most of that time watching Eliza as she slept.

He certainly hadn't been expecting this when he had returned home, filthy and bedraggled after his adventures on the streets of the East End. And he certainly hadn't expected it for a tense moment as he rose from his bath for her to discover that his left arm was not all it should be. She had given a startled gasp and taken a step back as she took in the alien limb.

But then to give her her due, she had soon got over the shock and had drawn close to him again, shaking off her own clothes, her hands continuing to caress his body, finding him responsive to her ample charms.

Ulysses supposed that she had seen all sorts of things in her line of work, and had to deal with all manner of strange requests, even perversions, from all manner of obese and aging clients. With so a handsome man in his mid to late thirties with a toned body, even if he did have one rather peculiar arm, his good points outweighed the bad.

But then, reminded of his malformity, Ulysses had felt uncomfortable and unappealing. It had been Eliza who suggested he cover it up again, and so he had donned the gown, even going so far as to pull on the glove over his left hand.

From that point on, as soon as the primate's hand was covered up, he had relaxed, easing himself back into the moment. Besides, it had turned out that Eliza had thrilled to the feel of the leather stroking her skin.

He combed his other hand through the sweep of his hair, mercifully clean now after the bath he had enjoyed – in more ways than one – the night before.

Once again her took in the shapely mound the girl's buttocks gave to the sheet partially draped over her, the small of her back, the crease in the taut skin of her back following the line of her spine up her shoulders, along her slender arms and down to the subtle suggestion of the swell of her breasts beneath her. He savoured the delicate line of her swan-like neck, the fall of her dark hair across her back and the wonderful coffee-coloured pigment of her skin.

Eliza stretched and turned to face him but her eyes remained closed.

His smile turning into a devilish grin, he sat up suddenly, the sheet falling from him. Pulling it from Eliza as well, exposing her perfectly formed bottom, he gave the sleeping prostitute's rump a playful slap.

"Come on, old girl!" Ulysses announced, jumping out of bed, "up and at 'em!"

The whore opened bleary eyes and grunted something incomprehensible.

"Wakey wakey, rise and shine!"

The girl stretched again and made a small, soft sound like a little moan of pleasure.

"What time is it?" she mumbled, still without opening her eyes.

"Eleven o'clock, or there abouts."

Eliza's eyes snapped open. "Eleven? You're kidding me!"

"No, I'm not. Don't forget we went to bed late, and got to sleep even later," he grinned again, flashing the girl his pearly whites. "You were obviously tired."

"Oh, you know," she said, closing her eyes again. "Run off my feet all day, I was."

"Off your feet all day, eh? I can well imagine, Eliza Do-Alot."

"I mean, chasing after dandy ne'er-do-wells like you, Mr Lah-di-dah," she countered, blinking drowsily.

"Come on, there's no time for sleeping now."

"Oh yes?" Eliza said suddenly coquettish, sliding a hand under Ulysses' gown. "Feeling frisky, are we?"

"No, no time for that either," Ulysses said, swinging himself out of bed and away from the whore's caresses before circumstances beyond his control changed his mind. "But maybe later."

"So what's the big hurry?"

"We're going out," Ulysses said, striding across the bedroom to the walk-in wardrobe on the other side.

"Out? Where?" Eliza called after him, rolling onto her side, the dark nipples of her breasts stiffening as they were exposed to the air.

"If I were to tell you, that would spoil the surprise." Ulysses popped his head round the door of the wardrobe, unable to wipe the schoolboy grin off his face as he savoured the sight of her pert, young breasts. "Now tell me, my dear. Have you ever ridden in a Rolls Royce?"

Ulysses opened the car door and climbed out, offering Eliza a hand and helping the young prostitute out of the Silver Phantom after him. "Thank you, Nimrod," he said, poking his head back inside the car. "You coming in, old chap?"

"I won't, if you don't mind," his manservant replied, regarding Ulysses through the rear view mirror. He hadn't said a word the whole way there, as they drove from Mayfair to Southwark.

"Suit yourself. Wait here then." Ulysses sighed as he closed the door.

He knew Nimrod didn't approve of his new lady friend, but then he never really approved of any woman Ulysses got to know on an intimate level. Eliza was a step too far, as far as the faithful family retainer was concerned.

Ulysses paused, looking up at the classical facade of the hospital, with its pillared entrance and domed cupola roof.

"So, what is this place?" his companion asked him, in her oh-so-blunt and to the point way.

"This, my dear 'Liza, is Bethlehem Royal Hospital for the mentally deranged."

"You must be bloody joking! You've brought me to Bedlam? What is this, are you going to have me locked up or something?"

Eliza began to shuffle away from Ulysses.

"What for? Moral insanity?"

Eliza looked at him aghast. "You're not getting me in there, I'll tell you that for nothing!"

"But aren't you even a little bit curious?"

"What? What do you mean?" Eliza pouted, watching him warily now.

"Aren't you at all interested in the meaning of the message you so graciously passed on to me, last night? 'The bugger went to Bethlehem'?"

"None of my business, is it? It wasn't for me was it?"

"You don't fool me," Ulysses grinned. "You're an intelligent girl, I can see that. I can see it in your eyes. Part of you can't wait to get through those gates and have a look inside."

Eliza's expression of wary apprehension didn't waver but she did dare a glance at the facade of the hospital.

"Looks like a palace," she said distantly.

Ulysses looked again at the structure that lay beyond the wrought iron gates, so like the British Museum in design – but then the two buildings were both the work of the architect brothers Sydney and Robert Smirke.

"Yes. Yes, I suppose it does."

He turned to watch Eliza's confused reaction to the palatial lunatic asylum as she tried to resolve in her mind how such a magnificent building could be so synonymous with Hell.

"Magnificent, isn't it?"

"Yeah, I suppose so," she agreed grudgingly. "I'm just finding it hard to imagine how such a wonderful building can be the home of madmen." She turned from her study of the hospital to return Ulysses' gaze and smiled coquettishly again. "But then all those other magnificent London buildings, like the Houses of Parliament, are full of madmen too, aren't they?"

Ulysses couldn't suppress his laughter. "Yes, I suppose they are. Yes indeed."

He offered her his arm.

"Shall we, my dear Eliza?"

She hesitated for only a second. "Yes, why not, Ulysses," she said, affecting an upper class accent.

And arm-in-arm they admitted themselves to the hospital grounds.

Bedlam; well it deserved that name.

From as early as the fourteenth century there had been a Bethlehem Hospital. This first incarnation of one of London's grimmest institutions lay outside the city walls as Bishopsgate, where Liverpool Street Station stood now. Its remit was to care for 'distracted' patients, as the insane had been euphemistically described at the time, and although it bore the name 'hospital', it was little better than a prison. Those same 'distracted' patients were kept under lock and key, supposedly to keep them out of harm's way. But the truth of the matter was that they were detained there to keep them out of the way of all right-minded people. If the inmates made a nuisance of themselves – which, being mentally ill and denied their freedom, many of them invariably did – they were whipped or even ducked, in an effort to teach them a lesson, that many were incapable of ever learning.

The asylum was moved from its Bishopsgate site, in the latter half of the seventeenth century, to more palatial buildings at Moorfields, designed by the noted polymath, Sir Robert Hooke. Bedlam became one of the sights of London, its inmates exhibited as if they were specimens in a human zoo, to be jeered at by the visitors, who paid well for the privilege.

It was common practice during the eighteenth and early nineteenth centuries to visit Bedlam, as it was by then commonly known. Visitors paid good money to view the freaks of the 'show of Bethlehem', laughing at their unseemly sexual antics and spectating at outbreaks of violence among certain inmates, as if they were enjoying a boxing bout.

However, the hospital and its 'unfortunates', as the inmates were referred to, moved again to Bedlam's current location at St George's Fields in Southwark, a new building constructed in the classical style, after the Moorfields hospital fell into disrepair to the point that it was deemed unsafe for anyone, even the insane, to remain there. It was this incarnation of the hospital that Ulysses and Eliza now approached.

The dandy's crown-authorised ID got the two of them past the doorman-drudge and into the office of one Professor Rufus Brundle, the hospital's current director.

"A cockroach, you say? Yes, I know the man of whom you speak," the professor said, regarding Ulysses over steepled fingers.

Eliza was staring at Ulysses too, in disbelief. "A bleeding cockroach?"

"Now, now, my dear," Ulysses chided under his breath, barely opening his mouth and never once taking his eyes from the bespectacled man behind the desk, the size of which only seemed to emphasise how small he was. "You are here as an observer only. Let the professor speak."

"The patient of which you speak was brought here ten days ago."

"By whom?"

"An unmarked ambulance delivered the patient at around seven on the evening of the third."

"How did you feel when you got to examine the patient for yourself?"

"The same as every other time."

"Can you enlighten me further?"

"Surprise at first, of course, but not so much now. Pity, curiosity, a morbid fascination, a desire to understand what such an extreme physical change can do to a mind."

"Who signed the admission papers?"

"The ambulance driver."

Ulysses thoughts suddenly strayed from the Professor's office to another office, hidden deep below the capital and a big man on the other side of a huge desk, but this one in scale with his imposing height, bearing and commanding presence.

"Where is the patient now?"

"With the others."

"What others?"

"I thought you knew," Professor Brundle said as he led them through the east wing of the hospital, Ulysses striding along the corridors after the scampering professor, Eliza trotting to keep up with him. "Aren't you from the government?"

"How many of them are there?" Ulysses asked breathlessly, as he worked hard to keep up.

"Well, the patient of whom you speak was the twelfth to date."

"They've been twelve cases like this?" Ulysses said, unable to hide his astonishment.

"Yes, from right across the capital. Although only ten, that I know of, have survived," Professor Bundle threw him a confused look. "You are from Department Q, aren't you?"

"Department Q? How do you know about that?"

"Because it is the Department that gave me my commission."

They continued on through the next few galleries in an awkward silence until Ulysses dared ask, "Where are we going now?"

"To our – how shall I put this? – our 'special wing'?"

"Really?"

"The hospital is arranged over four floors, divided into two wings, separating the male and female residents, but there is another wing where our..." Brundle paused, as if searching for the most tactful way of expressing himself. "Where our noisier inmates are housed."

"And where is this 'special' wing?" Ulysses asked, as they continued at a brisk trot through the hospital, thinking that, at this pace, they'd soon being leaving again through the back door.

"It's in the basement."

Professor Brundle stopped at a painted iron door beside which stood a white-uniformed brawny orderly. He flashed his ID at the attendant and the shaven-headed man unlocked the door revealing a staircase descending into the musty depths.

As Ulysses passed the burly orderly, he noticed the baton tucked into the man's trousers, and the knuckledusters he was distractedly playing with in one hand. He couldn't help wondering whether all orderlies were so brutally equipped or whether it was just those set to guard Bedlam's more 'special' patients.

"I should warn you," Brundle said as he led the way down into the lantern-lit gloom, "that what you are about to see is not for the faint-hearted." He addressed this last comment to Eliza in particular.

"What do you say, my dear?" Ulysses asked. "Would you prefer to wait for us here, or do you think your constitution is hardy enough to continue our little tour of this establishment?"

Eliza shot him a sarcastic smile. "What do you think?"

"Very well, but don't say Professor Brundle didn't warn you. Lead on, Professor, lead on.'"

It was the smell of the place that unsettled Ulysses more than the green-lit darkness or the echoing drips of condensation or even the bare brick and stone walls of the basement galleries that made them seem more like a dungeon than a hospital wing.

It was a rancid, ammonia smell, like an abominable mix of urine and bile.

The basement was hot and humid and Ulysses could already feel his shirt clinging to his back. Eliza looked uncomfortable also, although whether that was down to the humidity or the nature or the place itself, he couldn't be sure.

"Here they are," Brundle said, unlocking the last iron-barred gate. "Keep to the right hand wall and don't – whatever you do – don't put your hands through the bars."

Taking a deep breath of the muggy air, Ulysses stepped over the threshold and entered the final stretch of passageway. Even though he had already come face to face with the human cockroach at the Daedalus Clinic, his mouth still dropped open in incredulous amazement. What he saw took him back to the moment when Wormwood's zeppelin had crashed into the newly-reconstructed Crystal Palace and all that had followed.

But it was Eliza who vocalised how both of them felt as she saw Bedlam's 'special' patients for the first time.

"Bloody hell! I think I'm going to be sick." But, to her credit, Ulysses thought, she wasn't.

"Your 'man', as it were, is in the first cell, here on the left."

"Who is he?" Ulysses asked as he stared at the giant cockroach scuttling over the slimy bricks of the wall on the other side of the cell.

"Who is he?" Brundle repeated, sounding surprised. "For all intents and purposes what you see before you is a six-foot long cockroach."

"Alright then, who *was* he?"

The professor opened the file he had brought with him. "Francis Bird, steam-velocipede manufacturer."

"What about his mind? Sorry, *it's* mind? Is that still human?"

"It's hard to say. That's what I'm trying to determine."

Ulysses took another step along the passageway and recoiled as he came face to face with an enormous praying mantis. It watched him with its head cocked to one side, its long upper limbs moving with jerky, staccato movements as if it were conducting an orchestra.

"What about these others?" he asked, morbidly fascinated by the mutated inmates and yet, at the same time, feeling his gorge rise as he watched something that looked like an over-grown bluebottle vomit on a platter of mouldering fruit, before sucking up the resulting syrupy soup through its proboscis. "Do they have anything in common?"

Professor Brundle raised his eyebrows at Ulysses and pushed his spectacles back up the bridge of his nose. "That praying mantis there was a wealthy banker until a week ago. Fifty-three years old. Wife, three children, lived in Kensington with a weekend bolt-hole somewhere in the Cotswolds. The fluke-worm in that tank over there was a chimney sweep from Deptford.

"There are men and women of all ages, all socio-economic backgrounds and ethnicity – Chinese, Irish, English, Polish. There's even one – that weevil down there at the far end – that we suspect to have been a child of no more than ten when the change took place. And no two have regressed to the same biological antecedent."

"I beg your pardon."

"Each of them is a different species, and not one of them is of the genus *homo sapiens* anymore."

Professor Brundle turned to him and suddenly Ulysses saw how fatigued and defeated he looked. "You ask if they have anything in common. The only thing they have in common is that they are all here and that they are all like this."

"Fascinating," Ulysses breathed, observing the cockroach again.

"The Department want me to find a connection and basically work out what's going on."

"And we shall, Professor," Ulysses said, never once taking his eyes from the hypnotic dance of the cockroach. "Together, we shall."

CHAPTER TWELVE

The Crucible

"Ladies and gentlemen," the Host began, rising from his chair. "I call this meeting of the Crucible to order."

An expectant hush descended over the chamber as all eyes turned to the Host.

"Let me begin by thanking you all for coming, at such short notice."

"Like we had any choice," one man remarked, muttering loudly to himself. Several of the others shuffled uncomfortably within their chairs at the man's disrespectful attitude. Many of them shot anxious glances at the imposing figures standing in the shadows behind the Host, as if hoping that this dissent wouldn't put them all out of favour.

"You always have a choice, Mr Galsworthy."

The unhappy Galsworthy glowered at the Host, but his angry frown was met with nothing less than a patient smile. The smile silenced him more effectively than any retort could have done.

The Host played the part of the civilised gentleman perfectly, from his slicked back black hair, exuding the strong smell of lacquer, to his smoking jacket. Every word that came from his lips was enunciated within an inch of its life, in his slightly shrill, patronising tone.

"Now, to business," the Host announced, surveying those seated around the circular table.

There were thirteen places arranged around the table. Each of the society's members – with two exceptions – sat at one, the Host occupying the thirteenth position. At the centre of the table stood a smouldering brazier, with the symbolic crucible being heated upon it suffusing the air with plumes of incense smoke.

Two of the seats at the table were unoccupied. As the Host took in each member in turn, his sparkling, jewel-like eyes lingered on those two empty spaces, his smiling expression heavy with meaning.

"Where are Mandrake and Seziermesser?" another of those present asked anxiously.

"I am sure you are all wondering why you have been asked to attend this meeting." The Host said, ignoring the man's question.

"Yes, why have we been summoned here like common criminals, made to feel like disobedient children?" Galsworthy asked, his dander up.

"Perhaps because that is precisely how the Alchemist feels some of you have been behaving."

"I have never been spoken to like this in my life!" Galsworthy fumed, rising from his seat. "I will not sit here and be subjected to this!"

"Very well then," the Host said coolly, "remain standing."

"Why, I've never been so insulted in all my life! I don't know who you think you are, but I have had enough and I want out of this meeting and this damned society of yours!"

"Oh, not of mine, Mr Galsworthy, as well you know. I am merely the Alchemist's eyes and ears at these meetings, and my companions," he indicated the hulking creatures lurking in the shadows behind him, "are the instruments of his will.

"So sit down, Mr Galsworthy, and listen to what the Alchemist wants you to hear. And after that we can discuss your membership of the Crucible if you so wish."

A rumbling growl came from out of the shadows behind the Host's chair. Shoulders sagging, not daring to take his eyes off the things standing statue-like in the gloom behind the Host, Galsworthy sat.

"Someone has been careless." The Host quickly scanned the room. It was as if he fully expected their guilt would betray them, whoever it was that had been 'careless.'

"In what way 'careless'?" another man asked.

"Every one of you here present has made use of the Proteus serum that has been so generously provided by the Alchemist."

Some of those in attendance nodded in agreement.

"At a price," Galsworthy muttered under his breath, unable to help himself.

"Of course at a price," the Host railed, "but the Alchemist's offer to each of you has been more than generous. The price you have had to pay has only ever been a fraction of the money each of you could make from your own enterprises. What the Proteus serum can help you achieve in your own specialised fields is priceless!"

"That is why each of us chose to join this secret society though, is it not?" It was Doctor Pandora Doppelganger who found the confidence to speak up now.

"I must correct you on that point, Doctor Doppelganger. None of you *chose* to join. You were all *invited* to join. You were chosen by the Alchemist that he might help each of you achieve all that you could only have dreamt of, without the aid of the Proteus serum.

"But, as I was saying, some of you have betrayed that trust and have acted carelessly."

He pointed at the empty seat to his left. "First there was Mr Mandrake, hoist, we suspect, by his own petard. Then there was Herr Seziermesser, the over-reaching schemes of his and his accomplice Josiah Umbridge resulting in their mutually assured destruction."

"I read about that in the paper. I thought Umbridge died in a house fire at his place up in Yorkshire," a woman said, looking confused.

The Host gave her a withering look, as a parent might a naive child.

"Oh, I see," the woman muttered, breaking eye contact with the Host in embarrassment.

"And as we step closer to the dawn of the twenty-first century, already this year we have people changing into insects all over the city. The unfortunate incident that occurred at the Daedalus Clinic has only served to highlight how big a problem this has become."

Nobody said anything, but all shot uncertain glances at their fellow Crucible members.

"The Alchemist is unhappy with how some of you are using his serum. He is concerned that you risk discovery in pursuit of your individual passions. And if one of you is discovered you endanger us all.

"The very anonymity of the Crucible is being threatened. One of you, present here today, has been careless and such haphazard practices cannot go unchecked."

As he spoke, the Host's eyes picked them all out in turn. He finished speaking, his eyes on the scientist Galsworthy.

"What? What is this? What are you saying? That I'm the one responsible for this current state of affairs?"

"I do not remember making any specific accusations, Mr Galsworthy."

"Then why are you looking at me?"

"What is the matter? What is troubling you, Mr Galsworthy? A guilty conscience perhaps?"

"Look here. This has *nothing* to do with me, do you hear me, you pompous arse? *Nothing!* And I don't see you accusing anyone else."

"Correct, but then I am not accusing anyone, Mr Galsworthy. I am merely relaying the Alchemist's concerns to you, that is all."

"How do you know it's not..." Galsworthy glanced at the faces of his fellow confederates. "Her?" he said at last, finally settling on Doctor Doppelganger.

"How dare you?" The woman spat, the harshness of her words accentuated by her German accent. "I have never been so insulted! Do you have any idea what it is I even do?"

Galsworthy withered in the face of Doctor Doppelganger's wrath.

"Experimental cloning, isn't it, doctor?" the Host said calmly.

"How...? How do you know about that?"

"The same way I know that Madame Wong" – here the Host indicated the middle-aged Oriental woman sitting beside Galsworthy – "is using Proteus to cultivate a new strain of opium poppy, that will grow faster and yield even more of the Empire's favourite recreational narcotic."

Madame Wong gasped, looked like she was about to speak, as she threw suspicious glances around the table at the other Crucible members, and then thought better of it.

"And that Dr Gallowglass is using it to help him in his research into rare disorders of the blood. Just to pick a couple of examples at random."

"That is top secret information," Dr Gallowglass railed.

"Do not delude yourselves for a moment; the Alchemist knows about all your dirty little secrets. And in this matter, none of you is above suspicion, Doctor Doppelganger," the Host said, suddenly turning to stare at the German doctor again. "And none of you has climbed so high that you cannot be brought crashing down into ignominy."

"So, if no-one is willing to tell the truth, what are you going to do?" Madame Wong asked, daring to speak up for the first time.

"Yes, how do you propose to resolve this situation?" said Dr Gallowglass.

"I don't," the Host said flatly.

"Then why bring us here?" Galsworthy fumed.

"The Alchemist has a proposition for you all." The Host's mouth smiled, but his eyes did not.

"What sort of a proposition?" Madame Wong asked suspiciously, eyes narrowing.

"A gesture of goodwill if you will, on your part."

"Go on," someone else said.

The Host turned and beckoned one of the figures forward from the shadows. A number of those around the table of a less hardy spirit could not contain their surprise and disgust.

Up until that point the brute's grotesque appearance had been hidden from them by the heavy shadows, but now they could all see the thing with ugly clarity.

The brute was naked from the waist up, his exposed, hairless, flesh a ghastly, pallid white, looking like kneaded clay riddled with knots of purple veins. It seemed likely that he had been a large man to begin with, but something had been done to him that had swollen his physique beyond what would be considered normal, so that he now stood eight feet tall, on swollen legs like tree trunks. His left arm was huge, bulging muscles and tendons writhing beneath the leathery skin, but his right-arm was of another magnitude altogether.

The meat of the limb was shot through with steel cables and pieces of tarnished metal that looked like they had been bolted directly to his skeleton beneath. All of this augmentation served to turn his arm into something like a robotic limb or crane hoist. The additional muscle and machinery needed for the brute to be able to even move the arm meant that his right shoulder was a mound of flesh and metal that had become merged with the right-hand side of his head.

But the artificial enhancements did not end there. His mouth had been transformed by the insertion of a pair of huge steel jaws and a red light flashed atop a gleaming metal box that had been clamped onto the brute's neck.

As the gathered members of the Crucible stared at the monster in appalled fascination, the brute lifted a doctor's bag from the floor and dropped it onto the table in front of the Host, the contents clattering inside.

"To put it simply," the Host said, the others still unable to tear their eyes from the monster standing slack-faced at his side, "the Alchemist agrees to keep providing you with what you need."

Unlocking the clasp on the bag he opened it, revealing the unremarkable stoppered glass bottles inside. He removed them one by one – there were ten in all – and then extracted a bundle of documents from a pocket and slid a sheaf of papers across the table to each of those present.

Curiosity getting the better of them, the Crucible members began to read the documents.

"However, you will notice that the payments you each make to the Alchemist in appreciation of his help with your work has just gone up," the Host continued.

"But this is daylight robbery!" Galsworthy announced, his face reddening. "I can't afford this."

"You are being provided with a unique compound with unique properties, which will allow you to accomplish great things that you never could have without its aid."

"This is blackmail!" Dr Gallowglass protested.

"The Alchemist prefers to think of it as an insurance policy."

"But this is too much!" Doctor Doppelganger said, adding her opinion to the discussion.

"The Alchemist understands that this arrangement might not suit all of you. This is, after all, a very exclusive group. If you feel that it is not for you – Mr Galsworthy, Doctor Doppelganger – then feel free to walk away, no hard feelings."

"Damn right I'm walking away! I'm not paying this!" Galsworthy announced. "I want out!"

"Very good, Mr Galsworthy. That is your choice. Please, one of my colleagues will show you to the door."

Galsworthy got up from his chair, suddenly looking less than certain that this was what he really wanted to do.

"Please, Mr Galsworthy, this way," the Host said, gesturing to a different door to the one by which they had entered. The hulking brute moved with lumbering steps to accompany him.

Galsworthy threw his fellow Crucible members one last uncertain glance, but they were all too busy digesting the new terms of their agreements with the Alchemist.

Cautiously, Galsworthy accompanied the heavy to the door. The brute, the expression on its face still showing no hint of any emotion or even suggesting that it possessed anything more than a rudimentary intelligence, let Galsworthy through the door before squeezing through after him.

The door closed quietly behind them.

Silence descended over the room. A second later it was shattered by a scream that turned bowels to water and blood to ice.

The expressions of horror on the faces of those present left no doubt as to what had just happened but no-one dared say anything, although Madame Wong stifled a cry within her handkerchief.

The Host smiled at them in the same dead-eyed way as before. With a look that could have been described as nothing more than innocent enquiry, the Host gazed at each of the remaining nine in turn.

"Would anyone else like out?"

CHAPTER THIRTEEN

On Entomology

"That's the last of them," Professor Brundle said, placing another bundle of case notes on the reading table. "That's the twelfth."

"So," mused Ulysses distractedly, still skimming a crime report from the last sheaf of papers the professor had placed before him, "that's my friend the cockroach, is it?"

"That's it. That brings you right up to date with all the recorded cases that have ended up here."

"It says here," Eliza suddenly piped up from the other side of the table, "that this Delaque girl turned into a giant moth. I means, how's that even possible?"

"Hmm?" Ulysses looked up slowly from the case notes. "Wait a minute, you can read?"

"I'm not just a pretty face, you know."

"I know that," Ulysses said, adding under his breath, "you have a great arse too."

Eliza glanced up from her scouring of the papers and gave the dandy a cheeky grin.

"What was that?" Professor Brundle asked, from his seat at the end of the reading table.

"Sorry, Professor?" Ulysses bluffed, "did you say something?"

"What? No. I thought you did."

"Oh, probably just thinking aloud. You know what it's like."

The three of them were ensconced within the hospital library. It truly was the most incredible space, made all the more remarkable when one considered that it was located within a hospital for the insane. It was lighter and airier than the professor's rather stifling study, and gave them more space in which to spread out all the papers associated with the metamorphosis cases, as Professor Brundle referred to them.

"So this is him," Ulysses said, opening the file Brundle had just presented to him. "This is our roach problem." He looked down at the photograph of a gaunt-faced man in his mid-thirties – not so different in age to Ulysses himself – taken, it appeared, specifically to go with his Daedalus Clinic notes. "This is Francis Bird."

Thumbing through the file, Ulysses pulled out a photograph. Eliza, peering over his shoulder, recoiled in disgust. "Eugh!"

"That's right. The metamorphosis appears to have occurred incredibly quickly." Professor Brundle said.

"The cockroach shows no signs of de-evolving any further?"

"No, none at all. Its new genetic form appears to be stable."

Ulysses was quiet again for a moment, one hand to his mouth as his eyes darted from one pile of open case notes to another.

"And this one," he said, pointing at a photograph of an elderly woman – whom he took to be a grandmother, surrounded, as she was, by her extensive brood – grinning through a mouth missing half its teeth, "was the first?"

"No. Not quite."

"But didn't you say that Ethel Partridge, widowed butcher's wife, seventy-four," Ulysses said, now reading from the case notes in front of him, "was the first to be admitted?"

"Yes, but she wasn't the first victim."

Ulysses fixed the professor with an intense, penetrating stare. "So who was, and what happened to them?"

"This was couriered to me here yesterday," Brundle said, picking up a carefully folded pile of hole-punched paper. "This is a printout of the police report that concerns one Carlton Smithers, late of Bedford Park, Chiswick."

"I've heard of him," Ulysses said, his face suddenly lighting up. "I read about the incident in *The Times* last week. Butchered the whole family with a kitchen knife, before turning it on himself, didn't he?"

"Then you only read the official version as put out by the Department."

"Do tell."

"Well, as you know, the story that made it into the papers had him going on a homicidal rampage, killing his wife, their five children, the children's governess, the maid and the cook, all with a kitchen knife, after he lost the family fortune when stock in the Carcharadon Shipping Line sank overnight –"

"Rather like their flagship," Ulysses couldn't help adding under his breath.

"– murdering them as a mercy to save them from a life of ignominy and destitution. But that version of events was nothing more than a hasty cover-up."

"So what really happened?" Eliza asked.

"Oh, Smithers did it, there's no doubt about that, but it wasn't the Smithers who friends and neighbours all described as a loving husband and father, and a good God-fearing Christian who went to church every Sunday with always a good word for everyone. No, it was Smithers the giant deathwatch beetle.

"The neighbours heard a commotion and called the police. When they finally managed to force entry to the house, and found the monstrous beetle feeding on the corpse of Mrs Smithers, a terrified constable shot it six times."

"I see," Ulysses said slowly, considering the enormity of this revelation.

"No one had any idea it *was* Smithers until they found his clothes shredded in his study, and not a drop of blood on them."

"Did anyone examine the body, I mean the beetle?"

"Yes. I've got the results of the autopsy here. But it doesn't tell me anything I didn't already know."

"So then there's Ethel Partridge who is now enjoying a new lease of life as an overgrown praying mantis," Ulysses said, "and third, and the second to end up in Bedlam, was little Tommy, the boot black boy."

"That's right."

"Little Tommy Shoeshine," Ulysses repeated sadly, picking up a slim file. There was no photograph of Tommy as he had been, aged ten, before he turned into a spider with a six foot leg span.

"Used to escape to the gin shops after his shift, before the beadle would drag him back to the Old Montague Street Workhouse. He was discovered vomiting into the bins out the back of the Sisters of Mercy of Orphanage. He had already started to change by the time a doctor was called."

"And he's now a web-spinning arachnid."

Ulysses picked up the printout relating to the Smithers case and made space for it at one end of the table. Next to that he placed the case notes relating to Ethel Partridge and then made space for the report on Tommy Kettlewell beside them.

"So, number four?" Ulysses said.

"Clementine Umbel," Professor Brundle answered.

"Ah yes, the Covent Garden flower seller." Eliza passed Ulysses the correct set of notes.

"The next to be admitted was Joyce Hurst," Brundle said, placing the relevant bundle of papers next to the flower seller's file.

"The board school teacher from St John's Wood."

"That's right. Fifty-two, divorced, no children."

"Number six is Alexander Kostov, the Russian immigrant omnibus driver from Bethnal Green," Ulysses recalled from his perusal of the case notes. "Believed to be in his early thirties."

"Transformation occurred whilst he was at the wheel of the Number Sixty-Three, unsurprisingly causing the 'bus to crash. Captured because the giant wasp he had become was trapped within the wreckage."

"And then we have Magnus Tyson, the banker." Ulysses took the proffered file from Eliza. "Sixty-two, onto his fourth wife – more than thirty years his junior – heart condition – I'm not surprised! – found shut inside the pantry of his Bloomsbury townhouse, now a giant termite."

The banker's case file joined the arrangement on the reading table.

"You're going to run out of room," Eliza remarked, looking at how much space the ordered papers were taking up.

"No we're not," Ulysses countered, skipping past her and dragging another table from between the bookshelves and joining it to the one they were already using. "Number eight!" he demanded excitedly. He was buzzing now, possessed of a passion for answers that gave him a veritable adrenalin kick.

"That would be Marie Delaque," Brundle offered.

Eliza handed him the girl's file. "Poor little Marie Delaque," she said, genuine sadness in her eyes. "She's almost better off now."

It was a pitiful case indeed. From what Professor Brundle had been able to find out, her mother had been a French immigrant who ended up working as a prostitute at the Wapping docks. A gin-addict, she had died when Marie was eight years old. Five years later, when the girl's body turned into a cocoon from which emerged a huge moth with a five-foot wingspan, she too was one of Madame Bovary's girls, having followed in her mother's footsteps, joining the oldest profession in the world.

Noting Eliza's reaction, Ulysses wondered how she really felt about her own position in the world. There was no doubt that she was very good at her job, and he had thought that she had enjoyed the time they had spent together, but she was obviously an intelligent girl. Was the oldest profession in the world really the only one that she could have opted for?

"The ninth was the opium addict," Brundle thumbed open the relevant file. "Charlie Chin, mid-twenties, half-Chinese, from Stockton." He placed the slim file beside Marie's on the tabletop. "Now deceased."

"What happened to him?" Ulysses asked, his features knotted

in concentration as he desperately tried to find a link between the cases.

"Found on the Circle Overground Line. Looked like he had thrown himself in front of a train, probably when he realised he was starting to transform."

"Or he was in an opium-addled daze and didn't know what he was doing," Ulysses pointed out.

Ulysses Quicksilver might have given in to various temptations during his life, and opium might be the most widely used recreational narcotic in the empire, but the dandy and the drug had never been friends.

"And then there was Sergeant Reginald Hazlitt," he said, "late of her Majesty's Metropolitan Police, due to retire next month. Such a rum do!" Ulysses took the penultimate document from Eliza and placed it next to the sergeant's file. "Followed by 'Old' Bailey, the tramp from the Shadwell doss house. And that brings us back to Francis Bird, my friend from the clinic."

Ulysses stared at the ordered row of documents laid across the two tables in front of them.

"If things continue at this rate, the Department's not going to be able to keep a lid on these spontaneous transformations for much longer."

"No," Brundle agreed, "and these are only the ones we know about."

"What do you mean?"

"The Orientals have a curse that goes: may you live in interesting times. And the times we are living in could certainly be described as interesting. Not all people readily report every strange or untoward thing that happens to them. There might be other cases with these poor wretches being cared for by friends and family. Think of the stigma with which people still treat cases of physical and mental handicap, even within families. And then multiply that shame by one hundred when your cousin Wendy turns into a cockroach one night."

"It's possible, I suppose."

"If there's one thing I know, it's people," Professor Brundle pointed out. "And then there must be the cases that have escaped detection because no-one was there to witness the transformation. We only know of 'Old' Bailey because he was staying at the Shadwell Street Refuge when he changed. There could be countless others living on the streets, metamorphosing in the same way but then escaping into the sewers or the flooded Underground network and no one would ever know."

"You have a point, professor. You have a point."

He was quiet again for a few moments as he surveyed the piles of paperwork.

"So we've got Smithers in Chiswick – forty-three, businessman, Ethel Partridge in Spittalfields – seventy-four, grandmother, Tommy Kettlewell, aged ten, Clementine Umbel, nineteen, Covent Garden, a Russian immigrant, an opium fiend, a mangy old tramp..." Ulysses suddenly broke off from his musings. "But what's the connection?" he snarled, throwing up his hands in frustration. "They had nothing in common before this... before these transformations began, how many weeks ago?"

"Three. There is nothing in their backgrounds I can find linking them, no." Brundle said. "Age, socio-economic class, location; nothing. You've seen that for yourself."

"And there's nothing else? You're sure of it? Forget their backgrounds, is there anything else – anything at all?"

"Well," the professor began, "there was the same deposit present in the blood samples I took."

"What?"

"Something in the blood, a biological or chemical residue of some kind."

"And this is in all of them?"

"Yes."

"Why didn't you mention this before?"

"I didn't think it important," Brundle muttered.

"Not important? How could it be not important?"

"I just thought it was a by-product of the transformation process itself. Look, I'm a psychologist, not a blood specialist."

"So they do have something in common," Ulysses mused, "other than the unfortunate condition they now share!"

"But what is it? What can it be? Do you know?"

"I'm not a doctor of any description."

"But it sounds as if you might have some idea what it could be."

"An inkling, perhaps. Nothing more. Without having seen a lab report on a sample myself, I wouldn't like to comment. But I could have a pretty good guess."

"Then what is it, man?"

"Look, it's too soon to say. I don't want to lay my cards on the table just yet. I'd rather let someone else take a look first," he confessed. The professor looked suddenly deflated. "But I've seen something like this, yes. But it didn't work in quite the same way, didn't have quite the same effect."

"You're talking about the Wormwood Affair, aren't you? You're talking about the apemen."

"You know about that?"

"I know that the escapees from the high security wing of the Tower weren't just the usual inmates, if that's what you mean. I know that something happened to them – had been done to them – before they engaged in their attack on the jubilee celebrations and that it wasn't just a mass breakout."

"But that was what was reported in the press."

"Come now, Mr Quicksilver."

"I've got it!" Ulysses suddenly announced. "I thought it was a product of their transformation, or a rogue quality that had somehow made them susceptible to this transformation. But what if it was something they had taken, somehow, ingested perhaps, and it was that which triggered the change? Some unknown agent."

"And how are we going to find out what this agent is?" the professor asked.

"Don't worry," Ulysses said, giving the fretting professor a broad smile. "I know someone who can help."

CHAPTER FOURTEEN

Fleet of Foot

Blip. Blip. Blip.

Thomas Sanctuary looked up.

Blip. Blip. Blip. The sound came again, and this time he saw the corresponding oscilloscope ripple on the Babbage engine's screen.

Hurriedly placing the soldering iron back in its cradle, he jumped up and ran over to the desk, turning the cogitator's monitoring screen round so that he could see it more clearly.

Blip. Blip. Blip.

The transmitter he had managed to place on the Limehouse Golem, the last time he had encountered it, was working a treat.

The droid behind the attacks attributed to the mythical Jewish vengeance-seeker, the same automaton that he had sent to the bottom of the Thames, was still operational and was on the move.

Excitedly he flicked a switch on his Babbage engine console

and the waveform disappeared to be replaced by a map of the capital made entirely from glowing green lines. At the heart of the map appeared a pulsing red dot.

Using the engine's rotational arrow targeter, Thomas zoomed in on the area surrounding the winking dot. It was in the East End. Somewhere close to the river. He zoomed in. The emerald lines now came into crystal sharpness, and Thomas could immediately see that he was looking at the Southwark stretch of the Thames. He watched the progress of the dot for a moment, now shown to be travelling along the river itself. Somehow Thomas doubted that it had been hoisted onto a barge but rather suspected that the droid was slowly making its way west along the river, back upstream, following the path of the river-bed, trudging through the mud and sucking silt. Its circuits were obviously well-shielded to survive the unkind attentions of Old Father Thames.

And as long as the golem was operational, Thomas knew that his purpose was to hunt it down and put it out of action for good.

He estimated that, once he was fully kitted up, it would only take him a matter of minutes – perhaps quarter of an hour at most – to catch up with the droid again. He was glad that he had refuelled the jetpack as soon as he had risen that morning.

Thomas glanced at what he had been working on before the transmitter-signal receiver alerted him to the fact that the golem was on the move again. Work on the second, improved model jetpack would have to be put on hold for the time being.

He looked out of the window. It was still daylight. He had not taken his masked vigilante persona out during the day before. Doing so brought a whole new element of risk to the venture, and a new buzz of excitement too.

Thomas ran the length of the room to where the tailor's mannequin stood silhouetted against the conservatory windows and the amber sky of the Smog-laden late afternoon beyond, his eyes meeting the lifeless goggle-eyes of the suit, pleased with the improvements he had made, from the armoured plates and gauntlets to the powerful jetpack and ominous bat-winged cape folded behind it.

The addition of the body armour made the suit – and by extension Thomas – an even more imposing and threatening presence, giving him some of the more sinister aspects of the knights of old. This, combined with the image of the bat, that reminded the primitive, ancestor-inherited part of the psyche why people once feared the dark, worked to turn Thomas Sanctuary into Spring-Heeled Jack, as the press had christened his alter- ego. A sinister symbol of justice not bound by the law – a dark knight.

I really will have to think of a better name for myself, Thomas pondered as he strapped on the whole shebang once again.

The Man of Iron, he thought. *The Bat-wing... the Night Wing... Bat Knight...*

None of them seemed quite right, somehow.

"I've got it!" he shouted as he buckled the last leather strap on his suit. 'The Armoured Avenger!'

With boots and gloves on, the jetpack securely strapped to his back and the cape in place over that, Thomas picked up his fob watch. But it was a very different timepiece to the one he had been given by his father to commemorate his eighteenth birthday. He had made a few modifications to it since the last time he had been out.

It was now attached to a leather strap which went around his left wrist, which also bore a tiny radio receiver and battery. With clumsy gloved fingers, Thomas opened the outer casing of the watch. He checked the time and then turned the knob at the side. The watch face rotated to reveal a tiny screen, bearing the same glowing green lines and pulsing red dot as his Babbage engine monitor was currently displaying.

Having confirmed that the receiver attached to his watch was working and, having strapped it securely to his wrist, Thomas pulled the mask down over his face. A bloodstained vision of the world swam into being, the conservatory and the cityscape beyond appearing again as though through an angry red mist.

Thomas checked his utility belt, with its multiple compartments – that he had also added to since his last run in with the Limehouse Golem – especially the dispenser in which he kept a store of his own magnetic micro-mines.

He stepped towards the conservatory doors, calling to mind the previous two occasions he had gone up against the golem. The first time, outside the Palace Theatre in Limehouse, the golem had been the outright winner. The second time, he had triumphed, or at least had thought so, but he had only managed to achieve what he had with the help of the dandy adventurer and renowned agent of the throne, Ulysses Quicksilver.

Tonight the Armoured Avenger would face the Limehouse Golem once more in battle, and he was determined that it would be their final confrontation.

A flicker of traitorous doubt crossed his mind, sending a shiver of uncertainty down his spine and into the pit of his stomach.

Could he do it alone?

Perhaps it was time to admit that he needed an accomplice on his mission, and Ulysses Quicksilver seemed like the ideal candidate.

But how to get hold of him?

His gaze returned to the Babbage unit and memories of hacking cogitator systems the world over came flooding back.

Ulysses Quicksilver trotted back along the pavement from the decrepit home-cum-laboratory to where the Mark IV Rolls Royce Silver Phantom was pulled up at the side of the road.

When he had left his two companions – the butler and the whore – to make his house call on the cantankerous Dr Methuselah, Eliza had been sat in the back, not looking wholly at ease with her surroundings, grumpily staring out of the passenger window at passers-by, pointedly not talking to his manservant, while Nimrod had been sat at the wheel, staring out of the windscreen making a point of not speaking to the young harlot.

But now, as he approached the car he could see that the two of them were obviously in the midst of a heated debate.

Ulysses took a deep breath, preparing himself for the worst.

And it was then that his personal communicator bleeped from inside his jacket pocket.

"And you lost the signal here, you say?" Ulysses asked, peering into the gloom of the tunnel mouth that yawned before them.

A stench like the miasma that permeated the tunnels he and Nimrod had explored beneath the streets of Southwark in their search for the missing evolutionary biologist Professor Ignatius Galapagos gusted out in noxious waves.

"It must be because it's gone underground," the masked figure beside him said, his voice sounding deep and gravelly through the speaker-grille of the mask.

Ulysses looked back over his shoulder at his companions.

For the time being, his manservant appeared to be more unsettled by the presence of the vigilante in their midst than that of the prostitute – although his attitude was somewhat hypocritical, considering the sort of things he had got up to in his youth. Ulysses noted with a grimace that Eliza was also occupied with the new addition to the group, although, seeing the simpering smile on her face, for a different reason altogether.

The four unlikely looking accomplices were standing at the bottom of the culvert that lay between the river wall and the built-up ground beneath the north bank footing of Blackfriars Bridge. Grey water slopped and slapped on the stone piers at the entrance to the subterranean waterway only a few inches from where they stood, the percussion of the water amplified by the weird acoustics of the culvert.

Above them, the sky was, as ever, shrouded by the Smog, bringing a premature dusk to the city and deepening the shadows within the culvert.

The river mouth was barred by a rusted iron gate, or at least it had been. Something had recently wrenched the bars apart.

The fetid waters of the Fleet churned and boiled from the stone-vaulted tunnel, disgorging into the Thames, turning the water in the culvert into churning white eddies, stained a tarry yellow and covered in a stinking brown foam.

The Thames wasn't London's only son. As the settlement beside the greater river grew over the centuries, the Roman garrison town eventually became the teeming metropolis of today. Like Cronos, father of the Greek Gods, the hungry city swallowed many of its children. The Effra, the Walbrook and the Fleet had all been built over, over the years, becoming absorbed into the city's ever-expanding sewer system.

Ulysses grimaced, his nose wrinkling as the tunnel exhaled another gagging breath of fetid sewer air.

"So," he said, unenthusiastically, "if we're going to find our golem, we have to go in there?"

"That's about the measure of it," the masked figure said.

Ulysses looked the caped figure looming at his shoulder up and down. "Your rocket-pack's not going to do you much good down there, is it?"

"You're not exactly dressed for a jaunt into London's sewers either, are you?"

Ulysses looked down at his tweed suit and spats. He supposed he could return home and change into something more suitable but that would take time, and he suspected that time was a luxury they didn't have. He didn't want to risk losing the golem again.

"Someone has to keep Savile Row in business, don't they?" he said, smiling weakly. He could see that another visit to his tailor would be necessary once this was all cleared up. "Can you even see anything through those?" Ulysses tapped a knuckle against the red lenses of Jack's goggles.

"Perfectly, thank you."

"Right then," Ulysses said, slapping the shaft of his cane into his gloved left hand, "what are we waiting for?"

He looked from the gaping void of the miasmic darkness, back over his shoulder to where his indefatigable manservant stood at the ready, torch in hand.

"Come on, Nimrod, once more unto the breach and all that."

"Yes, sir," Nimrod replied, his icy manner giving no indication as to how he felt about entering London's stygian underworld again. Ulysses doubted he was overjoyed at the prospect, considering how ill their last sojourn into Bazalgette's sewer system had made the two of them.

"After you, then," Ulysses said to the suited vigilante.

Being carefully not to snag his equipment on any of the twisted bars, Spring-Heeled Jack stepped into the darkness below Blackfriars Bridge.

"What about me?" Eliza said, hands indignantly on hips.

"What about you?" Nimrod asked coldly.

"Get yourself back home now," Ulysses told her. "I'll be in touch again when this is all over. Promise."

"You don't get rid of me that easily!" the harlot huffed, full to over-flowing with self-importance.

"I beg your pardon?"

"I said, I'm coming with you! You don't think you can lead me on like this, giving me a glimpse into this other world of yours, and then not expect me to want to know more, do you?"

"This is no place for a lady," the vigilante pointed out.

"Well I ain't no lady, sunshine," Eliza remarked, and with that, hauled up her skirts, tucking them into the waistband to improvise herself a pair of pantaloons, "so it looks like you're stuck with me."

She barged past Nimrod, pushed past Ulysses and strode into the tunnel.

The motley band followed the course of the Fleet upstream as it continued its subterranean journey beneath the city. What little light penetrated the fog and the arched entrance of the tunnel soon gave out and they had to resort to using torches to proceed further, although the vigilante seemed to be able to find his way easily enough without the aid of any light, and led the way through the stygian murk.

The penetrating beams of Ulysses' and Nimrod's torches, revealed a dank underworld, the span of the broad-arched roof of the tunnel hung with ragged moisture-loving plants and mosses while other forms of vegetation thrived where the nutrient rich sewer water splashed the narrow ledge they were following.

They continued in this way – listening to the constant noise of the churning river, the splash of the water and the drip of moisture from the ceiling, feeling splashes of the fetid liquid landing on the exposed skin of their hands and faces – for what Ulysses judged to be a good hour. Their sweeping torch beam sent rats scurrying to their holes in the crumbling brick walls, their excited squeaking reverberating from their nests. They saw albino slugs oozing over beds of ferns and a myriad sparkling spider-webs covering cracks in the brickwork of the tunnel.

But what they didn't see, or hear was any sign of the Limehouse Golem.

Eliza gave a squeal when a rat dropped from a hole in the ceiling onto her head, before she managed to bat it away, and contributed the occasional unhelpful comment, usually regarding the smell, but in general they continued without anything in the way of conversation passing between them.

At last the tunnel they were following opened out into a large domed chamber, where the waterway merged with the other tunnels of the sewage system. More twisted passageways branched off from this, while the course of the Fleet continued on the other side. Here the ledge they had been following became a wider walkway.

"So, which way now?" Ulysses asked the vigilante.

Spring-Heeled Jack stopped and looked down at a device strapped to his wrist. "I've got a signal!" he declared, the excitement in his voice obvious even despite the distortion of the mask.

Pain flared in Ulysses' head.

"Look out!" he gasped, as he doubled up in agony.

Nimrod immediately went for his gun, while Spring-Heeled Jack tensed, fists raised.

As his brainstorm passed, Ulysses fumbled for his sword-cane, pulling the blade free of its scabbard, but by then they were already surrounded.

The figures seemed to melt out of the shadows, the tunnel walls and even the ceiling. None of them carried lanterns and none were wearing anything like the vigilante's dark-vision goggles, but somehow they had managed to surround Ulysses' motley crew without any trouble and only Ulysses' heightened sixth sense had given them away.

They wore dark, loose-fitting clothes and in their hands they carried staves, nun-chucks and metal throwing stars, and looked like they knew how to use them. Each of them had the same, disturbingly mutated appearance. Eliza screamed. Their faces were distinctly rat-like, from the warped rodent snouts right down to protruding chisel teeth and twitching whiskers.

"Don't try anything funny!" one of the rat-men squeaked. "We got you surrounded. You're coming with us!"

CHAPTER FIFTEEN

King Rat

Ulysses wondered if he should have at least tried to fight back against the rat-men, as the four of them were led, at knife-point, deeper into the warren of sewer tunnels that branched off from the central chamber. But, he tried to convince himself, such an action would have been futile. They had been wildly outnumbered and were disadvantaged by the poor visibility. Even Spring-Heeled Jack, who could supposedly see as well in the dark as in daylight, hadn't seen them coming. Not only were they stealthy and agile, they also looked like they knew what they were doing with the weapons they were carrying.

For a moment it had looked like the vigilante had been ready to bring the fight to the Oriental rat-men but Ulysses had stayed his hand. And although Nimrod had already unholstered his pistol, Ulysses knew that his manservant wouldn't do anything without receiving a direct command from him first.

There had been another opportunity when the four of them had been thrown into some stinking cellar for what had felt like hours before being moved again, cold having numbed them to the bone. But it still hadn't seemed like the right thing to do at the time.

At the back of Ulysses' mind was the fact that the rat-men hadn't actually laid a blow against them yet. There might have been some rough handling as they had been disarmed and shoved along the sewer tunnels but, if they had wanted to, they could have cut them down in the dark without any warning. As long as the rat-men wanted them alive, there was still a chance they could get themselves out of this nightmare relatively unscathed.

The fact that their captors were rat-men hadn't really surprised Ulysses, not after what he had seen back at Bedlam.

He had a pretty good idea of what could have wrought such a change upon them though he had not seen such a partial physical change since the night of the jubilee. Then, however, the apemen had lost all semblance of their former humanity, whereas these rodent-like individuals patently still had their faculties intact.

And they were totally unlike the insects of Bedlam. As far as anyone could tell, those poor wretches had transformed without retaining any of their humanity. At least, that's what Ulysses hoped. To still have your wits about you while trapped within an insect's body, that didn't bear thinking about.

Suddenly the line stumbled to a halt. Ulysses looked up. The rat-men, who could see perfectly well in the dark without the need for any artificial light, had confiscated their torches along with their weapons. But Ulysses could still see a little through the gloom, thanks to mats of phosphorescent moss clinging to the walls of the tunnel – enough to discern one silhouette from another, and at least enough to see that the leader of the pack had stopped to sniff the air.

Ulysses wouldn't have gone so far as to say that he had become used to the smell – the tunnel still stank like a thousand unflushed privies – but at least he had managed to resist the urge to gag for some time. However, he would not have wanted to take such a strong sniff himself, for fear of losing his stomach contents.

And if their captors shared more than merely a physical resemblance to the species *rattus rattus*, then their sense of smell must be just as finely tuned. If that was the case, how could they bear to inhale the noxious aromas produced by the festering filth of the city's millions of inhabitants?

The leader suddenly gave a shrill squeak which was briefly taken up by the rest of his pack. And then they were moving again, at double quick time. What was it that the rat-man had smelt, Ulysses wondered? What were they so afraid of?

And so they continued, Spring-Heeled Jack at the front of the line, surrounded by four of the lithely-built rat-men. Then came Eliza, being escorted by another group of four armed rats, which the dandy couldn't help thinking was a little excessive. Then came Ulysses and, lastly Nimrod, both being accompanied in the same manner as the other two.

Ulysses realised that he could see Jack and Eliza more clearly and he realised that there was, quite literally, a light at the end of the tunnel.

A miasma-fogged caged electric light illuminated a heavily-rusted circular iron hatchway ahead of them.

The rat-men led them across a rusted iron footbridge and up to the door. A turn of a wheel opened the hatch with a grating squeal of protesting hinges and star-bright yellow light spilled out into the tunnel, making all of them – especially the vigilante – recoil, momentarily blinded.

Ulysses felt the blunt end of a staff in the small of his back and he, like the rest of them, moved forwards into the light-filled chamber.

There could be no mistaking the influence the designers had been going for when they had set to work down here. The chamber was decked out to look like the Palace of the Jade Emperor himself. Large golden lion-dogs and dragon sculptures lined the room, forming an avenue of imposing figures with great red silk banners hung between them from the vaulted ceiling.

The throne room might be completely different in appearance to the sewer at the heart of which it had remained hidden from the world above, Ulysses thought, but it still smelt like one and no amount of jasmine incense was going to be able to change that.

Fretwork lanterns bathed the opulent chamber in their warm glow, the light sparkling from the gleaming golden statues and the impressive throne that stood at the far end of the room.

It was towards this that the rat-men led their prisoners, bowing and fawning like penitent supplicants as they approached the dais upon which the throne stood, and the less than imposing figure seated upon it. Ulysses remained standing tall, as did his three companions.

"Bow before the Emperor," the leader of the rat-men hissed at him, obviously appalled by his disrespectful attitude.

"I bow before no man," Ulysses said, staring into the impassive, wrinkled mask of the wizened creature dwarfed by the immense throne.

"Lao Shen is no man!" the rat-leader hissed again, shooting Ulysses a sidelong glance, whilst making sure he kept his head bowed and his eyes averted from the figure, almost smothered by his voluminous robes. "Lao Shen is a god!"

"What, him?" Ulysses mocked. "I see no god. I only see King Rat!"

"How dare you speak this way before Lao Shen!" the figure upon the throne suddenly shrieked. "You will *kneel!*"

With that, one of the rat-men struck Ulysses across the back of the legs, forcing him to his knees. Gritting his teeth against the pain, Ulysses stared defiantly up at the king of the rat-men.

He was small, even by the standards of the Chinese, but he commanded the reverent awe of those who had sworn fealty to him nonetheless. There was not a single patch of skin on his body that was not a collection of sagging wrinkles. His flesh was the colour of a thousand year-old egg and his long moustaches trailed down past the sides of his mouth, to rest upon his robe. The fabric was red silk, like the opulent chamber's drapes and banners, and seemed to be too big for him. Upon his head he wore a Mandarin's hat.

The others were forced to their knees behind Ulysses.

"Do we really want to be antagonising our captors?" Nimrod whispered at his shoulder.

"If we want some answers, yes."

"Silence!" the King Rat shrieked. "What are you doing here?"

Ulysses looked from the unusually quiet Eliza to his manservant and then, to the impassive expressionless mask of the vigilante, before answering: "I think you'll find that it was your men – if you can call them that – who brought us here."

"I know who you are," Spring-Heeled Jack suddenly spoke up, his amplified voice echoing around the room.

"You do?" Ulysses replied, surprised.

"Yeah, and me," Eliza gasped in sudden recognition. "I've seen his face all around London, specially the East End."

Ulysses was truly amazed. He still had no idea who they were dealing with, beyond the fact that he must be one of a dozen Chinese opium lords who vied to capture their own slice of London's criminal underworld activities, now that the Black Mamba and Uriah Wormwood were both out of the picture.

"It's that vaudeville magician." Eliza said.

"Lao Shen," Jack added.

"You are not fit to speak the name of Lao Shen" the rat-leader uttered, in appalled embarrassment.

"The one with the show at the Palace Theatre?" Ulysses said.

"That's the one!"

"You know of the attack on our theatre?" the magician said, eyes narrowing further in dark suspicion. "Was it you? Were you behind it?"

"I had nothing to do with it, I can assure you –" Ulysses began.

"I was there," Jack interrupted.

"It was you? You started the blaze?"

"No, but I know what did. It was the Limehouse Golem."

"But who sent it to kill us?" Lao Shen said.

"I don't know."

"But that's why we're here," Ulysses added, "or at least that's why we entered this stinking rat's lair of yours. We're hunting the golem."

"But why? What is it to you?"

"Why? Because its actions look likely to start a turf war the likes of which..." He broke off, feeling dizzy. "The likes of which..."

Ulysses closed his eyes against the pulsing pain throbbing in his temples with every beat of his heart. A regular *thud-thud-thud*, like approaching heavy footsteps, like the pounding of a steam-hammer, like the banging of a fist on a door.

He opened his eyes blearily and muttered something only half-heard by those around him.

"What did he say? Tell me!" the Chinese magician demanded.

"He said, 'It's coming'," Nimrod said.

The resounding clang of ceramic-covered iron against iron came a moment later. Startled, the rat-men moved away from their captives and turned to face the heavy iron hatchway.

Ulysses turned with the others, towards the door.

And then, with a rending of steel and the crack of stonework, the hatch was wrenched free of its mountings in a welter of brick dust.

As the dust cleared, bathed in the yellow light of the throne room, stood the golem. Eight feet tall and hunched, ready for battle, eye-lamps blazing white hot, a guttural metallic rumble emanating from its furnace heart.

The golem-droid's head rotated about its neck joint, its eye-beams sweeping the throne room as the rat-men leapt into action.

To Ulysses, it seemed as though it stopped when its gaze fell on him, something like recognition whirred and clicked inside its mechanical brain. And then, with a roar like a steam engine at full power, it came for him.

CHAPTER SIXTEEN

Bad Medicine

The seemingly unstoppable golem crashed its way towards Ulysses, pulling great silk streamers down behind it, as its huge shoulders snagged the drapes and dragged them after it.

The dandy was aware of the rat-men taking the fight to the golem, but not one of them, despite all their martial skill and weaponry, even made so much as a mark on the relentless automaton's ceramic shell. He was vaguely aware of the clangs of their blades striking its great bulk, the thuds of staves against its steam-powered limbs, but most strident of all he heard the terrible high-pitched squealing screams of the rat-men as the golem batted them aside or tore their bodies apart, sending sprays of blood splattering across the opulent decor of the throne room.

Ulysses reached inside his jacket, aware of how filthy the tweed had become during his recent travails. He felt the handle of his pistol against the palm of his hand and pulled it free, even though he already knew that it was a futile effort. He had seen what the golem-droid could do and a few bullets weren't going to stop it, but he had to do something.

He could hear Eliza's screams, the shouts of his manservant and the ricocheting pangs of bullets. Bullets fired from his own gun, bouncing off the kiln-hardened carapace of the metallic monster.

And then, out of the corner of his eye, he saw Spring-Heeled Jack pelting towards him, saw the vigilante throw something in the direction of the golem, before piling into Ulysses, sending him reeling out of the path of the steaming automaton.

As Ulysses hit the ground, the wind was knocked from his lungs and an explosion shook the subterranean chamber. In the close confines of the throne room, he felt as much as heard the blast, tensing in agony as the concussive shockwaves rendered him momentarily deaf.

All he could now hear was the desperate pounding of his pulse.

He felt strong hands on him, trying to haul him up. He looked up to see the grim visage of Spring-Heeled Jack looking down at him through his expressionless red goggle-eyes. He knew that the masked vigilante was trying to tell him something, because he could hear the humming rhythm of speech beneath the throbbing rush of blood in his head, but he couldn't actually make out any of the individual words.

He went with the vigilante, still reeling from the shock of the explosion, taking shambling steps, his balance unsteady.

Ulysses shot desperate glances over his shoulder, to see what had become of the golem. He saw a cloud of gunpowder-grey smoke, the sharp, acrid smell of cordite hot in his nostrils. Through the coiling wreaths of explosive discharge, he saw the golem-droid stumbling backwards, its ceramic carapace scorched black but still in one piece and still on its feet. The hulking automaton stumbled into a golden dragon sculpture, shattering it into just so much gold-painted matchwood.

For a moment, he wondered, hope against hope, if the vigilante's explosive devices had really done the trick. But then, his hopes were dashed as the colossal machine found its footing again, gyroscopic stabilisers helping it to regain its balance.

The baleful beams of its eyes fell on the shrunken figure cowering upon the dragon throne. There was a puff of pink smoke then that enveloped the chair and its occupant. When the cerise cloud cleared, the shrivelled figure of the Chinese magician had vanished. Something like a bellow of frustration escaped the maw of the droid.

Ulysses turned to Spring-Heeled Jack. "We have to get out of here!"

This time, when Spring-Heeled Jack spoke, Ulysses was just able to make out what he said. "I can stop it."

"With those explosives of yours? They barely scratched the surface. Come on, we have to get everyone out, lose the golem in the sewers." He froze as the beams of the droid's eyes fell on him. "Now, do as I say and run!"

With the golem stomping after him, Ulysses ran to where Eliza was turning circles in confusion, panic and fear in her eyes, his manservant trying to drag the girl to safety.

"Get out!" Ulysses yelled, stumbling over the broken body of one of the Rat King's warriors, grabbing Eliza by the arm.

"Sir!" Nimrod shouted and tossed something towards him. Ulysses instinctively snatched his sword-cane out of the air.

"Good show, old boy! Now, let's get out of here!"

Nimrod turned and made for the hole in the far wall. Ulysses caught glimpses of the encumbered vigilante running at his side, the black wings of his cape flapping behind him.

The golem had described a circuitous route through the Rat King's throne room, causing untold damage but also leaving the exit clear for the few that had survived its crazed assault. Those rat-men who had not dared take on the unstoppable juggernaut, with Lao Shen – their leader and inspiration – gone, had already fled.

Ulysses threw himself through the hole, brick dust, shaken loose by the crashing footfalls of the two-ton monster, showering down over him and Eliza.

The four of them sprinted along the footpath that ran along beside the steadily moving channel of the sewer. Nimrod's swaying torch beam revealed the way ahead, giving Ulysses glimpses of mossy walls crumbling red orange bricks and the impenetrable shadows of the tunnel's snaking depths.

And then the way ahead became much clearer, illuminated by the penetrating beams of the golem-droid's eyes, as the automaton exploded from the ruin of the Rat King's subterranean lair, sending a fresh cascade of broken bricks splashing into the effluent stream.

The escapees ran on, the crash and splash of the golem's footfalls drowning out the desperate beating of their own panicked hearts. The droid's bellowing engine roars rebounded from the curving tunnel walls, creating a painful cacophony of noise, that Ulysses could now hear all too well.

The great domed space, like a partially drowned cathedral, emerged from the gloom ahead of them. Somehow Nimrod had managed to lead them back to the branching of the ways where the rat-men had first ambushed them.

With a cry, Eliza tripped – her sweat-slick hand slipping from Ulysses' grasp. Close on their heels, it was all Spring-Heeled Jack could do to bound over her to avoid trampling her beneath his iron-shod boots. Ulysses skidded to a halt and spun round, rushing to help her.

The Limehouse Golem was piling towards them, its hulking frame barely contained by the tunnel.

Eliza clung to the path, nails deep in the grime, feet kicking against the befouled water below her.

Ulysses reached down with his simian left arm and pulled her up onto the path in one swift motion, Eliza's scream audible over the piston roar of the golem that was almost upon them.

Terror giving them the adrenalin kick they needed to make their escape, they fled before the inexorable advance of the robot, feeling the pathway crumbling behind the mighty blows from the golem's steam-hammer fists.

Then Spring-Heeled Jack was before them again, appearing out of the murk of the sewer, illuminated by the beaming headlamp eyes of the droid, reaching into a pouch on his suit's utility belt and taking out something small and dark, like a collection of iron pebbles.

Realising what the vigilante was planning, Ulysses threw himself past him, even as the other hurled his handful of tiny grenades at the droid.

The two of them skidded out of the tunnel and into the vaulted space of the domed chamber. Ulysses pulled Eliza around the corner, pushing her up against the mouldering brickwork, shielding her body with his own.

The explosion rocked the sewer, dust and brick and effluent gouting from the tunnel behind them amidst an eruption of flame.

As the echoes of the detonation died away, Ulysses dared to look up, shaking brick dust from his hair. By what little light permeated the cavernous space from the fire now burning on the water's surface at the mouth of the tunnel, Ulysses saw Eliza looking up at him, the whites of her eyes clearly visible, her cheeks running with silent tears. In the aftermath of the explosion, as the echoes died away, he heard the plop of stone fragments hitting the water, the wash and slap of the disturbed waterway against the brick walls, and the quiet crackle of flames.

And then there was another sensation, an insistent itching at the back of his skull.

"Move!" he commanded Eliza, pushing her ahead of him.

They hadn't gone more than a few yards when, with a ghastly, aching groan, a hundred tons of earth and rubble cam down on top of them as the roof caved in.

"Nimrod!" Ulysses shouted for the umpteenth time. "Can you hear me? Are you there?"

He listened intently for a reply, anything at all that might tell him that his manservant was still alive, trapped on the other side of the cave-in but alive nonetheless. But all he could hear was the slosh and surge of the Fleet as it continued to churn through the chamber, now forced to find another way out through the maze of tunnels.

"Jack? Anybody?"

"It's no good, I've told you already, they can't hear you," Eliza pointed out grimly. "If they're even alive at all."

Ulysses picked up a broken brick from the pile of rubble that had blocked of the chamber so effectively and hurled it away into the black water, giving voice to a frustrated, angry shout.

He looked like he was about to try to tear down the barricade with his bare hands, but then his shoulders sagged, the passion that had burnt within his eyes suddenly extinguished. Wading thigh-deep through the fetid soup of the sewer he returned to where Eliza sat on the ledge of the footpath, keeping her feet clear of the foul waters, her shawl pulled close about her shoulders, her arms folded across her chest.

"You really know how to show a girl a good time, don't you?" Eliza grumbled.

"It was you who insisted on coming with us."

"I know, and I wish I hadn't!"

"Well that makes two of us then!"

Clambering back onto the walkway, Ulysses turned his torch on the tunnel ahead of them and set off.

A disgruntled Eliza hurried to keep up.

"Where are you going now?"

"Getting out of here!" came his reply, echoing hollowly from the darkness of the tunnel.

"Here, slow down! I'm coming with you!"

The two of them continued in uneasy silence, following the course of the buried river for what felt like hours. They followed the twists and turns of the tunnel, sometimes having to leap across it to reach the path on the other side when the ledge they were following ran out, sometimes having to duck, as the ceiling sank lower to accommodate who knew what within the roots of the city above.

And then at last the tunnel widened as it entered a vast colonnaded hall, its roof soaring away above them, now resting on great pillars of stone.

Shining his torch into the massive subterranean chamber, Ulysses saw other pillars ten, fifteen, twenty yards away to both left and right, the waters of the Fleet filling this vast man-made cavern like a lake. A distant rhythmic hammering and the staccato clatter of ceaseless machinery could be heard coming from the far side of the vast space, the sounds of implacable industry reminding Ulysses of another underground complex he had visited, nine months before. He couldn't help wondering if he would find a connection between the two. He hoped that it wasn't going to be a repeat experience, but then, from everything he had seen so far he was beginning to fear that it might be.

Negotiating the cavernous vault by means of criss-crossing, corroded, rust-red walkways, they came at last to an arched opening that spilled muted light out into the chamber.

From beneath the entrance, five feet down in the brick built wall, a stone pipe protruded from the wall. From it spilled an oily liquid the colour of coffee, run through with streaks of lurid yellow and green. An acrid stench rose from the brown soup being vomited into the lake, the discharge creating a foamy residue that was then borne away by the flow of the Fleet.

Seeing movement, Ulysses looked down. He caught the impression of something like a rat, but with too many coiling limbs, slithered away over the mouth of the pipe, before plopping into the stagnant soup.

"This is the place," he muttered to himself, as if there had ever been any doubt.

"What place?"

"The place we'll start to find some answers."

"How can you tell?"

"How could it be anything else?" Ulysses said, pointing through the archway into the bottling plant beyond.

"I don't bloody believe it!" Eliza gasped as she stared through the brick archway.

Before them, in an underground hall the size of one of the East End's vast warehouse storage barns, a complicated arrangement of clattering conveyor belts, vast hoppers, brewing vats and endless miles of metal piping, worked tirelessly to one purpose and one purpose only.

"Incredible!" Ulysses gasped, a look of unadulterated amazement on his face. He stepped through the archway and down a flight of stone steps onto the factory floor.

"Here, what do you think you're doing?" the strumpet hissed after him.

Ulysses paused and looked back up at her. "Taking a look around. What does it look like?"

"But what if somebody sees you?"

"Take a look for yourself!" he said, shouting to be heard over the noise of the machines, making Eliza shoot anxious glances left and right, fearful that he might give them away. "Do you see anybody here?"

Eliza peered along the aisles before her, at the platforms and grilled iron walkways above. Ulysses was right; she couldn't see anyone.

"It's fully automated. There doesn't *need* to be anybody here."

The noise was incredible, an unending rattling, crashing, whooshing, whistling, thudding cacophony of industry. And all of it was focused on churning out one innocuous product, a stubby brown glass bottle. Miles of snaking conveyor tracks ran the length of the vast hall, doubling back on themselves, coursing under and over in a never-ending circuit.

Fascinated by the rattling machinery and amazed by the scale of the operation, Ulysses set off along one of the broad aisles, between the massive hissing steam engines that powered it all, as he tried to follow the bottling process back to where it began.

To his right was the end of the line, groups of the stubby bottles being deposited, rattling, into wooden crates, which then jolted on their way, over a rollered conveyor, through an aperture to another part of the processing plant.

Tracing the progress of the bottles back from the packer, Ulysses came to the labelling machine. Before that the glass bottles were stoppered with corks, held in place with tightened wire cages.

"Look at this," Eliza said, now trotting along at his heels, lifting a bottle from the rattling production line, "my mate swears by this stuff."

Ulysses glanced at the garish label:

◇◇ DR FEELGOOD'S TONIC STOUT ◇◇

The beaming face of Dr Feelgood, with his gaunt features, half-moon spectacles and pronounced goatee beard, leered out at them from the gummed paper label, claiming that his patent panacea was a cure-all for:

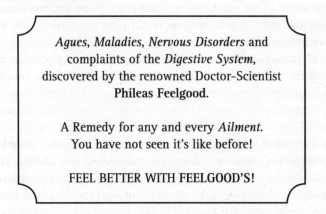

Agues, Maladies, Nervous Disorders and
complaints of the *Digestive System*,
discovered by the renowned Doctor-Scientist
Phileas Feelgood.

A Remedy for any and every *Ailment.*
You have not seen it's like before!

FEEL BETTER WITH FEELGOOD'S!

"Renowned Doctor-Scientist?" Ulysses muttered to himself, turning the bottle over in his hand. "I'd not heard of him before he started peddling his go-go juice."

There were no ingredients printed upon the label, as if he had really thought there would be.

"Your friend swears by it, eh?"

"Says it stops her catching the clap or getting in the family way."

"I have a feeling it does a lot more than that," Ulysses set off again, tracing the production line.

A bitter, hoppy smell permeated the hall. As Ulysses proceeded deeper into the bottling plant it grew stronger until it was a miasmic haze hanging in the air above a steaming vat from which, via a complicated network of plumbing, the bottles were being filled, before they rattled off along the line to be stoppered.

He paused to watch as a dozen bottles were filled simultaneously, pumped full of dark steaming liquid in a matter of seconds, before trundling on their way to make room for another twelve.

"Just how many bottles does this place produce?" Ulysses wondered aloud. "What *is* this stuff?"

"It's Doctor Feelgood's Tonic Stout, isn't it?" Eliza said, giving him a confused look. "I thought you were meant to be a bright spark."

"I mean, what is it *really*? Something tells me that it could be the missing link we've been looking for to connect those poor 'unfortunates' back at Bedlam.

"There must be another chamber, come on." Ulysses set off at a brisk pace, possessed by the spark of excitement again.

It did not take him long to find the arched entrance to the second hall beneath the wall of steaming pipes. Eliza scampered after him.

The dimensions of the second chamber were on a similar scale to those of the bottling plant. The hot, humid air smelt even more strongly here. The unpleasant, nose-wrinkling mix of chemicals and malted hops hitting them like a wall as they entering the brew-house, making both Ulysses and Eliza reel and take a step back, blinking in the face of the heat.

Like the first, this chamber was also devoid of any human presence. And, like the first, it was packed with a forest of pipework, huge bubbling vats and clouds of noxious steam.

"Oh my God!" Eliza spluttered, unavoidably inhaling a great lungful of the noisome gases. "I can hardly breathe. Can we get out of here now?"

"Just give me a moment," Ulysses wheezed, almost choking from the noxious stench.

"But haven't you seen enough?"

But Ulysses was already distractedly gazing up at two of the vast vats steaming away in front of him, roaring furnaces beneath them making sure that the liquid was kept at a constant simmer.

And then he was away, up a metal staircase bolted into the brickwork of a wall, to the grilled walkway twenty feet above, from which he could look down into the bubbling vats.

Eliza staggered after him, dragging herself up to the aerial walkway. Thankfully up here the air quality was better. Whatever the miasmic gas-clouds were formed from, it appeared that they were heavy enough to sink to floor level, even through the warm air of the brewing chamber.

"What is it?" she puffed.

"Look!" Ulysses said with something like triumph in his voice, pointing at the vats.

The liquid inside the right-hand vat was a lurid, oily green while the brew in the left-hand cooker was a nasty jaundiced yellow, unpleasantly reminiscent of pus, the stirring paddles disturbing the iridescent sheen marbling its surface.

"There are two different substances being produced here."

"I can see that. What's your point?"

"Well the contents of this one," the dandy said, pointing to the right-hand vat, "is being pumped through these pipes" – his finger traced the route of the plumbing – "and into the bottling chamber."

"You mean that disgusting stuff ends up in Dr Feelgood's Stout?"

"I know, vile isn't it? But the contents of this container, this yellow gloop, is being transported elsewhere." He pointed to a different set of encrusted pipes that led through the opposite wall.

"So where's that going, then?"

"My thoughts exactly. I think it's time we took a look for ourselves, don't you?"

Ulysses turned, looking for a way through to the, as yet, hidden, adjoining chamber, and then froze. He looked at Eliza, a haunted expression on his face.

"Don't move," he said quietly.

It was then that Eliza heard the staccato pattering, like metal pins tapping on pipework. It was a tinny rattling sound, like she imagined robot crabs would sound scuttling on the hull of a sunken iron ship.

Unable to help herself Eliza turned, appalled eyes looking behind and above her, and it was then that the first of the approaching clockwork spiders launched itself at her face.

CHAPTER SEVENTEEN

Storm Warning

Giving a startled yelp, Eliza flung up a hand to protect her face as Ulysses grabbed her other arm and pulled her sharply backwards. The metallic spider clattered onto the walkway in front of the terrified girl and, in an instant, was on its feet again, looking up at Eliza with its single camera-lens eye. The rest of it was made up of a small steel box, containing the clockwork guts of the mechanism and from which sprouted multiple, steel legs. Each of these jointed steel limbs obviously utilised hydraulics in their construction and ended in machined dew claws that allowed the device both to cling to practically any surface whilst also providing them with the means to defend themselves or attack.

"This way!" Ulysses shouted.

As she staggered backwards, unable to take her eyes off the device, Eliza saw another set of steel limbs reach over the hand-rail of the walkway, like the flexing fingers of a mechanical hand. As the claws found purchase, a second spider-bot pulled itself up onto the walkway. Its single camera lens eye swivelled round to fix on Eliza.

A split second later, the spider-bot pounced.

Ready for it this time, Eliza ducked, pulling her hand free of Ulysses' grasp as she did so.

The device sailed over her head, the harlot giving voice to a wail of revulsion as one of its limbs caught in her hair for a moment, before landing on the walkway behind her.

She crouched and spun round in time to see Ulysses hoof the spider-bot over the railing, sending the strange automaton sailing into the vat of green goo. It remained trapped upon the surface tension of the stuff in the vat, limbs whirring and flexing pitifully, until a stirring paddle pushed it under.

Eliza felt a momentary flicker of relief until she remembered the first of the machines, still stalking her.

"Keep moving and don't look back!" Ulysses shouted, dragging her towards the far wall of the brewing chamber.

But she looked back nonetheless.

The original spider-bot was describing a zigzagging path across the walkway, scuttling from one side to the other, steadily closing the gap between them. The metallic tapping of its many legs provided a strange counterpoint to the ringing of their own running footsteps on the bolted iron sections beneath their feet.

It suddenly dawned on Eliza that there were too many drumming footfalls for even something with seven legs. The tapping was coming from all around them now, a hollow knocking against the pipes, from the walkway, the railings, even the deposit-encrusted boiling vats.

Eliza looked up, and immediately wished that she hadn't.

Crawling along a vast pipe running the length of the walkway above them were half a dozen more of the spider-bots.

Each one was slightly different from its fellows, but every single one had the same cyclopean stare and a disproportionate number of legs.

Their polished carapaces glittering with the reflected iridescent lights of the brew-house, the clockwork creepy crawlies scurried towards the whore and the dandy.

Another flash of reflected electric light caused Eliza to look down.

Clinging to the underside of the walkway were yet more of the scuttling horrors. They were completely surrounded.

One of the arachnid-automata launched itself at Eliza.

Screaming, Eliza instinctively made a grab for the 'bot before it could latch on and scratch out her eyes with its sickle-tipped limbs.

Its metal body felt cold and heavy as it wriggled within her grasp, legs spasming as it tried to get even the slightest grip on her. She could hear servo motors whirring and gears grinding in mechanical frustration. And always that single camera eye squealing as it zoomed in and out, trying to focus on her face.

At last, with an almighty heave, she hurled the spider-bot away from her. It clattered against a railing, knocking another of the advancing automata clear, sending it plummeting to the factory floor.

But now another spider-bot was running towards her and, this time, Eliza didn't think that she'd be quick enough to defend herself.

The retort of the pistol was loud in her ear, making her jump. Sparks burst from the metal shell of the advancing spider-bot. The second shot shattered the lens of its single camera eye. Its legs went rigid, and the spider collapsed onto the floor of the walkway.

"That's three down," came Ulysses voice from behind her. "Now, how many times do I have to tell you? Get moving!"

Ulysses ran, dragging the panicking girl after him. He could hear the clatter and crash of the spider-bots landing on the walkway behind them and Eliza's stifled screams told him when one was getting too close.

He twisted round and brought down another of the scuttling automatons with a deft shot. Through the 'eye' seemed to be the way to do it.

His attention was drawn to the reflected gleam of light cast by something scuttling along a pipe upside down above him. In a split second he had taken aim and fired. The 'bot clattered onto the walkway twitching and sparking, its clockwork guts spilling out, pieces of precision-engineered internal mechanisms dropping through the gaps in the grille to rain down onto the stone-flagged floor in a hard shower of cogs, gears and springs.

They were disturbing creations. Most automata were given some manner of human appearance, to make them more acceptable to those who worked and lived alongside them. But these things were totally alien. He wondered what manner of machining process could create such utterly unique creations when every other large scale automaton producer replicated robot after robot to an accepted design.

Ulysses fired again but this time missed his target by a hair's bredth. His next bullet took the spider mid-leap, before it could grab hold of Eliza's shawl. The shot entered through its base-plate, between the joints of its six legs. And then he was out of bullets and there was no time to reload.

But the end of the walkway was in sight now and he could see another stone archway at the bottom of the flight of stairs. He sprinted for the staircase and down it, forcing Eliza to stumble after him.

The girl screamed as a 'bot latched onto her. In a state of shock she missed a step and fell onto Ulysses. The two of them tumbled to the bottom, a handrail giving way as both of them fell against it.

They landed in a heap, the sundered pole of the handrail beneath them, Eliza screaming as Ulysses struggled out from under her. Scrambling to his feet, he saw the automaton clinging to her back as well as the growing scarlet patches now soaking her ruined blouse.

Grabbing the droid in both hands, Ulysses yanked it free. Eliza gave an agonised wail as the spider's hooked feet tore free of her flesh.

The clattering of metal on stone told Ulysses that other spider-bots had started dropping from the walkway. Hurling the automaton in his hands as far as he could, he pulled the bleeding and moaning Eliza to her feet, turning towards the stone archway. There, in front of him, another spider was descending the wall, ready to pounce.

At the periphery of his vision Ulysses could see others approaching from all sides now, but none of them had attacked yet. He could almost believe that they were waiting, somehow communicating silently with one another, combining their efforts to bring the invaders down.

Ulysses fumbled for the box of bullets he always kept close to his pistol. As, with shaking fingers, he forced a bullet into an empty chamber, the spider lurking above the archway leapt. Ulysses ducked.

The shout of "Yahh!" took him completely by surprise, but not as much as the whoosh of something heavy slicing through the air inches above his head and the resounding clang that followed half a second later.

"Take that, you bastard!" Eliza roared as she sent the spider-bot flying with a wallop from the length of railing she gripped tightly.

The automaton struck the wall before landing several feet away, its camera eye twisting wildly as it struggled to stand, two of its legs flapping uselessly from their mountings.

Ulysses spun round, a look of sheer astonishment on his face. "Remind me to look you up if the Old Boys' Cricket Team's ever in need of a twelfth man!

"Look out!"

Eliza spun round, blocking the next spider-bot's attack with another powerful swing. The droid went spinning away, its ruined internal clockwork making a harsh grating sound.

Eliza gave a *harrumph* of delight, her former panic replaced by the adrenalin-fuelled thrill of the kill.

"Now, for the last bloody time, let's get out of here," Ulysses said.

The two of them entered a dark, unlit tunnel. At its far end, thirty yards away, Ulysses could see the dull amber glow of electric light. They backed away slowly along the tunnel. Ulysses shot any 'bots that entered the tunnel after them, while any who escaped his bullets met with the edge of Eliza's steel pole.

And then, at last, they reached the end, entering another gloomy subterranean chamber. This one was nothing like the factory works of the bottling plant or the brew-house. it was significantly narrower and had a broad arched ceiling, disappearing away into the gloom as far as Ulysses could see. But now wasn't the time to stop and have a proper look round.

The only thing Ulysses was really interested in at that moment was the heavy steel door that had been left open at this end of the tunnel.

"Quick!" Ulysses commanded Eliza. Once she was inside he started to push against the door, putting all his weight against it. "Help me with this."

The girl joined him, but as the door began to close, with painful slowness, feet could be heard echoing from the walls of the tunnel as the spider-bots made their final assault.

Spurred on by fear, they managed to slam the door shut, snapping off a number of silvery limbs that had managed to gain purchase on the doorframe.

Ulysses leaned against the steel and gave a sigh. "Thank God that's over!" And then he saw the ball of steel limbs unfold itself as the only spider-bot to make it through sprang.

But Eliza was there with her improvised bludgeon again, batting it away with a gleeful grunt of effort. The spider hit one of the caged lights that lined the passageway. The bulb shattered and the automaton's limbs became entangled within the wire frame of the cage, a surge of electricity frying its internal components.

Eliza let the pole fall from her aching fingers with a resounding clang.

For a good few moments, the only sounds were the heavy breathing of the two exhausted escapees, the sputtering crackle of the spider-bot burning, and the glug of chemicals being transported away up the tunnel through another massive pipe.

"So," Eliza panted, still doubled up, hands on knees, the back of her blouse saturated with blood, "where are we?"

Ulysses tore his gaze from the smouldering carcass of the

burnt-out spider-bot to peer into the stygian gloom ahead of them.

"I don't know. But I have a feeling, if we follow that pipe we'll find out, eventually. "Come on," he said for the umpteenth time since they had embarked on their adventure underground, flashing her a devilish grin, "this way."

Ulysses Quicksilver and his latest female companion stood together, the open man-hole cover behind them, and stared at the emptiness of the vast hangar before them. Other than for a few abandoned crates, oil-drums and coils of rope, the place was deserted.

"It's gone," Ulysses said in stunned disbelief.

"What has? What's gone?"

Ulysses didn't answer, but instead started to pace slowly towards the middle of the hangar. Dust rose from the floor in flurries around his feet and sparkled like spun gold in the shafts of morning sunlight that pierced the high windows. He was momentarily reminded of another hangar-like space he had found himself in eight months before, although that one had been anything but empty.

Disheartened and bone-achingly weary after his night-time exertions, for a moment Ulysses simply enjoyed the fact that he was free of the cloying chemical miasma of the factory tunnels. They had walked for miles, negotiating the labyrinthine tunnels of the sewers as they had followed the outflow pipe from the processing plant to the hangar on Hampstead Heath.

They had seen two different chemical compounds being concocted within the underground factory. One was the secret, wholly stomach-churning, ingredient of Dr Feelgood's Tonic Stout. The other had been pumped miles underground to the site where Prime Minister Valentine's glorious *Jupiter Station* was being put together ready for its launch day, although it was no longer there.

"What's the date?" Ulysses suddenly demanded, spinning on his heel and sending another cloud of dust into the mote-shot air.

"Pardon?" Eliza responded, shaken from her exhausted reverie, the dull ache of the wounds left in her back by the spider's claws sapping her of strength.

"Today's date! What is it?"

"All right, all right. Keep your hair on. It's the fourteenth, I think."

"Damn!" Ulysses struck the palm of his left hand with the shaft of his cane.

"You mean you didn't get any cards either this year?"

"It's today!"

"I know it is, but that's not what you're talking about is it?"

"I hadn't realised we'd been so long underground."

Ulysses took out his fob watch, rubbing its face clean of mud and sewer slime. But the muck had got into its workings.

Instead to gauge the time, he looked up at the sunlight filtering through the windows.

"It's still early, which might mean that it's not too late."

"I would ask what you're talking about," Eliza complained as Ulysses removed a brass and teak device inlaid with enamel keys from a jacket pocket, "but it doesn't look like you're interested in answering my questions."

He flicked open the personal communicator and the tense grimace on his face relaxed slightly as he heard the hum of a signal tone when he put it to his ear. He wasted no time in keying in a number.

Eliza watched, having seated herself upon an upturned barrel, arms folded across her chest as Ulysses waited for someone at the other end to pick up.

"Quicksilver. Ulysses Quicksilver... I need to speak with De Wynter... Well where is he then? Yes, I'll hold..." Eliza could read the anxiety on Ulysses' face quite clearly. "Well try again!" he demanded after a minute's silence. "Tell him the launch has to be stopped. Do you understand? He has to stop the launch. The *Jupiter Station* cannot be allowed to take off!"

With a grunt of annoyance Ulysses took the communicator from his ear and immediately began to key in another number.

"Who are you calling now?" Eliza asked.

Ulysses ignored her question.

"Nimrod?" he said loudly, with obvious joy and relief. "Thank God you're alive... Yes, yes, we're fine. Now listen up, old boy. Pick us up from Hampstead Heath, would you? It's a long story. We need a lift to Hyde Park... Yes... Yes, that's right... We have an official function to gatecrash!"

ACT THREE

Metamorphosis

February 1998

My name is Ozymandias, King of Kings:
Look on my works, ye mighty, and despair!

(*Ozymandias*, Percy Bysshe Shelley)

CHAPTER EIGHTEEN

Jupiter Ascending

To the cheers of the assembled flag-waving faithful, tethers were loosed, anchors withdrawn, mooring clamps blown and finally, after long months of preparation, the *Jupiter* Weather *Station* ascended gracefully into the Smog-bound London sky.

Prime Minister Devlin Valentine stared out of the observation deck window at the colourful jostle and bustle of the crowds – his grateful people – dwindling before his very eyes, a benign smile on his face, as the *Jupiter*, with its complement of invited dignitaries on board, ascended heavenwards. As he watched the paths, fountains and flowerbeds of the park diminished as it was swallowed up by the crowding buildings of Marylebone. He saw the familiar face of London form as they rose high above it, its features formed from the streets and railway lines, the ornate public buildings and the haphazard slum tenements, its parks and its waterways, the Thames, cutting through it like a serpent slithering through the greatest city on the face of the Earth, or beneath the seas, the river glittering in the morning sunlight that was burning through the pall of pollution.

"My lords, ladies and gentlemen," the smooth baritone of a crewman came over the tannoy, "we are currently ascending to our operating height of ten thousand feet at a speed of approximately ten feet per second. Once there we will fire up the elemental engines and give you a short demonstration of the *Jupiter*'s capabilities before the dirigible-ferries arrive to take you back to the ground to rejoin the celebrations taking place in Hyde Park. The weather over London is fine, with a wind speed of three miles an hour. Enjoy the ride."

This was the beginning of something special, the dawning of an age of enlightenment and accountability and awareness for all. And at its head was Devlin Valentine, visionary and altruist, a new kind of hero for a new age. An age of tolerance and understanding, in which Magna Britannia, and Londinium Maximum, would become the utopia it had always had the potential to be, as the greatest empire the world had ever known entered the twenty-first century.

Valentine was only sorry that Her Majesty Queen Victoria was not been there to bear witness to his crowning achievement. But the Widow of Windsor had not left Buckingham Palace since the Wormwood Affair and the debacle that had consumed her 160th jubilee celebrations the previous year.

A purple-faced dignitary, wearing the finest handlebar moustache Valentine had ever seen and holding a champagne flute, approached him. Valentine turned to face the toff with a look of unalloyed joy on his face, beaming broadly.

"Marvellous achievement, old chap," Colonel Russen said, chinking glasses with Valentine. "What? All this? Bloody marvellous. Now let's just hope the damn thing works, eh?"

"Oh, have no fear, Colonel. The technology utilised by the *Jupiter* Station is cutting edge, state of the art, making use of the very latest in cavorite gravitic-repulsion systems, atmospheric excitation inducers and cyclonic dissipaters."

"And what does that mean when it's at home?" Colonel Russen laughed.

"It means, it'll work, Colonel, it'll work."

"Ah yes, but *will* it work?"

Tapping his nose with one finger whilst winking about as subtly as a Covent Garden tart, the Colonel marched off again across the public viewing gallery. It was here that the dignitaries had been contained, mainly to keep them out of the way of the crew.

It was an impressive space, beautifully wrought from steel and glass, as fine an example of the ironsmith's art as Oxford's Natural History Museum or the atrium hall of the London's own Natural History Museum. However, where the former was decorated with beaten metal foliage, here the metalworkers had based its decoration on recognised weather symbols, from shining sun discs and clouds to snowflakes and lightning bolts.

It really was incredible, Valentine thought. Here they were rising thousands of feet into the air and yet the ride was smoother than if they had been on board ship on a calm sea. There was almost no sensation of movement at all, certainly nothing that was likely to cause a bout of air sickness amongst any of the passengers.

White jacketed waiters moved between the great and the good, bearing platters of *vol-au-vents* and crudités, and topping up champagne glasses.

Valentine realised he was being selfish keeping himself to himself. He needed to make sure he shared his own company with those grateful souls whose lives he was about to transform forever.

Valentine turned to study the reactions of his guests.

They were, all of them, to a man and woman, caught up in the wonder and the spectacle of the moment. It was as if the Wormwood Affair had never happened all those months ago. Devlin Valentine had succeeded in wiping it from the nation's mind with the new wonder he'd bestowed upon the beleaguered capital that, only ten months ago, had seen the dinosaur herds of London Zoo running amok through its streets. Although, of course, if Wormwood hadn't almost brought the nation to its knees with his attempted coup, Devlin Valentine wouldn't have been standing here now enjoying the realisation of a long-held ambition.

All of those assembled within the viewing gallery were enraptured, all except for the one man who should be relishing this moment as much as Valentine; Halcyon Beaufort-Monsoon.

Monsoon sat in his wheelchair a little way from the other guests, guarded by his fierce nurse.

There was something about the two of them that unnerved him – the way they were looking out of the window distractedly, the way they weren't conversing with the rest of those on board, or the way they kept giving each other stern-faced looks that obviously spoke volumes.

Every now and again, one of the launch party dignitaries would approach them and be given short shrift. If Valentine wasn't careful, Beaufort-Monsoon's attitude could turn this whole carefully orchestrated public relations exercise into a PR disaster. There were even a number of specially invited men and women of the press on board and the Prime Minister wanted only positive headlines following the launch and not write-ups about how grumpy London's benefactor had appeared to be. Couldn't the man see what he was doing?

For someone who had effectively given away millions of pounds worth of goods and labour in gifting the *Jupiter Station* to the nation, the philanthropist was incredibly ill-tempered. Valentine would not have expected that someone whose lifelong dream it had been to improve the state of the nation would have been such a cantankerous curmudgeon.

Valentine was stirred from his reverie by the approach of the Leader of the Opposition.

"Very impressive, Prime Minister," his opposite number said, making no effort to hide the sneer on his face. "You are to be congratulated, Valentine. You and this Beaufort-Monsoon chap."

"Why thank you Sutherland."

"Funny thing though."

"And what's that?"

"Well, it's just that I've never come across this Monsoon chap myself before." Sutherland let that thought hang for a moment. "Funny that, considering all my contacts in the world of industry." And with that the rival politician moved on to talk to Lady Imelda Brize-Rose of the London Clean Air League.

His brow furrowing, Valentine gazed at the receding rooftops and the splodges of green that marked where the public parks lay, as he struggled to put the nagging doubts from his mind that Sutherland's remark had stirred up.

And he had been having misgivings for some time now, ever since their joint venture had begun, if he was honest with himself. It was strange that Sutherland should mention that he hadn't heard of Beaufort-Monsoon until the commencement of the *Jupiter* project. Up until that point, no-one had.

The ailing industrialist had turned up at just the right moment, or at least his people had, offering Valentine the prize that would see him win the election, after Wormwood's forcible removal from office. A device that promised a better, cleaner London for everyone. The launch of the *Jupiter Station* was also just the sort of spectacle that he needed to make sure his tenure as Prime Minster would never be forgotten.

But he wasn't going to let Sutherland put a dampner on things for him. Yet, still the doubts persisted.

Valentine didn't know much about London's saviour, other than what was written in the official press release – his childhood in India, his first job in a ball bearing factory, working his way up from gopher to managing director, his move into manufacturing and construction work, the undersea cities boom, a fortune made practically overnight, investment in new technologies. But then, he hadn't met anybody who had come across Beaufort-Monsoon before six months ago either, which surprised him. In fact, it worried him. Somebody didn't get to be as rich and successful as Halcyon Beaufort-Monsoon appeared to be without attracting some media attention.

Despite his best efforts to put the concerns from his mind, doubt was now gnawing at the pit of his stomach. It was nothing but the product of nervous excitement, that was all. Nothing was wrong. Nothing was going to go wrong. Nothing was going to spoil this moment for him.

He hadn't known what to make of Beaufort-Monsoon at their

first meeting, and he certainly didn't relish the prospect of having to make conversation with him now, but he had to be seen to be doing the right thing.

Taking a deep breath and turning on his most ingratiating smile, he strode over to the wheelchair-bound philanthropist and his attendant nurse, saluting Beaufort-Monsoon with his champagne glass.

"To you, Mr Beaufort-Monsoon!" Valentine said with all the bravura born of years of electioneering and political rhetoric. "Soon to be *Sir* Beaufort-Monsoon," he added in a hushed tone. "How do you like the sound of that?"

"I am not doing this for the prestige or for some poxy title," Beaufort-Monsoon growled, fixing Valentine with a withering stare from behind the bottle-bottom lenses of his glasses. His hair was swept back in a thinning widow's peak, his skin paper-thin and dotted with liver spots.

Age had not been kind to Halcyon Beaufort-Monsoon, and Valentine found himself wondering how many years he had left. Perhaps that was why he was so keen to help the people of London, hoping that it would somehow ensure him his place in heaven.

"No, no, of course not," Valentine backtracked hastily. "I understand that. Only it's rare to meet someone as generous and as selfless as you, Mr Beaufort-Monsoon. London is truly blessed. The people of Magna Britannia will never forget you."

For the first time since Valentine had been in the old man's company, Beaufort-Monsoon smiled. It was one of the most unsettling things Valentine had seen in a long time.

"Oh, I'm sure of it," he said. His expression was the smile of a hungry cat and it only served to bring Valentine's reservations to the fore again. But it was too late to be having doubts now, far too late.

Uncharacteristically lost for words, wanting to be anywhere other than where he was right at that moment, Valentine turned his gaze away from Beaufort-Monsoon and his predatory smile, and gazed again out of the viewing port. And as he stared down at the dwindling towers and pinnacles of the cityscape, and the complex spider's web of the Overground rail network, he wondered what the true cost of his premiership was to be and how he would really be remembered by the people of Londinium Maximum.

Through the lower cirrus wisps of Smog he saw the gleam of silver and watched as a car – a Rolls Royce, by the looks of it – drove into Hyde Park at speed, pulling up in front of the excited crowds. A man leapt out of the car and immediately craned his head back to watch the *Jupiter's* departure.

Feeling the blood drain from his cheeks, Devlin Valentine wondered what sort of a fate he had condemned his city to, a cold knot of fear tightening in his guts.

Ulysses Quicksilver opened the door and jumped out of the Silver Phantom before Nimrod had even brought the car to a complete stop.

He gazed up at the rising *Jupiter Station*, the great ring of iron, steel and glass silhouetted against the sun. It was hardly the best day to demonstrate how the Weather Machine was going to rid London of its blanket of Smog and improve the notoriously miserable weather patterns.

"Hell's teeth!" he shouted, giving voice to his annoyance. Despite their best efforts to prevent the launch something had thwarted his attempts to signal De Wynter, who was now, Ulysses was surprised to see, pushing his way towards them through the crowd of flag-waving Londoners.

"Quicksilver?" the big man exclaimed as he elbowed his way through to the front of the official cordon holding the crowd back. "Good God, man, what do you look like?" he roared, taking the stub of a smouldering cigar from between his teeth.

Ulysses looked down at himself. "A dog's dinner, by the looks of things, but I didn't come all the way from Hampstead Heath for fashion tips."

"Then what are you doing here?"

"You mean they haven't got hold of you?"

"What are you talking about, man?"

But Ulysses was too busy examining his personal communicator to answer. He pressed a key and listened for a dial tone but, when he put the device to his ear, all he could hear was static.

"They must be jamming comm signals!" He looked up at the weather platform. "Probably from on board."

"Look, Quicksilver, are you going to tell me what's going on, or are we going to stand around here all day with no-one having the foggiest what you're talking about?"

"It's the *Jupiter Station*! I wanted you to stop the launch."

"But whatever for? Has it got something to do with this state you've somehow managed to get yourself in?"

"You remember the cockroach from the Daedalus Clinic?"

De Wynter looked at Ulysses, his bushy eyebrows beetling in bewilderment. "Yes, of course. But I thought you said this was about the *Jupiter Station*!"

"Bear with me. I think I know what caused his degeneration and that of the others you've got locked up at Bedlam!"

"How do you know about that?" De Wynter railed.

"I have my sources," Ulysses said, glancing at Eliza – still laid out on the back seat – out of the corner of his eye. "But the point is, what turned them is only half the formula. Dr Feelgood's Tonic Stout has been laced with the stuff. Don't ask me why it only turned those few, I don't know, but there's another component to the potion."

"Formula? What formula?"

"That I don't know. The important thing is I'm pretty certain the other half is on board that thing. Gallons of it. Thousands of gallons, if I'm not mistaken."

De Wynter turned, giving a dry snap of his fingers, and suddenly the hunchbacked form of the elderly Agent Penny Dreadful came hobbling out of the crowd.

"Yes, sah?" she croaked, appearing to try to come to attention but her dowager's stoop making it impossible.

De Wynter had his personal communicator out now. "Get someone to jam the signal that's jamming the ether-waves and then get a message to the *Jupiter*. I want that thing out of the sky and back on the ground now!"

"My lords, ladies and gentlemen," came dulcet tones over the tannoy again, many of the dignitaries breaking off their conversations to listen, Prime Minister Valentine among them.

He hoped this announcement – whatever it was – wasn't going to take long. He was looking forward to the demonstration of the *Jupiter's* power – anything to take his mind of his increasing concerns, really – and then he had to board the first dirigible-taxi off this thing, ready for a meet and greet with the great unwashed in Hyde Park, before heading off to the Palace of Westminster again for a select committee hearing on... he couldn't remember precisely what now, but suddenly he wanted to be there more than he where he actually was.

"We are now at our operating height of ten thousand feet," the voice went on.

The crewman's words were punctuated by the rhythmic trotting footsteps of aeronautical auxiliary force-issue boots on the polished floorboards of the viewing gallery as other members of the crew – in their smart blue and white and uniforms – entered and arrayed themselves along the hub-ward side of the chamber.

"If you would all like to make your way over to the viewing window, we will begin our demonstration shortly."

Valentine gazed out of the window across the curving face of the city. He realised the *Jupiter Station* had stopped rising. He could see the Smog beneath them, spread out like a gauzy blanket over London, shimmering with an iridescent oily sheen that clung to the looming towers of the Upper City. He felt greasy just looking at it; but all that was about to change.

Valentine looked around him, taking some pleasure again from savouring everyone's wonder at his extraordinary achievement; his and Halcyon Beaufort-Monsoon's. His searching eyes found the philanthropist and his striking red-haired nurse. While everyone else was gazing in awe out of the viewing window, picking out famous landmarks just about visible through the Smog, the two of them were the only ones looking *into* the room, at the ordered line of crewmen.

"And now, my lords, ladies and gentlemen, the moment you have all been waiting for."

Hearing the *click-clack* of slides being racked and bolts being thrown, Valentine turned to observe the crewmen as well. What he saw made him feel sick, all doubt suddenly gone to be replaced by cold realisation and abject fear.

"The *Jupiter Station* is now under the control of the Darwinian Dawn and you should all consider yourselves our hostages."

"What?" one man fumed. "What is the meaning of this?"

"This is an outrage!" stormed another.

"You can't do this!"

"You can't treat us like this!"

"Now look here," Colonel Russen began, turning from the window and making for the line of armed crewmen, a stern finger raised in admonishment.

Several guns pointed in his direction. Somewhere within the crowd of dignitaries a woman gave a moaning cry and swooned.

"Get back over here, Colonel!"

Valentine snapped his head round in surprise. It was Beaufort-Monsoon who had spoken.

"Leave this to me, Monsoon," Colonel Russen persisted. "I'll deal with this. You can't take any nonsense from these types. Soon as I show them who's in charge we'll have no more trouble, mark my w-"

The pistol shot was loud in the confined cabin of the viewing gallery. Several people screamed. Valentine's looked from the sprawled body of the Colonel, his head shattered like an egg, and followed the sound back to its source amidst the confused crowd of clustered dignitaries.

A gap was forming at the centre of the group and at its centre was Halcyon Beaufort-Monsoon's wheelchair, his nurse standing behind him, one hand on a handle of his chair, the other holding the smoking gun.

Valentine stared at her, mouth open in shock. The old man was still smiling his cruel shark's smile.

"Thank you, my dear," Beaufort-Monsoon said. "The Colonel was becoming most irksome."

His nurse returned the gun to a thigh-holster, revealed by a split in her skirt and, without uttering a word, rolled her employer's chair forward to join the line of armed crewmen.

"I would suggest that no-one else tries anything foolish," he said, peering myopically at the guests. "That would be most rash. No, it is time to face facts, my lords, ladies and gentlemen. You should now consider yourselves hostages, my insurance policy if you will. And in a few minutes we will begin the little demonstration I have planned for you and all of London."

"They're not responding to hails, sah!" Penny Dreadful informed De Wynter as Ulysses listened in, appalled.

"I knew it," he hissed. "I just knew it! Damn it all to hell!"

"Have our boffins managed to cancel out that jamming signal yet?" De Wynter demanded.

"Yes, sah! We 'ave radio communication on the ground again, but we are still unable to raise those on board the *Jupiter Station* itself, sah!"

"So what happens now?" Eliza chipped in, an expression of dull shock etched onto her face.

"Now, young lady?" De Wynter replied. "Now we put Plan B into action."

"And what's that?" Ulysses asked.

"We shoot it down."

"What?" Ulysses railed. "You can't be serious?"

"We cannot afford to have another incident like the one Wormwood engineered. You said yourself the city's in danger. Besides, the British government does not negotiate with terrorists!"

"That's right, sah!"

"But desperate times call for desperate measures," De Wynter went on. "Get me General Templesmith."

"Okay, so you shoot it down," Ulysses reasoned. "And then what? If my suspicions about what's onboard are correct and you shoot that thing down, you're going to send a deluge of toxic chemicals of Biblical proportions down over the city, the outcome of which will make the mass breakout from the Tower of London look like a teddy bears' picnic!"

For a moment De Wynter said nothing, fixing Ulysses with his penetrating stare as he took a deep draw on his stinking cigar.

"Dreadful, delay that last instruction."

"Yes, sah!"

"So, Quicksilver, here's your chance. Show us the cut of your jib, put your money where your mouth is. Let's see if you're all talk and no trousers, shall we? What do you suggest we do now?"

"If I could just get on board –"

"And how do you plan on doing that?"

His own words were cut short by the roar of a rocket hurtling by overhead. And then everyone – from the assembled crowd to the conspiratorial huddle beside the Silver Phantom – was looking up, only this time it wasn't at the *Jupiter,* as a bat-winged shadow flashed across the park.

With a roar of retro-thrusters, and startled gasps from the crowd, the masked figure landed heavily in the middle of a bed of roses, the impact throwing up great clods of soil.

"Have no fear," the vigilante said, "Spring-Heeled Jack is here!"

CHAPTER NINETEEN

The Taking of *Jupiter Station*

"And what are you supposed to be?" De Wynter demanded, giving the new arrival a disdainful look. "Some sort of human bat?"

Before the masked man could answer they all heard a voice shout from the crowd. "All my born days, I don't believe it! It's Spring-Heeled Jack! I tell you, Maggie, it's only ruddy Spring-Heeled Jack!"

"Is that right?" De Wynter challenged the vigilante.

"Some call me by that name. I prefer to think of myself as London's Dark Chevalier, the city's Cloaked Crusader."

"Is that so?"

"It's him all right," Ulysses confirmed.

"Good Lord! Is that some sort of a rocket-pack?" De Wynter asked.

Jack followed the crowd's gaze to the tiny speck of the *Jupiter* hovering high above the city.

"So, I take it that you're stuck here, down on the ground, but you want to be up there?"

"That's about the sum of it," Ulysses agreed. Beneath the crust of dried on sewer filth and brick-dust, Ulysses' eyes were ringed with tiredness, but the sustained adrenalin high of the moment was allowing him to keep going, pushing his body to the limit. A part of him knew that he would pay for it later – if there was to be a later.

"Right you are then," the vigilante said, holding out his hand to Ulysses.

"I'm sorry?" Ulysses said.

"What are you waiting for? *Tempus fugit*, Mr Quicksilver."

"You mean that pack of yours can carry the weight of more than one man?" De Wynter said.

"I don't know, yet. But I should think so. I can cross London in less time than it would take you to drive across, so I don't see why that thrust won't allow me to carry a passenger as well."

"So long as you're not planning on taking part in an aerial stunt show or doing any loop the loops." Ulysses said.

Something like a laugh emerged emitted from the speaker of the vigilante's mask. "No. I was just planning on going straight up, if that's all right with you."

"That'll be just fine."

Ulysses wasn't afraid of heights; no-one could accuse him of that after he had given such fearless demonstrations as train-top knife fights and his death-defying battle with the nefarious Black Mamba high above the jagged peaks of the Himalaya Mountains.

"All right then?" Jack asked again.

"Yes. Fine," Ulysses said. "Let's do this before I change my mind."

"Very well then," Jack stepped up behind Ulysses and took hold of him under the arms of his ruined jacket.

"All right," De Wynter addressed the two of them. "You've got half an hour. Any longer than that, or if there's any obvious sign that you've failed, I'll command the Battersea Battery to shoot that thing down, hostages or no hostages. Do we have an understanding?"

"And if, perish the thought, this actually works?" Ulysses said.

"Give me a sign – a clear sign. Launch a flare or something, anything you can lay your hands on, or get this chap here to get a message to us on the ground. You got that?"

"Clear as the skies over London," Ulysses quipped.

De Wynter glowered in the face of his brevity and growled something under his breath.

"Are we ready?" Spring-Heeled Jack said.

"We're ready," Ulysses said, feeling for the loaded pistol holstered under his arm and taking a firm hold of his sword-cane.

Eliza stepped forward, grabbing Ulysses' face between her hands, kissing him fully on the mouth. "For luck."

Ulysses simply smiled in grim acceptance of his fate, knowing that he may well never see her again.

"Hold on tight," Jack said.

"Isn't that your job?" Ulysses said, and then, before he could say anything else, the hiss of the jetpack's pilot-flame became the deafening roar of engines igniting. With a scream of sound and light Spring-Heeled Jack blasted back into the sky, taking the startled dandy with him, and leaving nothing behind but a blackened circle on the immaculately-kept lawn.

Ulysses had thought himself prepared for the rocket ride, but the reality of being fired into the air like a human missile was like nothing he had ever experienced before.

Although he had been into space, when, as a young man, he had undertaken a three-year Grand Tour of the Solar System, seated in a luxury seat as the interplanetary liner drifted heavenward, even there one didn't experience the tremendous G-forces that Ulysses was having to endure now.

The wind whipped through his hair, and forced him to part close his eyes against the slipstream created by their hurtling ascent. But the voice of the wind in his ears was drowned out by the fiery scream of the jetpack. Everything was passing him by in a blur.

He looked down at the ground, disappearing at a rate of knots beneath them, the anxious, upturned faces of the crowd merged into one homogenous mass gathered upon the painstakingly kept lawns of the Hyde Park.

Having thought that he had left his stomach behind, Ulysses was surprised at how nauseous he felt as a terrifying, vertiginous feeling threatened to overwhelm him. Feeling the pinching pain of the hold Jack had on him, helped him to forget about his rising gorge.

Rather than look at the ever-increasing distance he had to fall if Jack lost his grip, Ulysses forced his head up and, despite the pressure of the wind against his face, peered at the yellow-painted Smog layer above them, the silhouette of the Weather Station dominating his field of vision as they drew closer to it.

The *Jupiter Station* was an impressive piece of work and no mistake, a credit to those men who had toiled long and hard to bring Prime Minister Valentine's vision to fruition. The torus must have a circumference of over a thousand yards, Ulysses considered. He had no idea what this outer ring contained, but he assumed that hidden within was the esoteric technology that would allow the *Jupiter Station* to alter London's weather. And, of course, somewhere within the Weather Machine there was stored thousands of gallons of whatever it was the chemical plant had been set to produce. And there, at the back of his mind, was the fear that he knew precisely who had taken control of the station.

The Weather Station was only a matter of a few hundred yards away now. Then it was only fifty, and then Spring-Heeled Jack was soaring past it. For a moment Ulysses thought he saw desperate faces, pressed up against the glass of a broad viewing window, and he hoped that their approach wasn't being tracked.

Now that he was seeing the *Jupiter Station* from above, as well as a proliferation of aerial and other, curious antennae, he could see jutting walkways, landing stages and dirigible tether-points. It was as wide across as two rugby pitches were long, the myriad glass panels in the steel-framed sections of its outer ring sparkling like diamonds against the sun-washed sky beyond the pollution belt of the ever-present Smog.

The Jupiter was designed to be manned twenty-four hours a day, seven days a week, month in and month out, its crew constantly monitoring the changing weather patterns over the capital and using the station's advanced technology to influence the weather as necessary, the intention being to eventually rid London of its permanent pall of Smog. Crews would spend a week on board at a time, rotating shifts during that time, with a permanent crew of eight. When it was time for a shift change, the work-teams would be swapped over by dirigible ferry.

"Prepare for landing," Jack shouted in his ear.

Ulysses wondered just precisely how he was supposed to prepare for landing when the only thing holding him up in the air in the first place was Spring-Heeled Jack's sure grip. Double-checking his grip on his cane, he tensed his body, knees bent ready to absorb the shock.

He heard the pitch of the jetpack's engines abruptly drop as Jack adjusted their speed. However, they were still hurtling towards the *Jupiter*, the brass handrail surrounding one particular pier rushing to meet them.

Ulysses tensed as his feet barely cleared the railing and Jack let go.

He crashed down onto the pier, his momentum bowling him forwards into the opposite rail. For a moment he lay there, on his back, one arm dangling off the side of the platform, staring up at the cerulean bowl of the sky.

A bat-winged shadow soared above him, as Spring-Heeled Jack turned and made his own approach.

Having taken a few good deep breaths, Ulysses scrambled to his feet as Jack cut the power to the engines and dropped – the wings of his cape extending on either side of him – landing on the pier in a crouch.

At the far end of the pier stood the massive curving side of the *Jupiter*, an ornamented iron door giving access to the vessel beyond.

Ulysses could really begin to appreciate just how big the Weather Station was, now that he was on board it.

"This way," he said, setting off at a trot, buffeted by the strong winds making themselves felt up here.

The door was not locked, but then why would it be? Whoever it was that had taken over the *Jupiter* hadn't been expecting any uninvited guests.

Ulysses opened the door and stepped into the gloom of an entrance pod. After the glare of the sunny spring day outside, he found himself in almost total darkness. What he could make out was the narrow corridor that led off from this space, connecting the access hatch with the main arterial passageway running throughout the body of the craft.

And although he could see little other than the gangway ahead, his finely attuned sixth sense screamed danger.

"Get down!" Ulysses shouted, hoping Jack would hear him over the keening of the wind, as he threw himself flat.

At that moment, a pair of uniformed crewmen turned into the passageway, guns raised. Either they had heard the intrusive noise of the wind through the open hatch or they had felt the accompanying draft. Whatever the reason for their presence, their eyes fell first on Ulysses – scrabbling to free his pistol from its holster as he rolled out of their line of fire – and then on Jack, suddenly clearly silhouetted in the open doorway.

They opened fire.

Ulysses looked on in horror as the vigilante was hit twice in the chest. Jack staggered backwards, reeling, and then fell, the buffeting wind sending him tumbling over the side of the air-pier and out of sight.

As appalled acceptance of the vigilante's fate hit him, a split second later Ulysses realised the true extent of danger that his heightened senses had been alerting him to. It hadn't been the crewmen, something else was hiding in the darkness.

Eyes blazed in the darkness and, with a grating of gears and the roar of furnace power, a massive shape unfolded from the gloom and his blood ran cold.

Ulysses trained his pistol on the metal behemoth and let off a couple of shots, which spanged off the stone-like surface of the droid's carapace.

A massive hand closed over Ulysses' own, bending the gun barrel out of shape, and he could feel the bones inside his hand grating together as the automaton lifted him clear of the floor.

Just when he thought his hand was going to be crushed to a pulpy mess, a tinny voice – as if heard over a tannoy – spoke through the automaton.

"Stop! Bring this one to me."

And as Ulysses stared into the golem-droid's face once again, and despite the hot pain blooming in his hand, he couldn't help thinking that there was something strangely and unpleasantly familiar about the voice.

But surely it couldn't be, he thought, his mind suddenly awhirl, for it was a voice he had thought he would never hear again.

It was the voice of a dead man.

CHAPTER TWENTY

Rainmaker

Spring-Heeled Jack clung to a metal rung on the underside of the Weather Station as he carefully fixed another of his limpet mines to the superstructure. No bigger than the palm of his hand, the mine was held in place by a powerful electromagnet. Once activated, a red light on the device informed him that it was armed.

Thomas Sanctuary reached into a container on his utility belt and, finding it empty, tried the next. He didn't have many of the magnet mines left. Glancing back along the length of the *Jupiter Station* from his precarious position slung beneath the vessel, he could see a string of twinkling red lights. He was going to have to make the last few mines count.

He had planted the devices in several strategic positions – from the great turbine fans positioned beneath the outer ring of the station and cavorite-shielded ballast tanks, to the seams where the pre-fabricated sections of the ship had been bolted together. Unlike the small grenades he had made use of in the sewer tunnels, each of the mines was set to detonate remotely, the trigger unit attached to the vigilante's utility belt.

Thomas's intention was that each of the explosions would have a domino effect on the structure. A strategically blown joint could result in a whole supporting arm tearing away from the central Hub. A small detonation underneath a fuel store would cause a chain reaction of larger explosions that could cause the station to disintegrate entirely.

But the total detonation of the mines was only to be initiated as a last resort if the mission of wresting control of the *Jupiter Station* from whoever had taken it failed. Thomas hoped that, right at that moment, Ulysses Quicksilver was inside the craft, putting that very plan into action. But when he considered the attack by the crewmen that had could so easily have sent him plummeting to his death, somehow he doubted it was going to be quite as simple as that.

He looked down at his dented breastplate. The two concave impact marks were clear to see. He couldn't pretend that his chest didn't hurt – he imagined that when he finally got the chance to remove the suit he would find that the bruising covered much of his chest. But without the armour plating he would have been dead.

After being shot, momentarily stunned, he had dropped a good few hundred feet through the Smog layer before he had been able to extend his cape and pull himself up out of his death-dive. He had then been able to reactivate his jetpack and return to the Weather Station.

He was glad that he had taken the opportunity to return to Sanctuary House after escaping from the Fleet sewer and recharge the jetpack's fuel tanks, as well as emptying his store of micro-mines.

Gunning the throttle of the jetpack, Thomas swung himself free of the underside of the Station, coming up slowly on the outer face of the ring, well away from any viewing ports. Of course he didn't know what other manner of detection devices there might be on board. But, if the terrorists were tracking him, they hadn't sent anyone to deal with him yet.

Moving cautiously towards another landing stage, cape outstretched to give him greater control over his approach, Thomas came down on the *Jupiter Station*. Another ornamented iron door awaited him at the hub-ward end of the airship mooring point.

Giving the distant ground one last glance – barely able to make out Hyde Park through the pall of the Smog now – his pulse pounding inside his head, he approached the door, one hand hovering over the grenade pocket of his utility belt.

It was time to play the hero once again.

With the Limehouse Golem's massive hands clamping his arms to his sides, Ulysses Quicksilver was carried onto the bridge of Weather Control, at the heart of the *Jupiter Station*.

He found himself looking down into the centre of operations located at the bottom of the Hub. The control room was surrounded by a panoramic window, giving those working within – monitoring weather patterns and striving to influence them accordingly – a three-hundred-and-sixty degree view of the city beneath, seen through a network of glass and steel that reminded Ulysses of the great glasshouses of Kew.

The golem came to stand at the edge of a curved platform that ran around the entire circumference of the control room, three equidistantly placed iron grille staircases leading down into Weather Control itself.

Beneath Ulysses stood three banks of equipment made up of what appeared to be a combination of Babbage Engine consoles and monitoring equipment. It was obviously from here that the meteorologists hoped to be able to influence the weather, dispersing the clouds on a rainy day to bring sun to the shadowed streets beneath, or cool breezes when there was a sweltering heat wave.

At the centre of the room atop a raised dais stood the station commander's throne. Sitting upon it now was a hunched elderly gentleman, apparently relishing his chance to laud it over everyone. As the golem-droid entered the chamber, the old man looked up and gave a gasp of delight as he caught sight of Ulysses trapped within the monster's clutches.

"Excellent, you're here at last," he old man said with manic glee. He steepled his fingers before him, elbows resting on the arms of the commander's chair. "Now we can make a start."

"You've been expecting me?" Ulysses asked.

"No, not precisely. But seeing that you *are* here now, you can bear witness to my final triumph. And I can proceed in the certain knowledge that there is nothing you can do to stop me this time."

It was that voice again. But could it really be him? Was this twisted figure really Uriah Wormwood?

They never had found a body, and although Ulysses had hoped that the former Prime Minister, and unrepentant megalomaniac, really had died in the airship collision with Tower Bridge, a part of him had half-expected that this moment might come. All the same, it didn't stop Ulysses from feeling shocked to the very core of his being.

That shock was doubled as his eyes darted from the old man to the flame-haired nurse at his side.

It was all starting to make sense. Ulysses had been certain that the late Professor Galapagos' de-evolution serum had been the catalyst for the insect regressions but he had barely even entertained the idea that his arch-nemesis would be behind it all. But considering the DNA-warping effects of the serum, coupled with the identity of the voice he heard speak through the golem-droid and the presence of Kitty Hawke, who had also seemingly risen from the dead – although not entirely unscathed, judging by the ostentatious patch covering her left eye – it could only mean one thing. The unthinkable – the end of the world as he knew it. The end of the empire.

Ulysses quickly took in the control room's occupants, hostages and hostage-takers alike.

Even though he hadn't at first recognised Uriah Wormwood there was no mistaking Kitty Hawke. Her hair might be a fiery shade of crimson now, rather than auburn, but he would have recognised that figure anywhere. She was a femme fatale of the first order; the last time they had met, she had tried to kill him.

She was wearing the most outrageously provocative white and red medical uniform, that made her look more like one of the girls from the Queen of Hearts' Temple of Venus rather than an actual member of the nursing profession. It was all high heels, fish-net stockings, short belted dress, unbuttoned at the front to create a plunging neckline and expose far too much of her cleavage.

She was smiling at him provocatively, the eyebrow above the scarred orbit covered by the clinical white eye-patch arched suggestively. Her skirt was split at the side to reveal a small pistol holster above her stocking top, the holster for the same small pistol she was toying with carelessly in her right hand. The demure Miss Genevieve Galapagos, that had been her creation, was long gone!

As he watched her intently, she blew him a kiss from her pouting, full red lips. "Hello, lover," she said. "It's been too long."

"Not as far as I'm concerned," Ulysses growled in reply.

A lab-coated scientist was manning the main instrument panel below the command position, with a crewman – whom Ulysses took to be the pilot – at the console next to him, standing behind the ship's wheel. Two further smartly turned out crewmen manned the two remaining consoles. But there was no indication that these men were being coerced to work for Wormwood. So Ulysses could only assume that they were in on the whole thing.

A third of the way around the walkway on which the golem stood, stood the Prime Minister Devlin Valentine, an armed guard at his side.

"Good morning, Prime Minister," Ulysses said, nodding at Valentine.

Devlin Valentine threw him a look of annoyance. "Quicksilver, isn't it?" he said, as he took in Ulysses' dishevelled appearance.

"Yes, sir. It's a pleasure to meet you at last."

"And I you. I only wish it was under more convivial circumstances. I have followed your exploits with interest."

"Enough!" the old man shouted. This was his moment and he

wasn't going to let anybody ruin it for him. "When you two are quite ready we can begin!"

"Begin what? What's going on Beaufort-Monsoon?" the Prime Minister demanded, the fear that his crowning glory was about to come crashing down about his ears furnishing him with the courage to challenge the old man.

"Oh, I think we know each other well enough now, Valentine, that we can dispense with such formalities."

"What do you mean? What formalities?"

"I think we can dispense with aliases now, don't you, Wormwood?" Ulysses chipped in.

The old man bristled, the dandy having stolen his thunder.

"Wormwood?" Devlin Valentine gasped. "*The* Wormwood? *Uriah* Wormwood?"

"The very same!"

"I had hoped you were dead," Ulysses said.

The man Valentine had referred to as Beaufort-Monsoon, had dispensed with his bottle-bottom glasses and was now peeling the last of the latex rubber mask from his face.

Although he was now recognisable as Ulysses' former government contact and Prime Minister Valentine's predecessor, it was not the same face Ulysses had last seen aboard the zeppelin that had carried them both away from Hyde Park and the jubilee debacle. Half the flesh of his face had melted like wax and reset in a knot of raw and twisted tissue.

"Hardly charitable of you, Quicksilver," the old man chided, sounding smug at the same time, "but as you can see I am very much – what's the expression? – alive and kicking."

"Hardly kicking though, are you?" Ulysses remarked, with a nod towards the old man's wheelchair.

"Ah, do not let appearances deceive you. That always was your problem, as I recall." He stood up.

"So how did you escape the zeppelin?" Ulysses asked, trying not to appear too startled by the old man's latest revelation.

"As you can see," Wormwood said, pointing to his scarred face, "I didn't escape unscathed."

"There was no coming back from that inferno."

"And yet here we are."

It was clear to Ulysses now that everything that had happened since Prime Minister Valentine came to power had all been part of Wormwood's plan. In the last eight months he had simply picked up from where he had left off.

Ulysses considered everything he had discovered over the last few days: the de-evolution to an insect-like state of various members of London's populace brought on, in part at least, by the consumption of Dr Feelgood's Tonic Stout, a drink that had taken the capital, and beyond, by storm; the secret chemical production plant where Feelgood's patent panacea was manufactured, and combined with Wormwood's secret formula; and then there was the second solution that had been pumped all the way to the *Jupiter Station's* hangar on Hampstead Heath.

The chemical plant must have all existed before Uriah Wormwood was ever exposed as the mastermind behind the Darwinian Dawn. It had all been waiting there, in the shadows, ready to be brought into play as necessary, to further Wormwood's master-plan to force the British empire to change for, what he believed to be, its own good. And now Ulysses saw the true scale of Wormwood's operation, the extent of his ambition, how great an empire he had built for himself, hidden at the very heart of the stagnating monster that, after one hundred and fifty years, Magna Britannia had become.

"Things have come full circle," Wormwood stated, an icy smile on his face, and Ulysses felt the bottom drop out of his world. Trapped in the clutches of the madman's droid, with Spring-Heeled Jack having fallen to his death and Nimrod too far away to help, there really was nothing more that he could do.

"Shoot it down! *Shoot it down!*" Ulysses hissed under his breath, as if De Wynter might somehow hear him and have time to act before the whole of London paid the price for Wormwood's revenge.

How much time was left until their mutually agreed deadline? Had De Wynter uncharacteristically cut them some slack and allowed them longer to complete their mission? Ulysses sincerely hoped not.

"What's that?" Wormwood said with a cruel chuckle. "No-one's going to shoot us out of the sky when I have so many very important people on board! They wouldn't dare. Especially not since their precious Prime Minister is stuck up here with us. I doubt those on the ground will even know anything's awry up here, until it's too late."

"That's what you think."

"It matters not! Whatever they have planned, they'll be too late!"

"Do they really know what's going on up here? Those on the ground, I mean?" Valentine asked softly.

"Indeed they do, sir," Ulysses replied. "Indeed they do! And right now there's a whole squadron of zeppelins on their way to liberate the *Jupiter*."

A harsh bark of laughter cut through the tense atmosphere. "Helm, is there anything on the scopes?" Wormwood asked.

"No, sir," the helmsman replied. "There's nothing. The skies are clear."

"You're bluffing!" Wormwood snarled at Ulysses.

"What are you going to do?" Valentine asked Wormwood, his voice rising in desperation. "What is it you want? Is it money? That's why you've taken hostages isn't it?"

"No, it isn't. What I want is change, the opportunity to wipe the slate clean, if you will, and start again. I want nothing less than the total destruction of Londinium Maximum, the city that has so far spurned my very best efforts to drag it kicking and screaming into the twenty-first century. I want to force it to evolve. I want the chance to re-build, to start again. To rule!

"And now things have come full circle, and it seems almost poetic that you are here to witness my triumph, as I witness your minds shatter, as you are forced to accept that everything you have fought for has all been for naught!"

"Is that what this is?" Ulysses shouted. "A competition? A test to see who's the best? If you want to have this out with me, let's do it, here and now!"

"Don't flatter yourself. This isn't about you. What, you think that you've become my... my nemesis? You are not worthy of the title. Look at you. You're a nobody. You're nothing but a ridiculous fop with a monkey's arm, an over-inflated sense of your own importance and delusions of grandeur. You couldn't stop me before and you won't stop me now. How does it feel, Quicksilver," the old man gloated, "to know that you only managed to delay the inevitable, that all you have struggled for has been for nothing?"

Ulysses was barely aware of what was happening around him on the bridge as the control room became a bustling hive of activity.

He was roused from his shocked stupor by a commotion on the far side of the deck, as a pair of armed crewmen marched into the Hub, a tall, black-suited figure held forcibly between them.

"Sorry to interrupt, sir," the bolder of the two began, "but we found this character snooping around the storage tanks."

"Excellent. Excellent." Wormwood crowed. "The more the merrier. Now, take a look all of you," he said, taking in the view beyond the panoramic windows, "and marvel at what science and a superior intellect can achieve!

"Gentlemen, the time had come. Activate the Weather Station. Initiate cloud-seeding. The command is given and the command is 'Rainmaker'!"

As the white-coated scientist and the crewmen operating the controls set to work a deep, bass hum rose to fill the control room, the steel plates of the walkway vibrating in sympathy with its harsh harmonics.

"Look on my works, ye mighty, and despair!" Wormwood pronounced in a loud voice over the rising hum of esoteric machineries. "I'd say it looks like rain."

CHAPTER TWENTY-ONE

Valentine's Day

With a great grinding of gears, grilles opened in the bottom of the Weather Station's outer ring. Preceded by a hollow gurgling, with a gushing roar that reverberated throughout the vessel, a chemical torrent pumped from the reservoirs of storage tanks, along the twisting pipework intestines of the *Jupiter*, and a moment later it started to rain.

The oily yellow downpour cascaded from the outlets all around the underside of the torus. Ulysses could see the chemical shower quite clearly, the droplets steaming acidly as they came into contact with the Smog layer below. And he fancied he saw something else through the toxic rain; a smattering of blinking red lights.

As Ulysses and the others watched, thousands of gallons of the sickly yellow liquid rained down upon the stubborn cloud cover. The fat, greasy raindrops gave off acrid puffs of vapour as they came into contact with the pollution-suffused clouds.

As the chemical shower continued, Ulysses could see discoloration occurring within the Smog, filthy trails darkening the surrounding morass, a shimmer of oily iridescence rippling across it.

At last, the steady shower began to slow until it finally stopped, the last few droplets still clinging to the mouths of outlet pipes. A noisy gurgling, as of a cistern emptying, belched through the pipes located above the control room.

"Cloud-seeding complete," Wormwood's pet meteorologist announced.

"Excellent! Then commence ionisation of the atmosphere."

Switches were activated and levers were thrown and, slowly, the *Jupiter Station* began to spin. The motion was surprisingly smooth, Ulysses noticed, but the whole of the Weather Machine was turning, like a wheel – there could be no doubt of that.

"Charging hull," a crewman announced.

As well as all the other sounds echoing throughout the Weather Station, Ulysses could now make out a crackling hum. As he continued to gaze helplessly out of the vast panoramic window he saw lightning crackling from the underside of the *Jupiter* – like St Elmo's fire from the mast of a tea-clipper. In response he discerned a darkening of the sky around them. Before their very eyes, water vapour was condensing out of the air, forming ragged scuds of cirrus that were then spiralling towards the rotating Weather Station, merging to form great grey cumulonimbus conglomerations.

The rotations of the *Jupiter* continued, more water vapour condensing out of the ionised air. And it seemed that, the more clouds appeared, the more continued to appear with every rotation. Cloud cover over the city was increasing exponentially. The electrical discharge had spread beyond the Weather Station now, fitful flickers of lightning skittering across the darkening sky in a spectrum of colours.

The Smog appeared to be rising, drawn towards the rotating wheel of the *Jupiter*, metallic pinks and greens, like a beetle's wings, flashing through the massing storm, the morning sky now the colour of beaten pewter.

A rumble of thunder rolled overhead. The gravity-defying Weather Station shook.

Kitty gasped, looking all around her, scanning the storm massing beyond the glass and steel walls of the control room.

"Have no fear, my dear," Wormwood told her. "The *Jupiter* is designed to withstand hurricane force winds and its insulated hull can withstand a direct lightning strike."

They appeared to be right in the middle of the massing thunderheads now, the spinning Weather Station dwarfed by the boiling black clouds. Thunder boomed directly overhead, so loud it seemed to shatter the sky, and sheet lightning, as bright as supernovae, sliced the sky apart. With another cacophonous crash, the heavens opened and the downpour commenced.

A deluge of Biblical proportions fell on the darkened city below.

It fell on parks and gardens. It fell on chapels and churches. It fell on the homes of the rich and the slums of the East End. It fell on the Overground and the omnibuses, horses whinnying as the sudden cloudburst took them by surprise. It fell on the building works at the Tower of London maximum security prison and on St Paul's Cathedral. It fell on the British Museum and the Palace of Westminster. It fell on the confused crowds gathered at Hyde Park. And where it fell, it changed people.

A businessman, running for shelter, his copy of *The Financial Times* over his head, the pink paper disintegrating under the pounding acidic rain, collapsed at Oxford Circus, the contents of his dropped briefcase spilling across the pavement and into the gutter. A huddle of women passing by, running to get out of the rain themselves, muttered to each other that he was "falling down drunk" and "a disgrace." They did not hang about and so did not see the transformation that suddenly overtook the spasming wretch.

As he lay there, face-down in the street – legs kicking

convulsively at the paving slabs, hands flailing in puddles of oily rain – the back of his coat suddenly lifted and shredded, as wing cases tore from his shoulder blades, the flesh falling from his arms and legs to reveal chitinous limbs, a third pair of limbs thrusting through the sides of his body as ribs re-shaped themselves into something altogether more befitting a cockroach.

A woman screamed, frozen in terror at what had befallen the man, the mutating rain spilling down her face. Her shrill scream became a descending moan as her own face re-shaped itself, her jawbone fracturing and peeling back to become the chittering mouthparts of a giant insect.

A tramp sheltering beneath London Bridge, the rain pounding the shingle of the river-beach, watched as the pilot of one of the myriad steam-ferries that criss-crossed the Thames – hour after hour, day in day out – lost control of his craft as, his whole body shaking, he fell onto his back and began to change. The boat, now out of control, collided with one of the piers of the bridge, the current swinging it round so that it blocked the central span of Blackfriars.

The tramp, too intoxicated on cheap gin to understand what was going on, knocked back another slug of the strange brew from the brown glass bottle that he had been sharing with his dog – the image of a bearded man leering at him from the label. The laughter provoked by the ferryman's unfortunate situation died on his lips as the canine's head split open like an overripe tomato, the flesh of its muzzle tearing apart as the dog-sized bluebottle pulled itself free of its dog-skin pupa.

The rain dropped its deadly payload on the Old Montague Street Workhouse.

Governor Trimble liked to think of himself as something of a social reformer. He saw it as his duty to make sure that those sent into his care improved themselves in body and mind during their stay, so that they might eventually leave and become useful members of society. It had been with this driving purpose in mind that he had invested a goodly sum of the money given to him by the government to run the facility each week, in Dr Feelgood's Tonic Stout, distributing the patent panacea to the inmates every Thursday, encouraging them to take a measure of the tonic at every meal break.

On the morning of the fourteenth of February, three hundred and sixty-one inmates were out in the exercise yard taking part in a compulsory PT session – another of Governor Trimble's initiatives, part of his over-arching 'Think Fit' philosophy.

By the time the cleanup crews reached the Old Montague Street Workhouse, nothing was found of Governor Trimble other than his false teeth.

In the garden of their home in Holland Park, the Pevensey children huddled together inside the tree house their father had built for them. They watched, eyes wide in shock and dread, as Nanny Goodison's face melted beneath her bonnet and became a nightmarish mass of feeding tendrils, as their baby brother's skin split to allow the pulsating caterpillar to escape from within.

Nanny had always shown Baby how he should take his medicine, taking a spoonful herself first, first thing in the morning and last thing before bed.

Iron hoops scavenged from broken barrels to become children's playthings, bowled and bounced along the gutters of cobbled streets as the urchins that had been playing with them lost the ability to even comprehend what play was, as they too de-evolved into something even lower down the social ladder than the orphaned children of working class slum dwellers.

The train running on the southbound section of the District Line failed to stop at Paddington and ploughed into the platform at Bayswater killing fourteen people instantly, as the driver, exposed to the wind and the rain in his cab, became a limbless gastropod, a half-finished bottle of stout still in his canvas bag lying on the floor at his feet.

"Open fire!" De Wynter bellowed into the personal communicator. "Open fire on the *Jupiter*! Captain? Captain!" he roared, but he obviously wasn't getting any response from whoever was at the other end of the line.

Eliza looked from the big man squeezed into the front passenger seat of the Silver Phantom to Nimrod, sat behind the wheel, staring at the rain-lashed windscreen.

"Damn it all to hell!" De Wynter raged.

"What happened? What's going on?" the young tart asked, tears streaking her cheeks. She couldn't quite believe that De Wynter had given the order to fire on the Weather Station, even though Ulysses, the vigilante and half the empire's most important people were still on board. The blow he had laid against her, as she had tried to stop him, had split her lip and she could feel a bruise swelling on her cheek.

Nimrod turned and looked at her with a mixture of sadness and sympathy, and was it her imagination or were his eyes also glistening with the rumour of tears?

"I would imagine that the Battersea Battery is suffering the effects of the rain, just as the poor wretches caught out in the open here," Ulysses' butler said.

"Thank God for that," Eliza murmured as she turned to gaze out of the window, watching the figures flopping and twitching in the quagmire that the carefully manicured lawns of Hyde Park had so quickly become.

From their vantage point aboard the bridge of the *Jupiter Station*, Wormwood's prisoners could do nothing but watch as chaos consumed the streets below.

Devlin Valentine stared slack-mouthed at the broiling clouds as the rain continued to fall, with no sign of it stopping – or so it seemed to his overwrought mind. All that he had worked for, the symbol he had wanted to give the nation, and the world, to demonstrate that Prime Minister Valentine meant business, the means by which he had hoped to make his mark upon the face of London, had all gone to wrack and ruin. The will of a madman had turned his greatest achievement into the worst disaster to befall the city since 1666.

He had hoped that this day would go down in history as the day he left the capital changed forever. Well, he had certainly managed to achieve that. His own pride and over-reaching ambition had proved to be not only his downfall but also that of the city of which he was so proud.

Of course that had been Halcyon Beaufort-Monsoon's intention as well. The seemingly beneficent Beaufort-Monsoon had once said something along those lines, in fact, that he wanted to give something back to the city that had given him so much. Little had Valentine known then that what London had given him was a disfigured face, crippling injuries, and an unrivalled desire for revenge.

Valentine looked helplessly from the grim-faced Quicksilver to the masked vigilante. Despite all the guilt and regret that was consuming his mind, there was still one small part – the part that remembered that he was a politician – that was looking for a way out of this mess, searching for some way to turn the apparently hopeless situation to his advantage. This small part of his mind realised that the curiously-apparelled individual was the vigilante who had been terrorizing the Limehouse district, the one the press had dubbed the new Spring-Heeled Jack and who, at that moment, might well be the only one who could rescue them from their seemingly hopeless situation.

If Spring-Heeled Jack was capable of only half the things the papers claimed he could do, then he might still have his part to play, if only he wasn't being held prisoner. It really seemed as if Uriah Wormwood, disgraced former Prime Minister had won and stolen Valentine's moment of glory.

Somewhere deep within him a spark ignited and the words of a small, calm voice echoed inside his skull: "We are not beaten yet."

He might not have martial arts skills, prescience or a jetpack-powered flying suit, but he still had his intellect and his politician's cunning. His quick-thinking had got him out of enough tricky situations before – usually during debates in the House of Commons – and had helped make him that man he was today. Why shouldn't it save him now?

And he wasn't alone either; he didn't have to do it all by himself, did he? All he needed to do was topple the first domino, then he was sure the others would follow, falling under the weight of destiny.

Giving voice to a feeble moan, Devlin Valentine collapsed in a dead faint. The crewman watching him was taken momentarily by surprise. But a moment was all Valentine needed.

As he dropped, he kicked out behind him, catching the crewman across the shin. Losing his balance and surprised by the pain, the man doubled up, bringing his gun within Valentine's reach. Grabbing the barrel of the weapon Valentine sprang up, pushing the pistol up and out of his guard's hands. Valentine then brought the butt round hard, smashing it into the man's nose. He heard the wet crack of cartilage shattering and, with a stifled wail, the crewman went down.

All this had taken only a matter of seconds but now everyone else's attention was fully on him.

"Stop him!" Wormwood screamed, but Valentine was already moving. He was a sitting duck, exposed on top of the gangway. Even though he had a gun, this was simply a by-product of his assault on his guard, it hadn't been the main objective of his plan. All that was on his mind now was that he needed to even the odds. What he needed now were reinforcements. Dropping the pistol, he turned and ran.

A shot rang out, the bullet panging off the grilled floor of the walkway, but he was already two strides ahead of it. And every bounding step brought him closer and closer to the looming presence that was the motionless golem-droid. The only thing about the automaton that indicated it was still operational was the weakly pulsing glow of light behind its headlamp eyes.

Another shot sent sparks flying from the walkway in front

of him, but Valentine didn't falter in his frantic sprint to reach the robot. He heard Wormwood scream for his men to stop shooting and get after him.

And then he was there, gasping for breath, the hulking automaton and the captive Quicksilver before him.

"My sword!" the dandy hissed at him, craning his head in an effort to see behind him as crewmen left their work stations and moved to stop the valiant Prime Minister. A siren sounded, accompanied by the pounding of feet moving along adjoining passageways. "It's in my cane. Take hold of the bloodstone. Pull it free!"

Valentine had no idea how strong the droid's self-defence subroutines were, how it might react if it found itself threatened. Well, he was about to find out.

Quicksilver still had a hold of his cane in his left hand, although with his arms pinned to his sides, he had been unable to do anything more with it. But Valentine could.

Grabbing hold of the bloodstone, as Quicksilver had instructed, he pulled hard. As he reeled backwards, the keen rapier blade slid free of the black wood shaft.

For a moment, Valentine thought he saw the light within the robot's eyes pulse and he felt ice water trickle down his spine. There really was no time left to lose. He either acted now to save the day – and died a hero into the bargain – or he did nothing and would be remembered for all eternity as the architect of the atrocity consuming the city below.

Valentine danced around the droid as another poorly-judged shot rang from its ceramic carapace. It would only be a matter of seconds before the approaching crewmen caught up with him.

And then he saw it. Forcing the blade into the cavity beneath the droid's arm, he caught the bundle of hydraulic cabling against the edge of the sword and pulled down sharply. There was a pop followed by the hiss of fluid escaping and the droid's huge right hand flexed open.

Only one hand had opened but it was enough. Using the colossus' other arm for leverage, Ulysses forced himself free, clenching his teeth in pain as the remaining vice-tight steel and ceramic claw scraped the skin from his back and chest.

With a clattering of cogs and gears, the golem powered up again and a rumbling roar rose from within the depths of its furnace heart.

Ulysses dared risk a glance up at the mechanical behemoth behind him. His first priority had to be to get out of reach of its still functioning left hand, and then stay out of reach.

"Come on!" he shouted at the Prime Minister. "This way!"

With Valentine close on his heels, Ulysses made for the nearest exit. He took the approaching crewmen by surprise as he ran straight towards them, intent on reaching the passageway before they thought to risk using firearms again.

It was now, or never.

With two of their supposed captives free, the crewmen holding Jack suddenly found their loyalties torn, not knowing whether to keep hold of their prisoner or aid in the re-capture of the two escapees.

The vigilante felt the pressure on his pinned arms ease, only ever so slightly but it was enough.

Tensing the muscles of both his arms, with a sudden jerk, Thomas pulled free of his guards' grasp long enough to activate the spring-loaded opening mechanism of his cape.

The glider-wing extended forcibly behind him, unbalancing the two crewmen and pushing them away. Properly free at last, he made a grab for the trigger at his belt.

In one fluid motion he flipped the cover free and flicked the switch. The illuminated button beneath turned red. He hesitated for only a moment, listening to his pulse pounding inside his head; but it was only a moment.

He hit the button.

The first explosion sent a tremor through the control room, the faces of all those present contorting in shock and surprise. But it was only the first.

CHAPTER TWENTY-TWO

Unfinshed Business

One explosion after another sent an ever-expanding shockwave rippling throughout the superstructure of the *Jupiter Station*. Detonations tore great holes in the glass and steel outer ring, sending diamond bright crystal shards spinning out into the storm, the tiny glass fragments reflecting back the bursts of light that flashed across the sky beneath the towering black thunderheads.

Where one mine failed to detonate, the flames from another explosion close by touched it off. The explosions produced by the mines themselves were not particularly large – punching holes in the metal skin of the Weather Station or destroying coupling brackets – but the secondary explosions they caused within fuel tanks, cavorite-shielded ballasts chambers and electrolytic power cells, were of another magnitude altogether. As the fuel supply for the station's huge turbine fans lit off, a sheet of flame erupted from the *Jupiter*, blasting a hundred feet into the storm-wracked sky.

Chemical residue boiled away in burning clouds of noxious green vapour. Antennae sheared off and the esoteric machineries needed for weather control shutdown as a wave of fire swept across the top of the Hub. But in actuality it was the Hub and the control room itself that got off most lightly. The vigilante had not planted any of his magnet mines on that part of the structure and so it only suffered superficial damage as pieces of twisted metal and spears of glass whickered through the air over the top of the central section of the huge Weather Station.

Finally the explosions ceased leaving only a few pernicious fires burning within the superstructure, a shower of silvery droplets rising from the cavorite ballast tanks housed in one devastated section of the outer ring.

The *Jupiter* had stopped spinning now, and was listing badly to one side where the eruption of the fuel tanks had destroyed a good sixth of the torus, exposing the end of one curving passageway to the raging elements.

Wind and rain rushed into the ragged opening, the howling gale screaming through the inter-linking passageways all the way to the Hub and into the control room.

Ulysses could hear distant screams over the shrieking vortex whirling around the chamber. They were coming from the nearest intact passageway leading back to the ruined outer ring of the station. The screams were underscored by the arrhythmic drumming of glass and metal rattling and spanging off the panoramic windows of Weather Control as flying debris from other parts of the vessel struck it.

On board the bridge of the *Jupiter* all was chaos.

The scene inside the control room, as the first of Spring-Heeled Jack's magnet mines detonated, had seen the glazed golem powering after Ulysses and Valentine as they fled, the dandy's rapier still clutched tightly in the Prime Minister's hands, the two crewmen the vigilante had sent reeling still trying to recover themselves as Jack leapt from the walkway, wings outstretched, Valentine's former guard still crawled about on his hands and knees, blood pouring from his shattered nose, while Uriah Wormwood issued orders in a panic, Kitty Hawke watching the progress of the escapees intently, her pistol trained on the swooping vigilante, as the technical team tried to remain focused on the task of maintaining the *Jupiter*'s place within the eye of the storm.

But as the wave of explosions continued, the whole structure of the Weather Station shook, sending those at their posts staggering, while those running stumbled and, in some cases, went sprawling onto the deck.

A crewman pursuing the escapees screamed as he landed awkwardly on the hard grille, his grunt becoming an agonised screech of pain as the golem crushed his spine beneath one huge iron-shod foot. The man's cry was abruptly cut off as the crushing weight of the two-ton automaton pulped flesh and bone, severing the wretched man's body in two.

Another explosion shook the *Jupiter* and the station lurched again. Ulysses suddenly found himself trying to run in mid-air, falling onto the circling gangway. Valentine somersaulted past him, tumbling through the space beneath a handrail, crash-landing hard on the grilled deck of the bridge below.

Ulysses caught sight of another crewman closing the distance between them, coming around the side of the chamber along the balcony walkway. And he could hear the crashing steps of the golem closing from behind.

At that moment, Ulysses' world tilted through forty-five degrees. As he started sliding backwards, he flung out an arm, the fingers of his right hand closing round the stanchion of a handrail. The approaching crewman suddenly found himself running down a steep incline, lost his footing and went sailing past Ulysses, wailing in shock. A resounding clang behind him told him that, thankfully, the golem had also been sent hurtling backwards to land against the panoramic window.

Still clinging to the metal pole, by one hand, Ulysses pushed himself onto his back and looked down at the sprawled bodies lying under the two-ton mass of the golem, the crushing weight of the automaton trapping them against the reinforced glass and steel.

He saw a twitching arm and leg and part of a white lab coat, and knew that Wormwood's pet scientist wouldn't be helping anyone anymore. Another crewman lay trapped by the brute monster, both legs crushed beneath its ceramic and steel body.

Halfway between Ulysses and the incapacitated bridge crew, the pilot still clung to the ship's wheel, although it was apparent that its movements were no longer affecting the course of the *Jupiter*.

Through the panoramic window, Ulysses could see the greasy mass of the Smog rising to meet the craft while, through the windows above, it was clear that with nothing binding them to the Weather Station any more, the looming thunderheads were dissolving into wisps of grey, the storm dissipating.

There could be no doubt now that the *Jupiter* was losing height.

Wormwood and his deadly accomplice were both clinging to the command chair, Kitty obviously unsure whether to try to stop Ulysses escaping or ensure that she and Wormwood made it off the bridge safely.

Lying slumped over one of the cogitator banks of a control console was Devlin Valentine, blood oozing from a gash on his forehead. Mercifully, Ulysses' precious sword-cane was still in his hands.

"Prime Minister!" Ulysses called over the creaks and groans of the disintegrating platform. "Can you hear me?"

Slowly Valentine raised his head. He looked up at Ulysses with half-closed eyes. He blinked, managing to focus at last on the dangling dandy.

"Are you all right?" Ulysses called down to him.

"I'm all right," Valentine said. He sounded drunk, as he slurred his words.

"I'll come down."

"No, no. I'm all right. I'll come up." With that, using whatever jutting protuberances came to hand, Valentine started pulling himself up the tilted floor towards the nearest set of cantilevered steps.

"Quicksilver!" a booming voice shouted. It was Spring-Heeled Jack. He was leaning out from the entrance to the access tunnel. "Come this way!"

Ulysses scrambled up the incline of the balcony until he was within reach of Jack's outstretched hand, the vigilante pulling him up the rest of the way.

Below them, Ulysses was aware of Wormwood struggling to cross the flight deck to another access tunnel, Kitty Hawke aiding the old man whilst still casting wary glances back to check on Ulysses' progress, while Valentine had made it to the bottom of the tilted staircase.

And then Ulysses caught the look in Kitty's eye and knew that her priorities had changed. Then the pistol was in her hand as she supported herself against a swivel chair, bolted to the floor in front of one of the control consoles.

Spring-Heeled Jack saw it too. "Look out!" he shouted, as he pulled Ulysses into the entrance to the tilted passageway. He then turned his back on the woman, shielding Ulysses with his own body. There was the crack of the pistol shot and Ulysses fancied he heard a dull metal thud.

Spring-Heeled Jack didn't move.

"Are you all right?" Ulysses gasped, staring at his protector in disbelief.

"I'm fine," Jack answered, his voice an emotionless monotone. "I'm like a cat, me. I've got nine lives, although I suppose I've used two of them up in the space of less than half an hour. They should call me the Black Cat."

"I think Spring-Heeled Jack suits you better. Now move out of the way."

"What are you planning to do?" Then Jack saw the gun in Ulysses' hand. "Oh, I see."

Ulysses took aim. The bitch was in his sights. She had tried to kill him once before and now it was time for payback.

Ulysses squeezed the trigger.

With a deafening shriek of rending metal, the bridge lurched again, briefly righting itself before tipping to one side. Ulysses stumbled backwards as he fought to keep his balance and the shot went wide, hitting a metal strut in the roof and ricocheting off.

He saw his target duck. But the continued collapse of the station had aided Wormwood and Kitty's escape, the cantilevered floor sending them skidding and sliding towards their exit as Ulysses and Jack clung onto the swaying structure.

For a moment, Ulysses looked like he was going to follow them. But then the decision was taken out of his hands. With a twisting groan of buckling metal, one of the ceiling beams came crashing down across the entrance to the tunnel, barring their way and preventing Ulysses from going after the megalomaniac and his aide.

With a clanging crash another girder came down as the Weather Station continued to shake itself apart, this time barely missing the stumbling Valentine as it landed only a matter of a few feet behind him. But the Prime Minister was on his feet again in a second, hauling himself up the iron staircase using both handrails. In a moment he had caught up to them.

"This way!" Ulysses called to the dishevelled Prime Minister, before setting off after the vigilante.

"Where are the dignitaries?" Ulysses panted as they ran.

"They're safe." the vigilante said.

"Are you sure about that?"

"They're all contained within the outer viewing gallery. I saw them there before I was captured."

"We have to get them out of here!" Ulysses said. "I don't believe that a place like this wouldn't have escape pods or dirigible lifeboats. You have to get the dignitaries off the *Jupiter*. Do you think you can do that?"

"Leave it to me. I doubt I'll meet much resistance, not now. What are you going to do?"

"I'm going after the bastard responsible for all this!"

The floor shook beneath them and Ulysses' words were drowned out by the clattering of another girder coming down across the entrance to Weather Control, the access tunnel itself buckling.

Ulysses looked round in horror. That last girder had come down between them and the Prime Minister, blocking Valentine's escape route.

"Come on!" Jack shouted over the clamour of the disintegrating craft. "There's nothing you can do for him now!"

"Just watch me," Ulysses said, fiery determination in his voice. And then he hesitated for a moment. "Have you got any more of those fireworks of yours?"

Jack pressed a button on a dispenser on his utility belt. A single, hemi-spherical magnet mine dropped into his hand.

"I'm almost out, but take this one."

"Wish me luck," Ulysses said, curling his fingers around the explosive device.

"Good luck," the vigilante said darkly and then turned out of the end of the passageway, heading for the viewing gallery and the beleaguered VIPs.

Ulysses sprinted back the way they had just come until he stood before the fallen girder, peering through the latticework of its structure, trying to see whether the Prime Minister was even still alive or how he was going to get through, all the while calling Valentine's name.

Ulysses put his shoulder to the beam and pushed but, as he had already suspected, to no avail. The steel was well and truly wedged. The only thing that was going to move it now was the magnet mine. Even then, he would have to make sure that he put it in just the right place.

Propping himself against one tilting wall, his mind working feverishly, Ulysses tried to work out precisely where he should position the explosive device.

With a scream of metal grating against metal, the girder heaved sideways and Ulysses took a shocked step backwards, fearing for a moment that the Hub had suffered some catastrophic damage and was about to plummet to the ground.

But it was worse than that he realised as a bolt of prescient pain seared straight through his skull.

The beam suddenly screeched to one side.

Cold dread gripped his body as Ulysses Quicksilver came face to face with the unstoppable juggernaut powerhouse that was the Limehouse Golem, one last time.

CHAPTER TWENTY-THREE

Wormwood Falling

The massive droid reached for Ulysses with its one working arm. Ulysses dodged sideways, throwing himself against the splintering mahogany panelling of the crumpled corridor. The monstrous automaton pulled back before trying again. Ulysses was forced to leap backwards as the golem smashed its wrecking-ball-sized fist to left and right within the mouth of the tunnel, and then took a step further into the passageway.

Ulysses felt suddenly defenceless. He already knew that trying to shoot the thing would be about as effective as a mosquito trying to bite an elephant to death, and he didn't even have his sword-cane to hand. The blade was still in the Prime Minister's possession and the golem stood between him and Ulysses. The dandy didn't even know if the Prime Minister was still conscious, or even alive.

The golem-droid took another lumbering step forwards. And that was all the opportunity Ulysses needed. As the thing lunged and grabbed for him, Ulysses kept to its right and threw himself forwards under the sweeping hand and between the automaton's widespread steam-hammer legs. As he slid across the smooth metal floor, he twisted and hurled the small object still clutched in his hands directly upwards.

Kicking his heels against the floor, he pushed clear of the droid and scrambled to his feet. There in front of him, Devlin Valentine clung to the top of a ruined staircase.

And then he was launching himself at the Prime Minister, grabbing him in a rugby tackle that would have seen him sent off the field, back in his schooldays at Eton, with a shout of: "Take cover!"

Ulysses' feet left the ground as he pushed Valentine back down the stairs. The two of them were still in mid-air when the magnet mine detonated.

The golem came apart in an incendiary ball of light.

The impact of the concussive wave hurled Ulysses and the Prime Minister over a fallen roof beam, to land in a heap behind the main control console.

Scalding shards of metal and tiny red-hot ceramic fragments whickered through the air, pinging against the glass of the panoramic window as twisted pieces of steel – that might have once been the cogs and gears of a servo motor – clattered onto the deck-plate around them. Amongst the debris was what looked like the fused metallic vertebrae of a robotic spine.

Ulysses cautiously raised himself from where he had landed on top of the Prime Minister. Something as large and as heavy as an anvil crashed down only a few feet away, the deck plate crumpling like cardboard beneath it.

Ulysses looked up again and found himself staring into the still-glowing eyes of the droid. The light behind them died, as the jerking neck and one shoulder, with the grinding stump of an arm still attached to it became still.

"Are you all right, Prime Minister?" Ulysses asked.

"Er, yes. Yes, I think so. Thank you," Valentine said, sitting up and brushing the dust and filth from his suit. "Thanks to you, I might add."

"Then I'd say we're quits, wouldn't you?"

Valentine smiled grimly. "If you say so. What now?"

"Well you're getting out of here as quickly as possible," Ulysses said, looking not at Valentine but at the vista visible through the panoramic window. The *Jupiter* had broken through the Smog now and the towering edifices of the Upper City were getting awfully close. The *Jupiter* could have collided with any one of them as it made its dramatic and unexpected descent, but by some miracle it appeared to be heading for a crash-landing in the Thames, somewhere between Waterloo Bridge and Blackfriars.

"And what about you?" Valentine asked as Ulysses helped him negotiate the smouldering wreckage of the golem's undercarriage.

"I'm going after Wormwood!"

Valentine risked a glance over his shoulder and the look of horror in his eyes said it all. "But there isn't time, man! We're going to hit the Thames!"

"Justice must be served," Ulysses said, leaving Valentine at the foot of the staircase again and making instead for the exit by which Wormwood and Kitty Hawke had, only seconds before, made their escape.

"But we're going down. You'll be killed!"

Ulysses had to shout to be heard over the sparking of sheared cables, the relentless metal moaning of the dying structure, and the howling wind circling the Hub. "Get out, now! You are our proud nation's greatest hope. I, on the other hand, am only a hero of the empire, and heroes are expendable."

"You *are* a hero, sir, a veritable hero, and I salute you!" Valentine declared, and then he was gone, as he set off along the buckled passageway, searching for signs that would lead him to the nearest emergency life raft.

"Heroes be damned!" Ulysses muttered under his breath as he entered the tunnel in front of him. Sprinting along it, as the *Jupiter* shook itself apart around him, he desperately hoped that he might still catch up with the fleeing Wormwood and Kitty Hawke before they managed to execute their own escape plan.

Sprinting along the sloping corridor, he could feel the full force

of the wind being forced through the falling Weather Station by
its dramatic descent.

Reaching the end of the corridor, where it joined with the main
curving passageway, Ulysses found a neatly printed, framed sign,
half hanging from the wall opposite, banging in the stiff breeze.
It read:

EMERGENCY LIFEBOATS
THIS WAY ☞

The wind grew stronger as he followed the passageway as it
continued to bear right, and then suddenly the corridor came to
an abrupt end where it had been sheared off completely by an
explosion, with nothing beyond it but the cold rushing air and
the rapidly approaching waters of the Thames.

Ulysses skidded to a halt, grabbing the handrail running the
length of the passageway and braced for impact.

The *Jupiter* hit the Thames with a great *whoomph*.

A wall of water was sent crashing over the traffic jam on
Blackfriars Bridge and across the Victoria Embankment and out
across the South Bank. The great wave put out a number of fires
that had broken out amidst all the chaos and confusion that had
resulted from the mutating downpour.

The filthy river water washed along the city street, knocking
people and their metamorphosing insect kin to the ground, and
sending a host of locust-like creatures droning into the air before
it. A wave, like a small tsunami, set the schooners, barges and
steamers rocking, and jostling against each other, as it swept
downstream.

Across the capital a number of omnibuses, steam-wagons and
hansom cabs were involved in collisions as – having already
survived the chaos resulting from the spontaneous metamorphosis
of a significant proportion of the city's population – their drivers
saw the *Jupiter* crash down in the river.

For a moment it looked like the station might actually

remain afloat, buoyed up on the scum-encrusted surface of the putrid Thames.

And then the *Jupiter Station* started to sink, a shower of rain rising into the air from the exterior of the craft as more of its discharged cavorite carried droplets of river water with it as it escaped. What was left of the toxic soup sloshing around inside the *Jupiter's* storage tanks discharged into the river, flooding the ancient waterway with a lethal cocktail of poisonous chemicals, that would continue to cause problems long after this dreadful day was over.

The foul waters of the Thames swirling into the open mouth of the passageway, lapping at his heels, Ulysses turned tail and ran. Following the curve of the passageway to the left now, as it wound slowly through the body of the devastated structure, he passed the access tunnel to the central Hub, and kept on round. He had soon left the rising waters behind, but he knew that it was only a matter of time before the entire vessel sank to the bottom of the river.

Ulysses wondered how deep the Thames was at this point, but that wasn't the biggest thing he had to worry about right at that moment. With the movement of the water washing the last of the toxic chemical waste from the craft's storage tanks and straight into a river already awash with the outspill from the subterranean Fleet factory, Ulysses didn't fancy taking a dip.

And then he ran into Devlin Valentine.

"Quicksilver!" the Prime Minister gasped, his face breaking into a delighted smile. "You're alive!"

"For the time being, at least. And I see you didn't make it to the lifeboats in time."

"I hate to say I told you so, but..."

"Tell me about it. Any sign of the other VIPs? Do you know what's happened to them?"

"I passed the viewing gallery where we were held prisoner on my way here, but that place was empty."

"Good going Jack. So they got away. Well now, let's see about getting you off this sinking ship, shall we?"

"What do you suggest?"

"As the water level's rising, it seems to me that the only way is up."

Ulysses started scanning the curved roof of the passageway above them. There had to be a way up onto the roof of the Weather Station.

"Come on," Ulysses said, setting off again along the corridor, "and keep your eyes on the ceiling."

It did not take them long to find what they were looking for. Ulysses led the way, his ape arm forcing the access hatch open. A telescoping ladder dropped down from the shaft and Ulysses scampered up it, Devlin Valentine close on his heels.

With the Prime Minister ensconced within the narrow maintenance tunnel within the roof space, Ulysses closed the access hatch.

"You first," he said, indicating the rungs of the ladder as they continued up to another wheel-locked hatchway above.

The death moans of the *Jupiter Station* reverberating all around them – the weight of water bearing down on parts of the wreck already starting to exert its own unwelcome influence – Ulysses felt disorientated by the continual pitch and yaw of the rocking station.

Muted daylight spilled into the near-dark of the shaft as Valentine heaved open the hatch and the two of them climbed, blinking, onto the sloping roof of the *Jupiter*.

Turning, Ulysses took in the view. The top of the Hub appeared like an island of burned and pitted metal above the choppy waters of the Thames, as the ancient river inexorably sucked the wreck down towards the sludge and silt at its bottom. The apex of the Hub, like some gigantic steel turtle shell, bore the scars of the Station's destruction. Its hull-plates were riven by great gouges and discoloured by the scorch marks. Aerials and antennae had been sliced clean through by winnowing blades of twisted metal, like so many cornstalks before the scythe.

There was little else visible above the hungry waters. The Thames was in turmoil, great bubbles rising to the surface from the sinking ship and agitating the leaking chemicals to create a frothing toxic soup.

With another spouting eruption of compressed air the *Jupiter* shifted and heaved again. So great was the lurching motion that neither Ulysses nor Valentine was able to maintain his balance. Both fell awkwardly onto the slick surface of the hull. Unable to arrest their sliding descent, they slipped over the curve of the roof dropping towards the river.

As Ulysses headed for the chemical spill surrounding the downed *Jupiter*, he saw a shadow streak across the sky above them, hurtling along on a cone of smoke and flame.

And then the shadow was on them.

Spring-Heeled Jack crashed down onto the metal roof, sliding towards Ulysses on his stomach, his breastplate kicking sparks from the metalwork.

Instinctively reaching out towards the vigilante, Ulysses' gloved hand found Jack's gauntleted fist. His fall was sharply arrested as the activated magnet mine in Jack's other hand clamped itself onto the surface of the drowning vessel.

Ulysses snapped his head round and saw Valentine slipping feet first into the foaming water. He had been only seconds away from entering the chemical soup himself.

Without thinking Ulysses plunged his chimpanzee hand into the Thames, after Valentine. He felt the acid burn of the befouled waters on the skin of his borrowed arm, as the long fingers of his left hand closed around something beneath the water.

With Jack pulling him back towards the top of the still sinking outer ring, Ulysses heaved and pulled a spluttering Devlin Valentine from the viscous, cloying waters of the grotesquely-polluted Thames. The Prime Minister's clothes were sodden, the left hand side of his body still covered in an oily yellow sheen.

As Ulysses looked down at the barely-conscious Valentine, coughing the stinking river water from his lungs, he saw the man's flesh begin to blister and redden, and felt the prickly stinging on the leathery skin of his chimpanzee's arm become an angry burning pain. He closed his eyes in agony and gasped for breath.

Feeling the *Jupiter* heave beneath them once again, Ulysses opened his eyes and saw the waters of the Thames rising ever higher. It could surely only be a matter of moments before they all entered the river for the last time.

"Sir!"

Hearing the shout, doing his best to suppress the pain in his arm by strength of will alone, Ulysses shot desperate glances all around him, trying to locate the source of the cry.

Then there came another shout, a woman's voice this time, and he felt his heart leap. "Ulysses!"

And there, coming alongside the sinking Weather Station at the prow of a small steam-launch was Eliza, the ever reliable Nimrod at the wheel.

"Coming aboard!" his indefatigable manservant called across to them.

As Ulysses and Spring-Heeled Jack lifted the now unconscious Valentine into the launch, without any apparent emotion other than mild curiosity colouring his voice, Nimrod asked: "Close call was it, sir?"

"Closer than you could ever imagine," Ulysses replied, staring down at the disfigured mess of a man curled in a foetal ball in the bottom of the boat. He looked from Valentine's blistered face to the reddening flesh of his own simian arm.

"Oh no, I can imagine," his manservant replied, a knowing smile playing about the corners of his eyes.

EPILOGUE

After The Rain

"So, Mr Quicksilver, what do you think?" Doctor Pandora Doppelganger asked as she unwrapped the last of the bandages and removed the gauze from his bicep. The pair of identical nurses assisting her watched for his reaction with hawkish interest.

If it hadn't have been for the subtle scar circling his arm just below the shoulder joint, and the fact that the skin of the arm itself was as pink and smooth as a newborn baby's he would never have known that it wasn't the one he had been born with.

He flexed his left hand, watching the fingers move, staring in child-like wonder as the digits opened and closed.

"Can you feel this?" Doctor Doppelganger asked, touching the points of a pair of callipers to his forearm. Ulysses nodded. "And here? How about here? Here?" Ulysses felt every single contact, the sensation sending a tingling electrical crackle throughout his entire body.

Behind where Mercy and Clemency were standing, Ulysses could see a stainless steel trolley. On top was a large kidney-shaped metal bowl covered with a green cloth, but Ulysses could still just see the tip of the half-simian, half-beetle-like limb protruding from beneath it.

"So fast too," Ulysses whispered. "It's incredible."

He looked up at Doctor Doppelganger. There were tears in his eyes.

"Thank you."

Two days later, over brandy and cigars in the Quartermain Room of the of the Inferno Club off St James's Square – ironically slipping into the pattern established by his predecessor, amongst others, as a way of meeting with clandestine agents of the crown – Octavius De Wynter completed his de-briefing of the dandy.

The Smog of blue tobacco smoke clouding the room was like the Smog that still lingered over the city. It was hot too. A fire was roaring in the grate, even though it was already the month of March.

"We found him, you know?" De Wynter said.

"Found him?" Ulysses perked up at mention of this. "You mean Wormwood?"

"His body was recovered from the Thames."

Ulysses felt cold shock sink to the pit of his stomach. It was the news he had been hoping to hear but now that it was fact, and no longer mere wishful thinking on his part, Ulysses felt somehow cheated. It should have been him that had put an end to the traitor. Wormwood should have died on the end of his sword or by a bullet fired from his gun, staring into the stony face of his nemesis, knowing that he had been made to pay for the intolerable crimes he had committed against Magna Britannia.

After all, Ulysses had been the one who had let Wormwood get away in the first place. He should have made sure he'd finished him off when he had faced him aboard his zeppelin as he and Kitty Hawke made their escape from the stricken Crystal Palace.

"You're sure it was him?" Ulysses pressed.

"I identified the body myself."

"But you're *sure* it was him?" Did Ulysses really secretly hope that Uriah Wormwood had got away at the last minute, so that the two of them might clash swords again one day?

"What about his accomplice?"

"You mean the assassin who goes by the name of Kitty Hawke?"

"Yes. Amongst others."

"Her body wasn't recovered."

"Then she's still alive." Ulysses said, with possibly a little too much enthusiasm.

"She could be alive or, which I think is more likely, she's at the bottom of the Thames."

But Ulysses clung onto the slim possibility that she had survived to fight another day. And despite what De Wynter thought, Ulysses had a feeling that their paths would cross again.

"So how's the clear-up operation going?" Ulysses asked, moving the discussion on.

"In a word, slowly. It's a painstaking business, I tell you, and every day the clean-up crews are finding more nests. Entire areas have been infected by the rain and, for the time being, have become veritable no-go areas, especially the area surrounding St Paul's."

Ulysses had heard those rumours himself. Sir Christopher Wren's great cathedral had a new congregation now. And it wasn't just St Paul's that had become a refuge for those who had been changed by the toxic rain. The fallout from Wormwood's attack had struck right at the heart of the empire and London would take months, if not years, to fully recover. It didn't help that the Wellington Barracks had also been hit badly by the rain, changing a good quarter of the troops stationed there, the poor bastards having to be summarily executed by their superior officers.

Dr Feelgood had managed to wheedle his way into hundreds of thousands of people's lives, from all walks of society, and Ulysses suspected that his influence would be felt for a good few years to come.

"So what of the PM?" Ulysses asked as he thought of those warped by the modified Galapagos serum. "How is he?"

"The Prime Minister will be taking early retirement."

"But is he all right?"

"He had been through a lot recently and its going to be taking things easy from now on."

Ulysses was about to ask again, but from the steely look in the other man's eyes he knew he would be wasting his time. "So what happens now?"

"Now? Now, it is time for every man to do his duty. To step up to the breach, and all that."

"And what will you do?"

"What needs to be done."

Thomas Sanctuary put down the welding torch and lifted his visor. The new headpiece was ready. He only needed to attach the gas re-breather and then he could make a start on the rest of the suit.

He looked from his handiwork to the plans pinned to the easel next to the work table, and from them to the original suit, now adorning its tailor's dummy. He wanted to make the armour integral to the suit in this new, improved version. And having thoroughly field-tested his father's creation, he knew that he needed it to be more flexible. By embedding the armoured plates in smaller sections within the layers of the suit itself he should be able to solve both problems in one.

Then there were the gauntlets. He wanted to incorporate both grappling claws and a bolt-launcher mounting them on the wrists. And then he needed to re-stock his utility belt. He needed more tracking devices and magnet-mines too, and he had thought of adding some gas-bombs also.

He looked at the original, and already obsolete, scuffed and torn costume hanging from the dummy. About the only parts that he wouldn't change, at least not yet, were the jetpack and the cape. He had been very pleased with how they had operated in the field.

But the suit itself had changed almost beyond recognition. And it wasn't only the suit. The destitute man who had arrived at the door to Sanctuary House, two months before – who wanted nothing more than to be revenged upon those who had stood by while he went to prison for a crime he didn't commit, and who smiled while his father died, a recluse, mocked and derided – that man was gone too.

He would still strive to see those responsible brought to account for their crimes in time, and it would still give him a sense of purpose, but the *Jupiter* disaster had seen him change from being a simple, narrow-minded vigilante to become something more. He had become a hero.

He glanced again at the front page of *The Times,* casually discarded on the corner of the new schematics, lying beside a barely touched plate of ham and cheese sandwiches. The banner headline read:

SALVATION FROM THE SKIES

Beneath it was a clear picture of him, fully suited up, soaring over Waterloo Bridge as he came to Quicksilver's rescue atop the sinking *Jupiter* Station. It seemed that, for the time being at least, the press had decided that he was a dangerous vigilante no more. He was the hero of the hour and right now the Empire needed heroes like never before.

He looked out of the conservatory windows at the Smog-stained sky to the east. For all Prime Minister Valentine's promises of improving things for all, the launch of the *Jupiter Station* hadn't made things better for anyone. In fact, it had only made things worse – significantly worse.

The sun was setting and soon the swarms would rise again to hunt.

As if on cue, the mournful wail of the curfew siren sounded over the city, hastening people to their homes.

Uriah Wormwood had spoken of wanting to see Magna Britannia evolve and its capital, Londinium Maximum, most certainly had. It had changed from being a self-satisfied, corpulent monster into a paranoid, bristling beast, which considered the best form of defence to be attack.

Oh yes, Wormwood had changed things all right.

Thomas lifted the steel-plate mask from the table in front of him, looking from the eyeless mask now surmounting the tailor's dummy to the glass of its sinister red eyes. But all he saw was his own face reflected back at him from the ruby-red lenses.

He had a feeling that London would have need of Spring-Heeled Jack again. And, when it did, Spring-Heeled Jack would be ready.

The black-clad rat-faced man dropped to his knees on the rough planks of the warehouse, dark blood welling from the neat hole in his forehead. His yellow eyes rolled up into his head. His body remained where it was for several seconds, as if the wretch didn't know he was dead, and then it toppled forwards, exposing the back of the exploded skull.

White smoke curled from the muzzle of the pistol which was now pointing directly at the wizened old man. The sudden retort of the pistol had silenced his half-Chinese half-pidgin English tirade of curses, and he now sat cowering within his dragon-carved throne atop the raised dais at the end of the converted warehouse.

"Would anyone else like to challenge our authority?" came a voice as cold and hard as diamonds, carrying from the persistent shadows.

None of the rat-men said anything, and some took a few nervous shuffling steps backwards, away from the sinister party that had infiltrated Lao Shen's new base of operations.

The magician dared not take his eyes off the lethal markswoman. She wore tight-fitting practical clothes, favouring breeches and a jerkin over a more lady-like outfit, and her hair cascaded over her shoulders, a tumble of auburn tresses.

To top it all, the young woman's left eye was covered by an eye patch embroidered with a set of crosshairs. And still she had made the shot.

Behind her a bald-headed man hung from the ceiling via a grappling hook attached to the metal rig that enclosed his body and provided him with two more pairs of limbs, which twitched and flexed with a mind of their own. His eyes were hidden behind a pair of telescoping lenses. A number of camera-eyed spider-bots scampered and crawled over his inverted body, looking like newborn hatchlings crawling over the bloated body of their mother.

Over the gunwoman's other shoulder was an abomination worse than anything Lao Shen had encountered in the aftermath of the apocalyptic rainstorm. It looked like two unfortunate wretches had somehow been fused together during the devastating deluge, but the old man knew that this freak of nature had been created long ago, within some accursed womb.

The creature had two arms, two legs and two heads. The twins were joined from shoulder to groin but where one was a thickset, muscled brute, his sibling was a shrivelled, hairless thing. Both were ugly as sin and the black tie get up they were squeezed into – which fitted neither half well – only made them appear even more ridiculous, as did the two top hats the heads wore.

The conjoined twins stood poised, ready to commit some debased act of violence by the look of it, the heavy, ham-sized right-hand fist punching the wasted, long-fingered left hand repeatedly, a grim expression on the bigger brute, while his brother looked like some slack-jawed zombie.

"Thank you, my dear," the last member of the party said, emerging from the shadows at the end of the warehouse.

"My pleasure," Kitty Hawke said, smiling darkly.

"I know you!" Lao Shen shouted, almost hysterical. "B-But it can't be!"

"I can assure you, Mr Shen, that you do not know me," the young man said, combing a hand through his hair. "But I know you. Oh yes, I know you all right. And I'm here to tell you that there's a new Kingpin in town. Limehouse is no longer yours."

"Okay," the pathologist began, speaking into the microphone hanging from the ceiling of the white-tiled autopsy room. "Subject is male, approximately seventy years of age. Suspected cause of death drowning. Making my first incision now."

Watched by his colleague, the green-frocked pathologist placed the tip of the scalpel against the soft grey flesh of the corpse's sternum and pressed down, pulling the blade back firmly to expose the breastbone beneath.

"Good lord!" the pathologist exclaimed as the blade parted the flesh.

"What is it?" his colleague asked, taking a step closer to the dissection table. And then he saw for himself. "What is that?"

"If I didn't know better I'd say it was some type of fungus."

For a moment neither of them said anything, as the implication of what they had discovered sank in.

The two men looked at each other anxiously, the colour draining from their cheeks.

The pathologist performing the dissection, was the first to speak. "Now, are you going to tell the boss, or am I?"

Elsewhere, behind closed shutters and heavy drapes, in an inconspicuous room in an equally inconspicuous building, within the comforting anonymity of shadowy gloom, the Star Chamber met.

"I call this meeting of the Star Chamber to order," came the commanding baritone, breaking into the warm peace and quiet of the secret chamber that, moments before, had only been permeated by the gentle ticking of a clock.

"So, Wormwood has succeeded after all," said a second voice, as rich as claret.

"After a fashion," the first replied.

"It will take some time for London to recover," came a third, crisp voice, its tone reminiscent of a snapping terrier, "and in the meantime the empire will be vulnerable to attack from outside."

"It is only by facing adversity and overcoming it that the empire can survive. Wormwood understood that."

"And what of him now? Has he been disposed of? Is he dead?"

The first cleared his throat, as if momentarily embarrassed.

"No. He is missing."

"But *not* presumed dead."

"No. Presumed very much alive, I'm afraid to say."

"Then he remains a threat to our enterprise," said a fourth, his aristocratic tone as sharp and to the point as a rapier's blade. "Does Quicksilver know that Wormwood escaped?"

"No," the first said. "As far as he is concerned, his nemesis is dead. And that is how it is to remain." The baritone bore all the barely suppressed ferocity of a tiger's roar as the speaker addressed the only person left in the room who had not yet spoken. "Do you understand, Venus?"

"I understand," came a gentle feminine voice.

"But without you he would not have made the Bedlam connection."

"I thought it expedient," the woman's voice replied calmly.

"It is not your place to make such decisions," the first growled.

"But I felt he needed a helping hand to see who was behind the *Jupiter* scheme. Without Quicksilver's intervention who knows how far things might have gone."

"The matter was in hand."

"Then accept my profound apologies, my lord Saturn. I understand the need to test and challenge the strength of the Empire, but I did not think the intention was to destroy her utterly."

"And what of the nation's great champion?" asked the claret rich voice, the jangle of a crucifix chain underlying his words. "What of Devlin Valentine?"

"An unfortunate casualty of the *Jupiter* disaster."

"As I see it, it is a significant set-back."

"His condition was an unfortunate side effect of the operation."

"Unfortunate?" That one word was pregnant with implied meaning.

"Collateral damage, nothing more. We are fighting a war, after all. Both within and without."

"Indeed. So what now, for Magna Britannia? Who will lead it

into its bright new future now that Valentine is gone?" challenged the fourth.

"Now?" the first repeated as if surprised that anyone would feel the need to even ask. "Now, it is time for every man to do his duty, to step up to the breach."

"But what will you do?" the fourth asked, suspiciously.

"What needs to be done."

The Royal Bethlehem Hospital.

Bedlam.

Well it deserved that name. Eternal prison for a thousand broken minds. And incarcerated within the dungeons beneath, more 'unfortunates', their broken minds trapped within twisted bodies.

And there, locked within its deepest cell, hidden furthest from the light of day, Bedlam's newest guest waited.

Squatting in the filth and squalor of a dank cell, walls running with moisture and thick with moss, sitting upon a bed of mouldering straw, altered limbs restrained by the straitjacket he was forced to wear, was something that was neither man nor insect; something that should not exist in any sane world. Which was why it had been placed here, with those other unfortunates 'changed' by Dr Feelgood's patent panacea.

Stiff hairs, as sharp as spines, poked through the material of the straight-jacket. The feet of a fly – but a fly the size of a man – emerged from the left trouser leg of the confining suit, other such alterations visible through the tightly-bound straitjacket, all the way up the left side of his body, until they reached his malformed head, rudimentary mandibles forcing his mouth open, much of the left side of the skull reformed into the compound eye of a bluebottle.

Over the chittering voices of the other 'unfortunates' confined to Professor Brundle's 'special' wing, his voice rang out loud and clear as he screamed his frustrations to the uncaring darkness.

"You can't keep me locked up down here!" he shouted, his

words distorted by the mandibles forcing open his mouth. "Don't you know who I am?"

The only reply was the buzzing of cockroach wings and the crunching sound of the mantis devouring the half a pig that had been left in its cell.

"I'm the hero of the hour! I'm this nation's last great hope. I'm the Prime Minister, you know! You can't keep me locked up like this, I won't have it!"

His furious ranting suddenly dissolved into hysterical laughter, which rang from the dank stone walls of the dungeon. "You hear me? I'm Devlin Valentine! The nation needs me, if it is to evolve and live on into the next century, and not stagnate and die! England expects every man to do his duty! Evolution expects! Evolution! Do you hear me? Evolution expects Devlin Valentine to do his duty! Devlin Valentine, Lord of the Flies! Evolution expects!

"Evolution expects!

"*Evolution expects!*

"EVOLUTION EXPECTS!"

> And the third angel sounded, and there fell a great
> star from heaven, burning as it were a lamp, and it
> fell upon the third part of the rivers, and upon the
> fountains of waters; And the name of the star is
> called Wormwood: and the third part of the water
> became wormwood; and many men died of the
> waters, because they were made bitter.
>
> (Revelation 8:10)

THE END

Ulysses Quicksilver will return in *Pax Britannia: Blood Royal*.

Jonathan Green lives and works in West London. He is well known for his contributions to the *Fighting Fantasy* range of adventure gamebooks, as well as his novels set within Games Workshop's worlds of *Warhammer* and *Warhammer 40,000*.

He has written fiction for such diverse properties as *Sonic the Hedgehog* and *Doctor Who*, and non-fiction books including *Match Wits with the Kids* and *What is Myrrh Anyway? Everything You Always Wanted to Know About Christmas*.

Evolution Expects is his fourth novel set within the alternative steampunk universe of *Pax Britannia* featuring the debonair dandy adventurer Ulysses Quicksilver.

If you would like to find out more about the world of *Pax Britannia*, set your Babbage engine's ether-relay to **www.paxbritanniablog.blogspot.com**

Conqueror Worm

Jonathan Green

Abaddon

Conqueror Worm

Jonathan Green

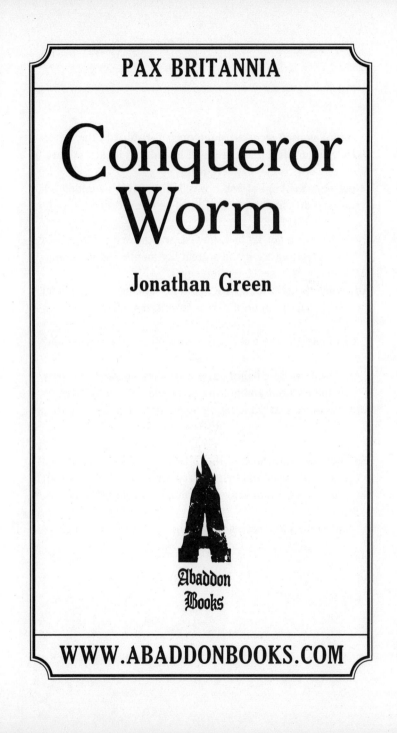

Abaddon
Books

WWW.ABADDONBOOKS.COM

John Lambton went a-fishing once, a-fishing in the Wear,
He caught a fish upon his hook he thought looked mighty
queer,
Now what the kind of fish it was John Lambton couldn't tell,
But he didn't like the look of it, so he threw it down a well.

Now the worm got fat and growed, and growed an awful size,
With great big teeth and a great big mouth and great big
goggle eyes,
And when at night it crawled about all looking for some booze,
If it fell dry upon the road, it milked a dozen cows.

This fearful worm would often feed on cows and lamb and
sheep,
And swallow little babes alive when they lay down to sleep,
So John set out and got the beast and cut it into halves,
And that soon stopped it eating babes and sheep and lambs and
calves.

So now you know how all the folks on both sides of the Wear,
Lost lots of sheep and lots of sleep and lived in mortal fear,
So drink the health of brave Sir John, who kept the babes from
harm,
Saved cows and calves by making halves of that famous
Lambton Worm!

(Traditional)

I

Stand and Deliver!

NOVEMBER 1797

The carriage raced on through the driving rain, into the gathering dusk, as though the very hounds of hell were after it. Iron-banded wheels rattled and bounced through ruts in the road, splashing filthy water from the overflowing hollows. The horses snorted with effort as they strained to keep the carriage moving through the sucking quagmire the road was rapidly becoming, foam flying from their flapping lips.

"Hi-Yaah!" the driver shouted, lashing the reins, leaning forward in his seat, glad of his high-collared coat in the face of this freezing November rain.

November in the north of England was as miserable a month as you were likely to find anywhere within the King's realm. But no matter what the weather, the coach's passengers had a pressing engagement to attend. Time was, as always, of the essence.

Although it was only just past sunset, it was already as dark a night as you would wish to avoid out in the wilds of County Durham, an area renowned for its brigands and highwaymen.

The driver peered at the road immediately ahead, keeping an eye out for pot-holes or fallen branches that could send them careering off the road – hazards possibly placed there by enterprising bandits – but saw little by the swaying light of the jolting coach-lamps.

And then another bobbing light appeared from out of the darkness, like some treacherous will-o'-the-wisp, its sour yellow glow approaching through the gloom. Fear took hold of the driver's stomach and twisted. This second light could mean only one thing.

Lashing the reins with an urgency born of a forbidding dread, the driver urged the panting horses onwards, in the vain hope that they might yet outrun the approaching menace.

The crack of a pistol shot exploded from out of the darkness and the sheeting rain close by – closer than expected. The horses whinnied in alarm, rearing up onto their hind-legs, the carriage slewing across the mud-slick road behind them.

The driver gave a weak groan and toppled from his seat, landing with a wet slap, face down in a puddle of black water. There was a cry of alarm from inside the carriage and a shrill womanly scream.

Two figures on horseback appeared from out of the darkness, their steeds trotting over to the carriage, the horses carefully stepping over the prone body of the wretched driver. Both figures wore water-proofed capes against the rain, which ran in a constant stream from the corners of their tricorn hats. One sat tall in the saddle, long-limbed and possessed of a certain breeding, judging by his stance, his features as sharp as a knife. The other was shorter and stockier, the pistol that had taken the driver down still smoking in his hand.

Someone inside the carriage fumbled the curtain that was draped across the window of the carriage door, and a middle-aged man's sagging face peered out, his mouth open in an 'O' of shock and surprise. On seeing the two dark riders, he gave a pitiful moan and pulled the curtain shut again.

The stockier of the two highwaymen directed his steed over to the carriage door and, grasping the handle firmly in one gloved hand, pulled it open sharply.

As well as the portly, middle-aged gentleman, his powdered wig askew, next to him, wearing a dress that was all ostentatious petticoats and over-fussy satin and pearls, a tight bodice and whalebone corset beneath, accentuating the swell of her breasts, was the dirty old man's considerably younger and more attractive female companion.

The highwayman's eyes sparkled as his gaze lingered on the young woman's heaving bosom. The girl whimpered again, fear writ large upon the delicate face.

"W-What is the meaning of this?" the portly gentleman spluttered, having at last found some modicum of courage and his tongue.

The brigand's eyes snapped back onto him and in an instant the flintlock pistol was raised and aimed at the man's jowly, fish-white face. He was sweating profusely, despite the cold.

"Oh yeah," the stocky highwayman said, as if suddenly remembering what they were there for, "your money or your life."

"Now, now, Mr Abershawe, there's no excuse for poor manners," his partner said, speaking for the first time as he too brought his horse closer to the open carriage door, "especially when in the presence of a lady."

Peering out from under the brim of his tricorn hat, this second gentleman of the road grinned at the young woman, and gave her a knowing wink. The light and shadows spread by the swaying lantern hung from a pole beside the driver's seat accentuated the man's strong bone structure, revealing a ruggedly handsome face half-hidden by a couple of days' beard growth.

Where Abershawe sounded like a man who had smoked too many pipes, the other's accent had more of the banqueting room than the bar-room about it – a cultured tone that was seemingly at odds with his chosen profession.

And the second highwayman's horse was just as striking; a roan stallion with a white flash on its muzzle.

"This is utterly outrageous!" the portly passenger jabbered. "Who are you, sir, and what is the meaning of this?"

"I, sir, am Richard Runyan esquire and this is my associate Mr Joseph Abershawe," the dandy highwayman said. "You might have heard of us, me in particular."

"No, sir. I have not, sir!"

"You haven't heard of 'Galloping Dick' Runyan?"

"No, sir!"

"Shame. But no matter. And I would have thought the meaning of this little escapade was apparent. As my colleague put it so concisely, your money or your life. We're here to relieve you of your valuables." He grinned saucily at the young woman again, "And I have to say there are a few other things I wouldn't mind relieving you of as well, ma'am.

"And now that we've had the decency to introduce ourselves to you, perhaps you would like to return the courtesy."

"I'll have you know, sir, that I am Sir George Sackville. And also let it be known that I shall see you swing for this."

In the silence that followed Sir George's foolish threat, the ratcheting click of Mr Abershawe cocking his pistol could be heard quite clearly over the drumming of the continuing downpour.

His voice like steel, the charming highwayman said: "I was asking the young lady."

"Cassandra. Cassandra Tyrrell," she replied, boldly.

"Tyrrell, eh? Not *the* Tyrrell family by any chance?"

The quaking Sir George shot his companion a bewildered glance.

"The very same."

"How interesting. Now, you must understand that we don't want to kill anyone, do we Joe?"

"What about him?" Cassandra pointed at the rain-washed body of the driver, his face sunk into the worsening quagmire of the road.

"He was unlucky," Abershawe rumbled.

"So if you would like to ensure that you hold onto what little good fortune you still have, perhaps you would be so kind as to place your valuables in this," Runyan said, passing a velvet bag through the open door of the carriage. "And don't forget your wallet, Sir George, or that fine pearl necklace, milady." The highwayman's gaze lingering on the shapely mounds of breasts once more.

Sir George didn't need to be told twice.

"And that pretty trinket of yours," Runyan reminded the girl, meeting her furious blue-eyed stare.

She put a hand to her bosom and fished for something hidden in her cleavage, a hankie, the highwayman supposed, to dab the startled tears from the sparkling sapphires that were her eyes.

Quick as a flash, she pulled her hand free again, only now there was a tiny lady's pistol there, fitting snugly in the palm of her hand, and it was pointing at Abershawe's chest.

The brigand barely had time to register his shock before the sound of the gun shattered the night around them. Blood sprayed in the darkness. The force of the shot threw the highwayman backwards out of the saddle. He landed heavily in the mud and didn't move again, black blood oozing from the hole cauterised in the middle of his forehead.

Abershawe's horse whinnied and shied, trotting backwards, away from the thunderclap crack of the pistol and the acrid stink of gunpowder. At this Runyan's steed shied too, rearing up on its hind-legs.

"Whoa, Quicksilver! Whoa there. Easy boy!" Runyan pulled on the reins with one hand while trying to calm the horse with a pat on the neck at the same time.

As the dandy highwayman struggled to soothe his skittish steed the young woman dropped the pistol on the floor of the carriage – its single shot discharged – and, grabbing hold of the sill above the door, she swung herself out of the carriage, into the driver's position and the pouring rain.

Taking up the reins, with a shout of "Yaah!" she whipped the horse between the traces into motion and the carriage pulled away into the encroaching night.

Galloping Dick Runyan was left reeling, watching as the carriage disappeared into the night, until the wildly swinging carriage-lamp was swallowed by the trees crowding the sides of the road.

Cassandra Tyrell dared a look back to where Sir George Sackville bounced and slid across the seat inside the carriage. His expression of abject terror and uncomprehending disbelief was illuminated for a moment by the fitfully swaying lantern.

"Are you alright, my lord?" she shouted over the drumming of the rain and the jolt and splash of the carriage wheels.

Sir George simply stared back at her, his mouth agape like a goldfish.

"W-Who are you?" he managed at last. "Who sent you?"

"Let's just say you have friends in high places, Sir George. Friends who want you to make this meeting."

II

All The King's Men

The already tired horses couldn't maintain the pace set by Cassandra as she fled with Sir George. But even though their initial burst of speed did not last for much more than a couple of miles, she kept the animals moving at a steady trot, flecks of foam flying from their bits, hoping that it was not far now and knowing that Sir George had to make the meeting. That was her prime objective. Everything else that might follow after hinged on that one fact.

The rain passed over, the clouds tugged apart by the rising wind, and the moon broke through, casting its monochrome glow over the rugged countryside. But there was still no sign of their destination, when the carriage crested another rise and Cassandra caught sight of horsemen on the road ahead.

She reined in the horses, slowing their advance to a gentle trot, but ready to lash them into a gallop again at a moment's notice.

Their silhouettes black against the grey pall of moon-washed clouds, shapes began to coalesce from the darkness. As she brought the carriage closer, brass buttons gleamed in the guttering orange glow of the carriage's lantern.

When the carriage was still a good ten yards from the waiting redcoats, a voice hailed Cassandra.

"Good evening, milady," the leader of the troop said, doffing his hat to the dishevelled-looking young woman in the driver's seat, unable to hide his look of surprise on finding a woman at the reins. "It is not the sort of night to be out on the road, is it?"

"Indeed it is not, sir," Cassandra called back.

The officer jumped down from the saddle and approached the carriage. He walked slowly past her, one hand stroking the horse closest to him, taking in her sodden state. Then he peered inside.

"Excuse me, my lord, but you must be Sir George Sackville. Am I correct?"

"You are, sir," the peer managed with something like his old assertive authority, born of a cultivated sense of superiority. "And who are you?"

"I am Lieutenant Riggs of His Majesty's First Royal Dragoons and you will be pleased to hear that we are here to escort you to Lambton Hall, where your attendance is anticipated. The roads aren't safe, you know," he added, taking in Cassandra again.

"We know," Cassandra said bluntly.

Another five miles along they came in sight of candlelit windows and, following the line of guttering torches that had been set out on the approach, Sir George Sackville's carriage entered the courtyard of Lambton Hall.

Waiting on the steps before the main entrance to the house, was an appropriately-attired steward with all the apparent charm of a sparrow hawk about him. Cassandra eyed him just as suspiciously as he regarded her.

"Welcome back, lieutenant," the steward said, as a footman scurried to open the carriage door. "And good evening, Sir George," he added as the still-shaken peer stepped down unsteadily from the interior. "I trust you had a good journey."

"No, I did not! Quite frankly, I'm just happy to be alive."

Before the peer could say any more, with a clattering of iron-shod hooves on cobbles, a second troop of red-coated cavalrymen entered the courtyard. Their commander – his athletic build obvious to Cassandra even through his uniform – jumped smartly down from the back of a white stallion and approached the steward, saluting him before speaking.

"As you know, sir, we are due to return to Durham tomorrow, but this night we have apprehended a dangerous criminal. We will take him back with us on the morrow to face the magistrates, but might we keep the blackguard incarcerated within some suitable cell for the night?"

It was only then that Cassandra noticed the man, strung between the two horsemen bringing up the rear of the party.

"But of course, Captain Drysdale," the steward said. "I am sure Sir William will be most gratified to hear that you have done such an effective job of keeping the roads safe for his guests. I am sure that we can find some suitable iron ring you can chain the rogue to."

"I will mention Sir William's cooperation fully in my report," Captain Drysdale said and ushered his men forward, the two at the rear dragging the prisoner between them.

Now it was Cassandra's turn to be taken by surprise, as the prisoner – covered from head to toe in mud – glanced in her direction and she found herself looking at the grinning face of Galloping Dick Runyan.

Captain Drysdale and his men dealt with, the steward turned his attention to the peer and his unusual companion.

"Please, Sir George, if you would like to step this way," he said, directing the peer up the steps towards the grand entrance as Cassandra climbed down from the carriage. "And perhaps your... driver would like to make herself comfortable in the stable block."

"This young woman is *not* my driver. In fact she saved my life. No, sir, she stays with me!"

"Very good, your lordship," the steward said, smiling

graciously and giving a sycophantic bow. "The other guests are this way." And with that, the steward led Sir George Sackville and his guardian into the house.

III

The Legend of The Lambton Worm

"Your guest suite is this way, Sir George," the steward said as he led them through the candle-lit halls and galleries of Lambton Hall, his shoes tapping on the polished marble. He turned to double-check that Cassandra was still following them and looked her up and down disdainfully. "Please try not to drip on the floor."

"So this is the legendary Lambton Hall," Sir George said, gazing at the paintings and displays of armour adorning the walls of the long gallery.

"Legendary is the word," the steward agreed. "Are you familiar with the story associate with this place?"

"Vaguely."

"What story?" Cassandra piped up.

The steward came to an abrupt halt that caught Sir George unawares. "Why, the legend of the Lambton Worm, of course."

"Oh, I do love fairy stories," she said with a delighted clap of the hands. "Do tell!"

"I would not presume to impose upon his lordship's time in relating the tale now," the steward said unctously.

Sir George shot him a disdainful glance. "Humour the girl."

"Very well, my lord," the steward said, the ingratiating smile back on his face in an instant. He cleared his throat and, as they resumed their slow amble along the galleried hall, the steward told his tale.

In his younger days, when he was still but heir to his father's great estate, Sir John of Lambton, later Knight of Rhodes, was a callow youth with little respect for the teachings of the Church and with little will to keep the Sabbath day holy. One Easter morning, when he should have been attending Mass, he went a-fishing in the Wear.

And while he sat beside the Wear, his line trailing in the water – cursing his bad luck and affronting those who passed by on their way to morning prayers – he felt his line go taut, for he had snagged a mighty catch, and battled to land what he thought was a great fish. But when he did at last pull his catch from the raging torrent, he was appalled to see that, rather than a trout or pike, he had hooked himself something more akin to a worm than a fish. It was an ugly creature, something like a lamprey or an eel, but its head was like that of a salamander, with nine holes on either side.

Disgusted by the unsightly appearance of the worm, believing he had caught the Devil himself, the heir of Lambton cast the creature into a nearby well and now, with a contrite heart, straightway sought to make amends for the wrong he had done Almighty God by profaning the Sabbath with his actions.

Having sought absolution for his sins from his father's confessor, and following a night during which he was plagued by the most terrible visions of the very pit of Hell itself, the next morning, the young Sir John embarked upon a perilous pilgrimage to the Holy Land, there to aid with the liberation of the Holy City from the heathen Saracen and the Turk.

Having taken up the sign of the Cross, for seven long years

he battled the infidel, forgetting his former life and earning many battle honours. But he also became disillusioned by the unending war, the unrelenting heat and the unnatural agues that bedevilled God's soldiers, and a deep sadness grew like a canker within his heart.

But during those seven long years, the devilish worm that he had caught and cast into the well had grown too, grown to a prodigious size having feasted on the livestock thereabouts until it was so large that it coiled itself about a certain crag, earning that benighted place the name of Worm Hill.

The monster held the lands of Lord Lambton in thrall to its terrible appetites. It devoured lambs and oxen both, and drained the milk of nine cows day in, and day out, which the people were wont to provide, lest it fall upon man to satisfy its unholy hunger.

Many had tried to slay the worm and many had failed, for if the monster's flesh was rent asunder by any blade, the wound, no matter how severe, would heal in an instant, flesh and bone would simply knit together, uniting the severed parts.

Having completed his seven years of penance, Sir John Lambton – now Knight of Rhodes – returned at last to that blighted place he had once called home, and with him hope returned as well.

Realising that he was to blame for the dire predicament in which his father's faithful vassals now found themselves, Sir John set forth to do battle with the fell worm.

He met the monster in battle at its hilltop lair but was thwarted by its unholy powers of rapid healing. Accepting that it was his duty now to put an end to the unnatural creature, he sought counsel from another creature vested of unnatural powers, and came at last to the dwelling of the Witch of Lambton.

And so, when next the Wear was in spate, Sir John scaled a rock that rose from the middle of the churning waters, clad from head to toe in armour bristling with blades, each as a sharp as a razor's edge. Having baited his trap, there he waited.

He did not have to wait long before the worm came that way, seeking to cross the river that lay between its hilltop lair and the drinking trough wherein was put the milk it supped upon daily. Seeing him, standing proud atop the rock, challenging its dominance, the worm fell upon the knight and the battle that ensued was as terrible as any had ever been.

In its rage, the worm fell upon Sir John, encircling him within its crushing coils. But as the blades that studded his armour sliced deep into its unnatural flesh, and the Wear ran red with the monster's blood, the severed pieces of its sinuous body dropped into the river and were carried away by the current before they could be reunited. Soon all that was left of the foul fiend was the monster's hideous head, then that too went into the river.

But the worm's defeat had come at a price, a price that could only be paid in blood. The witch had demanded that on slaying the monster, the noble knight must then also kill the first thing he met thereafter, be it man or beast. And so he arranged that, should he prove victorious, he would sound his hunting horn, that his faithful hound might come to him, and that the witch's bargain might be paid for with the dog's blood.

Climbing from the river, Sir John blew loud and hard upon his horn, but where Sir John had heeded well the witch's words of warning, his father did not, and the old Lord of Lambton ran to congratulate his son before his hound could reach him. Unable to kill his own father, so Sir John cursed the Lambton line for nine generations to come, his heirs meeting violent and untimely ends for his folly.

So all who would profane the Lord's Day and go fishing on the Sabbath, be warned.

"What a wonderful story!" Cassandra declared looking again at the dragon-like beast embroidered upon the tapestry before which they now stood and the spear-studded knight preparing to meet it in battle, with the river raging by, his sword raised high above his head. "Total nonsense, of course, but a wonderful story nonetheless."

"Oh no, madam," the steward said, turning on her suddenly, "it is no story."

"Surely, you can't believe it's true?"

"If it is but a story, then how do you explain this?" he asked, indicating the suit of armour mounted upon a plinth.

The armour was certainly an unusual and remarkable heirloom. To Cassandra's eyes it could well have dated from the time of the Crusades, but for one untypical characteristic. Protrusions like dagger blades or spear-tips had been added to the breastplate and vambraces.

"Remarkable," Sir George gasped.

"It's incredible!" his young companion declared. "It's just like the suit described in the legend. Then this spectacular piece must have been absorbed into the legend," she added under her breath.

"Or it is the same suit of armour worn by Sir John when he fought the Lambton Worm, which I think you'll find is more likely," the steward said.

"Remarkable," Sir George breathed again.

"The sword with which Sir John killed the worm used to adorn this wall also," the steward said. "Legend has it that it was fashioned from star-metal."

"Used to?" Cassandra said.

"Sir William, had it melted down and updated." Was that a hint of disdain in the steward's voice, at mention of his master's disrespectful attitude towards the legendary sword.

"Updated how?" Sir George said.

"Sir William had it re-made as a pistol and its accompanying shot."

"Fascinating," Sir George said.

"And where did this come from?" Cassandra said.

The steward stared at the object resting upon its velvet stand within the small glass display cabinet, and when he spoke again it sounded as if he was speaking from somewhere else, somewhere far away.

"That is another interesting story. There is another tale attached to this crystal skull," he said, his eyes sparkling with distant constellations.

"I thought there might be." Cassandra murmured.

"It was brought back from the Land of the Berbers by Sir John, when he returned from the Crusades."

"Who made it?" Cassandra said, peering at it inquisitively. It appeared to have been carved from a single block of crystal. Looking closer still, she could see tiny fault lines within the crystal that almost gave the skull the appearance of having blood vessels running through it. The candlelight illuminating the object was trapped by the crystal and refracted so that a golden glow suffused the brain pan.

"I-I don't know," the steward admitted, caught out, "but it is said that on stormy nights the skull can be heard to scream."

"Really?" said Sir George, completely caught up in the steward's tales of dragon-slayers and screaming skulls from heathen lands.

"Oh yes. It cries to be returned to the place from whence it came."

A clock chimed as a liveried footman trotted up to the steward and, having bowed respectfully to Sir George and his dishevelled lady friend, whispered something in his ear. The steward turned to Sir George, the ingratiating smile back on his face.

"I am sorry, Sir George, but time is pressing and I must ask that you come with me. I believe the guests are here now. It is time to join the gathering."

"Ah yes, of course. Very good. This way is it?"

Cassandra went to link arms with the peer but, before she could, the steward stepped between them.

"In the meantime, your companion will be shown to your bedchamber," he said, fixing Cassandra with a withering stare. "This way please."

Cassandra knew better than to argue; there was no point in causing a scene here. As the steward led Sir George she followed the footman up a broad flight of marble stairs to an opulently furnished bedchamber. Cassandra marvelled at the splendour of the room's decor and furnishings.

She heard the click of the door closing behind her and then the scrape of the key in the lock and the bolt being thrown.

The footman had locked her in. She was suddenly a prisoner of Lambton Hall.

IV

Abandon Hope All Ye Who Enter Here

Cassandra listened at the door for a moment, hearing the footman depart along the landing.

Alone at last she removed her soaking dress, took off her ruined wig – glad to be rid of its damp sheep's wool smell – and, loosening the laces at the back of her bodice, slipped out of her petticoats.

She paused, taking a moment to inspect herself in the dressing table mirror.

She pulled at the cloth of the shirt and trews she had been wearing underneath the dress, glad to be free of the constraints of the corset, and buttoned up the dark leather waistcoat her previous outfit had been hiding as well. And that was not all the layers of petticoats had been hiding.

Strapped around her waist was a bandolier, holding a brace of pistols, the powder and shot to go with them, and a double-edged dagger. With the bandolier now over her shoulder, and having taken the time to load both pistols, Cassandra took a moment to tie her shoulder-length blonde hair into a ponytail, using a ribbon from the rain-ruined dress, and then she was ready.

She turned towards the door.

The sound of chanting coming from beyond the window of the bedchamber caused her to stop and turn from the door again. Dousing the single lamp she moved to the window. Standing to one side she pulled the curtain back a fraction and peeked out at the gardens.

She saw a procession of figures in long scarlet robes bearing lit candles and torches, their faces hidden by golden cherubic masks, snaking its way through the grounds of Lambton. She counted twenty in all and, although the robes created a certain anonymity, she could tell that there were women as well as men among the group, several were of a considerable girth. Most corpulent of all was the figure that brought up the rear of the procession, the man waddling to keep up with the rest.

The rain had long since stopped, but a blustery wind still blew through the formal gardens. It tugged now at the acolytes' guttering torches, their flickering flames turning the shadows of the hedges and topiary into ghoulish phantoms.

The procession made its way towards the black mound of a hill that rose up out of the darkness.

As she watched, Cassandra listened carefully to the chanting. She could not discern the meaning of the words. Perhaps it was Latin or even a unique language invented by the cult.

As the party proceeded further into the darkness, all that she could see of them as they made their way towards the wooded crag that overlooked the deep scar of the Wear valley, were the flickering pin-pricks of the lights they carried and all she could now hear was the sowing of the wind in the witch-fingered branches of the leafless trees.

Cassandra turned back to the door, taking a set of metal tools from a pocket in her waistcoat.

Moving as stealthily as a cat the young woman slipped through the house and soon found herself outside. The cold wind tugging at her ponytail, she set off after the scarlet-clad figures.

Moving much more quickly than the cultists, Cassandra was

soon climbing the path up the side of the hill after them, and had to slow her padding steps so as not to catch up with the wobbling figure bringing up the rear.

She hung back, waiting half-way up the slope, and watched as the weird procession passed through the sculpted mouth of an ornate grotto in the side of the hill.

The last of the figures disappeared into the hillside, their chanting voices softened, becoming a murmuring echo rising from the depths of the hill.

With the coast clear, Cassandra set off after them, a burnt resin smell catching in her nostrils, the sweet taste of incense on her tongue. Her pulse quickening in anticipation, Cassandra passed beneath the arch of the cave mouth and entered what seemed like some mythical entrance to the underworld.

The grotto itself was not large but from it a set of steps, roughly-hewn from the bedrock of the hill, descended deeper. With every cautious step she took, the voices of the cultist grew louder, only now the cave added its own unsettling acoustics to the polyphony.

Following the curve of the steps, Cassandra suddenly found herself bathed with the light of a dozen torches, now placed in sconces carved from the limestone walls and the ruddy glow of smoking braziers that filled the air with billowing clouds of musky incense.

The stump of a stalagmite provided Cassandra with a temporary shelter. From behind the rock she was able to see what was taking place within the bowl of the cavern beneath her.

The chamber was almost circular and, in the very centre of the sandy floor, stood a well.

The red-robed cultists surrounded the well, each standing several feet from its black mouth, apart from one. Standing at the edge of the pit, peering down into the darkness was the grotesquely large individual Cassandra had followed into the hill, still breathlessly intoning the same monotonous chant, over and over.

Cassandra thought it likely that the man standing before

the well was the man she had been sent to stop, the traitor Sir William Lambton.

As the chanting continued, three figures stepped forward from the circle, each presenting what they carried in their hands to the leader of this bizarre rite. The magus accepted them; a brass gong, a golden beater and a silver knife. He laid each one upon the red cloth that had been laid out upon the smooth stone.

When everything was in place, the magus raised his hands, and the volume of the chanting rose, the sound reverberating from the walls of the cavern until Cassandra could feel her nerve-endings vibrating in sympathy.

As the repeated refrain reached the climax of its cycle, the golden-faced leader of the cult brought his hands together and, at that moment, the chanting stopped, the acoustics of the cavern singing the last syllable back into the chamber once, twice, three times, before it faded into silence.

Cassandra held her breath.

"Oh, conqueror worm," the Lord of Lambton intoned, "we come before you as penitents, shriven of our sins, our pride and our ambition, that we might become vessels for your holy godhead, to be bearers of your divine essence."

Raising the gong he struck it with the golden beater, the assembled cult responding with shouts and claps.

"Mighty worm, lord and master, divine agent of change. Come before us now, reveal yourself to us, that we might receive your blessing!"

The magus took up the silver knife in his right hand and calmly drew it across the palm of his left, letting the blood running freely into the darkness of the well.

There were more chants and whoops and cheers and then, at a signal from the cult's leader, silence fell like a thunderclap within the chamber. An atmosphere of nervous expectation hung over the gathering, the near-forgotten sowing of the wind across the entrance to the grotto barely a distant reminder of the inclement autumn night beyond the sanctuary of the cave.

And then Cassandra thought she heard something – a shuffling, scraping sound – rising from the well.

"Our lord, He comes!" the magus gasped in ecstasy.

Cassandra clamped a hand to her mouth to stifle her own gasp of horror as, eyes wide in abject terror, she saw something abominable emerge from the darkness of the well.

As the cult began to chant and cry and moan in ecstatic delight at the coming of their god, Cassandra turned from the perverse spectacle and vomited onto the rocks beside her.

V

With Vilest Worms to Dwell

The bulbous dome of the worm's head swayed blindly from side to side, as if it was sniffing the air. It looked like a repulsive amalgam of worm, leech and maggot. Its rippling, segmented body was covered in a sheath of slime and its white flesh was mildly translucent. Writhing pseudopods, like caterpillar legs, started half way down what could be seen of its grotesque body; its mouth, large enough to engulf a human being whole, and rimmed with tiny cutting teeth. Its head, bigger than that of a horse, loomed atop a body that was almost as wide as the shaft of the well. Not all of the creature had yet emerged from the well either, and what Cassandra could already see of it had to be at least twelve feet in length.

The worm's mouth worked constantly, but it made no move to attack any of the awestruck penitents encircling the well. And although it had no obvious eyes, Cassandra fancied she could see sensory pits in the side of its head. Not only that, but she could clearly see a series of puckered slime-oozing orifices in its squishy white larva-flesh – she counted nine on each side – running from the side of its head and down along the upper part of its body.

The worm's hypnotic rippling dance suddenly stopped. It had found what it was looking for.

The swollen head arched over the corpulent form of Sir William Lambton, the cherubic mask of the magus gazing up at the impossible creature, his eyes the only part of his face visible, stared at this abomination as if it was the most beautiful thing he had ever seen.

"My lord!" he gasped and pulled off his mask.

Cassandra could see the look of rapt delight on his jowly face, as well as the swollen goitre protruding obscenely from his neck, a mass of blue-veined fatty tissue.

"Step forward," Sir William said, tears of joy streaming from the corners of his eyes, "and abase yourselves before your lord and master."

What Cassandra saw next was almost too much for a sane mind to bear.

The assembled penitents threw back their hoods and approached the well, as if sleep-walking or in an opium-addled daze, unable to take their eyes off the monstrosity swaying before the magus. Their robes fell open, revealing their nakedness – pot-bellied or bony, obese or ill-proportioned – apparently uncaring that everything was now there for all to see.

Sir George Sackville was amongst them and Cassandra thought she recognised one or two of the others. But she would most definitely recognise them again after this; their horribly delighted expressions would be etched onto her memory for a long time to come.

When they were all standing beside the well the creature began to sway again but now its movements were more violent, the bulb of its head reeling in all directions. Rather than perturb them, this seemed to excite the cultists even more. The worm made not a sound as it convulsed but the cave rang to the orgasmic moans of the ecstatic penitents.

And then the curious, sphincter-like holes in the creature's neck opened, and a thick, vicious fluid oozed from each one, lubricating the orifices for what was to happen next.

Cassandra felt her gorge rise again as small white heads, the size and shape of cave-grown mushrooms, emerged from the tubular vents in the side of the creature's body. As the parent creature continued to convulse, its spawn – perfectly miniaturised versions of the mother worm – wriggled free.

In response to this, the cultists opened their mouths wide. Necks craned back, jaws stretched open as far as possible, the seemingly intoxicated men and women moved to receive the writhing young. One by one eighteen small worms wriggled free of the orifices in the gigantic worm's body to be swallowed whole by the eager cultists. Cassandra could even see the bulge of the creatures passing down the cultists' rapacious throats.

With the spawning complete, the gigantic worm slunk back down the well.

Cassandra had seen enough. Her masters in Whitehall had wanted to learn more about the Disciples of Dionin, the cult Sir William Lambton had established here at his ancient family seat, but surely they could not have begun to imagine that the truth would be anything like this.

Cassandra suspected that the danger this particular secret society posed the British Empire was like no other they had had to face before. The cult and its monstrous worm god had to be destroyed. But the nagging doubt remained at the back of her mind that she wasn't going to be able to accomplish such a feat alone.

Cassandra turned and began to scramble back up the rock-cut steps, heedless now for the need for stealth.

Her mind still reeling at the soul-shredding horror of what she had just witnessed, her fingers found a shoe rather than the solid stone of the next step. Slowly she raised her head, taking in the scarlet robe, dumb realisation now unclouding her befuddled mind. Eighteen had received the worm god's sacrament – the Lord of Lambton Hall had watched as they did so – but twenty had entered the hillside ahead of her.

She looked up into the sneering face of Sir William's steward a split second before she felt his fist connect with her face. A vicious kick to the chest followed, which sent her tumbling back down the uneven steps, to land in an unconscious heap at the bottom.

"Join us," Sir William said, the goitre beneath his chin wobbling as he spoke. His robe hung open, rolls of fat preserving what little modesty he had left. And, bizarrely, he appeared to be wearing a belt around his expansive waist. "Someone like you – an agent of the crown, no less – could be a valuable asset to us in our great work."

"Never!" Cassandra spat. Her head ached from where she had knocked it in the fall but she hadn't lost her senses so much that she would choose to join these freaks and submit to their abominable practices.

"Join us," the magus repeated, his voice barely more than a whisper, hypnotic, mesmerising. "Join us."

She felt her head yanked back sharply, the steward pulling hard on her ponytail, the fingers of his other hand pinching her nose shut, so as to force her to open her mouth.

"Join us," Sir William said one last time and then his head starting to bob backwards and forwards as if he was trying to regurgitate something in his throat. And then Cassandra saw his swollen goitre move. With Sir William's head craned backwards, the goitre slithered around his neck beneath the flabby flesh of his throat, and the Lord of Lambton opened his mouth wide, jowls quivering.

Fighting to keep her mouth shut, despite the desperate need to breathe, eyes wide in unblinking horror, Cassandra watched as a swollen maggot head pushed its way up and out of the magus' mouth, forcing the jaws apart unnaturally wide.

The worm emerged from the man's oesophagus as the goitre collapsed.

Sir William lowered his head and regarded Cassandra with malevolent hunger, the worm wriggling its way still further from his mouth. Its eyeless head and scissoring, leech-like jaws came closer, the creature's rippling movements hypnotic, mesmerising, almost alluring.

Her sixth sense screaming at her from her subconscious, Cassandra closed her eyes tight and pulled herself out of the steward's grasp. Kicking her way free and staggering to her feet, she put the steward between her and the magus, one of her brace of pistols already in her hand, cocked and primed and ready to fire, her finger tight on the trigger.

The worm-thing suddenly pulled itself back inside Sir William's mouth, and the man swallowed hard, the goitre slithering back into place.

Cassandra took a step back, keeping her pistol trained on the peer, and felt the lip of the well against the back of her legs.

"What a waste of a perfectly good vessel," the magus said, reaching inside his crimson cloak.

Cassandra pulled the trigger.

The acoustics of the chamber made the crack of the pistol painfully loud. Through the white cloud of gunpowder, Cassandra could see Sir William still standing there, smiling at her like some self-satisfied toad.

How could she have missed at almost point blank range?

Then Cassandra saw the bullet hole in his flabby chest, saw thick blood oozing from the wound as he took a step forwards, pulling his own pistol from the belt around his waist.

She hadn't missed. But the shot hadn't even slowed him down.

"Such a pity," he said and fired.

It felt like someone had punched her in the chest, knocking the wind from her. Cassandra felt suddenly, inexplicably cold. Her body crumpled and she toppled into the well, down into the darkness.

VI

Among the Hungry Worms I Sleep

Cassandra opened her eyes only to find herself in utter darkness. She lay on her back, not daring to move, trying to piece together what had happened.

Immediately, nightmarish visions of the disgusting white worm sprang into her mind. She remembered the horrific ritual in vivid detail, the abhorrent actions of the cultists, Sir William, the cult's magus, nothing more than the host for another of the vile creatures. She remembered shooting him and the bullet having no effect. She remembered being shot and then falling. She should be dead.

Only miraculously she wasn't. Cassandra lay there in the cold, damp darkness, cautiously testing her limbs, seeing if she could still move them, seeing if she had suffered any broken bones. But she could find nothing wrong, nothing beyond a few cuts and minor abrasions. She sat up. She had been lucky; things should have been considerably worse.

Cassandra's hands were pressing down on damp sand. The

bottom of the well was almost dry.

The air was musty with damp and the over-ripe smell of rotting carcasses. She wondered how large this particular underground chamber was. Her eyes were stinging. She squeezed them shut and rubbed at them, hoping the irritation would soon pass.

When she opened them, she could see something pulsing red in the darkness, something the size and shape of a man. He was lying face-down, his arms bound behind his back. She saw him as patches of warm colour, his head, his arms and legs, the trunk of his body; she could even see the pulsing beat of his heart inside his chest.

She gasped, putting a hand to her mouth, as she realised that what she could see was the man's body heat. Such a thing should not be possible.

And now that she was aware of the fact that there was another person down there in the dark with her, she could hear muffled breathing coming from the prone figure.

She thought Sir William's bullet had hit her in the chest. Carefully, she probed the area with her fingers and found the hole the bullet had made. Gingerly she felt beneath.

The breath caught in her throat as her fingers came back sticky with blood. Then she *had* been shot, but how had she survived her encounter with the magus of the Disciples of Dionin?

And then she became aware of a slithering, scraping sound, as of something large dragging its great bulk across the silt covered the floor of the cave.

She stared into the impenetrable murk before her and a mass of cold colours coalesced. There could be no doubt as to what this was. Even though she could only see the monstrous worm as shades of chilling blue, Cassandra could hear the wet slap and slurp of its slimy advance, as its rippling musculature dragged it across the cave floor on a carpet of oozing mucus. She could picture its eyeless head sweeping the darkness before it, homing in on her position by means of its own preternatural senses, hear its constantly working mouthparts masticating in gluttonous excitement.

Panic and the natural instinct to survive suddenly took over from cold, clinical thought, shaking her from her nerve-deadened stupor. Her heels kicking against the sandy floor, she began to back away from the slithering advance of the monster.

For a moment Cassandra wondered – nay, hoped – whether the monster might stop to feed on the bound man, now groaning as he started to come to. But then the great worm was past the lucky wretch and Cassandra was worrying at the second pistol still in its place on the bandolier.

Her hands shaking, she screamed in frustration as she fumbled for the weapon.

Finally she drew the pistol and fired. The bullet flew from the muzzle and into the spongy flesh of the worm's pulsating body. But like its faithful devotee, the bloated Lord of Lambton Hall, the wound didn't even cause the creature to recoil. It just kept coming, jaws working as it devoured the darkness between them.

The man was screaming now as he came to and found the abomination sliding over the ground beside him. Cassandra smelt the hot, ammonia stink of fear as he emptied his bladder.

Then the worm was practically on top of her. With its bulbous head and mashing jaws mere inches from her face, she put up her hands to defend herself. The pain of what felt like dress-makers pins pushing up through the tips of her fingers stopped her screams and made her open her eyes as she took a sharp intake of breath.

Cassandra could see the piercing wire tendrils bursting from her fingertips, pulsing the same hot red colour as her own flesh.

The tendrils kept growing, from every finger and thumb, like needle claws, until they pierced the pulsating offal-white flesh of the worm – and they didn't stop, even then.

And now it was the worm that was screaming. It was the first time Cassandra had heard it make any kind of sound at all, and dreadful it was too. A high-pitched shrieking that drowned out her own screams and the terrified howling of the bound wretch still lying on the sandy floor.

The worm started to convulse, twisting in on itself like a salted slug. She could feel it writhing between her hands, but she couldn't let go of its slime-slick flesh, no matter how much she might want to.

Its convulsions lifted Cassandra from the floor of the cave and hurled her against the low ceiling of the chamber, but still she held on, the wire finger-claws buried deep inside its body uniting the woman and the worm in an inseparable embrace.

Face to face with the screeching worm, through eyes that could now register colours beyond the visible spectrum, she saw the brightness of its body dim, seeing its flesh shrivel and blacken and turn to slime in her mind's eye.

Gasping for breath, she did not have enough air left in her lungs to scream now. Slowly the worm's piercing screams faded and died too and then, at last, its peristaltic writhing stopped.

Cassandra lay back on the floor of the cave, the liquefied flesh of the creature dripping from her wire-talons as it melted in a pool of stinking slime, bubbles forming within it, only to pop a moment later, releasing gusts of noxious fumes.

And then the only sounds that remained were the blasphemous curses of the terrified prisoner and Cassandra sobbing to herself in the darkness as the impossible claws drew back into her fingertips.

VII

The Screaming Skull

Cassandra stared at her hands in horror. The impossible metal claws had gone, but she knew that they had simply withdrawn back inside her.

"What just happened? In God's name tell me! Am I going mad? Is there anyone there? What was that thing and... and... what happened to it? Can you hear me? Can anybody hear me!"

The man's desperate shouts shook Cassandra out of her bewildered reverie and she realised that she knew that voice.

"Dick?" she gasped, her tears now tears of relief. "Galloping Dick Runyan?"

"Yes?" The highwayman's voice sounded suddenly small within the echoing acoustics of the worm's lair.

"It's me, Dick. Cassandra. Cassandra Tyrell, from the stagecoach!"

"Milady? Is that really you?"

"Yes, Dick, it's me. You're safe. You're going to be all right."

"What happened? I can't move my hands and my feet are bound."

"It's going to be all right. I'm going to get us out of here."

"I can't move."

"Don't worry," she said, feeling a knot of anxiety form within the pit of her stomach. "I think I have something for that."

The highwayman free of his bonds, old instincts taking over, Cassandra searched for a way out. She already knew that if she were to stop the cult she would need help and, under the circumstances, the highwayman seemed as good an ally as any.

She was pleased to discover that the well-shaft was not the only way out of the cave in which the monstrous worm had been kept. Following the circumference of the cave, they came upon a narrow cleft in the rock. It was far too narrow for the worm to have ever been able to squeeze even its boneless body into but it was big enough for them.

Cassandra and Dick followed it as it became a rough-hewn passageway which ended in a metal door which was, inevitably, locked.

But locked doors were something almost cosily familiar to Cassandra. She could deal with locked doors. Gigantic flesh-eating worms were another matter altogether. Taking her tools from a waistcoat pocket, in only a matter of moments she had the door open and they found themselves in a darkened brick-built passageway.

Cassandra surmised that they were in the cellars under Lambton Hall itself now, the tunnel they had followed having wound its way through the hill for quite some distance.

Having encountered nobody in the tunnels beneath the house, they climbed a set of crumbling stone steps to another door which, Cassandra suspected, would lead into the main body of Lambton Hall.

"Screaming," Cassandra said after having placed her ear to the door. She turned to face the highwayman. "I can hear screaming."

She carefully eased the door open and they entered Lambton Hall, following the echoing screams along the servant's passageway.

The house was in disarray.

Cassandra and her confused companion turned a corner only for a middle-aged woman, who was naked under the scarlet robe she was wearing, to run straight into them, howling like an animal. She fixed Cassandra with a wild, accusing stare, put the knotted claws of her hands to her head and screamed into the young woman's face.

"Make it stop! Please, make it stop!" she sobbed, snot running freely from her nose. And then she turned and fled back along the corridor.

The woman had been there at the ritual. Cassandra had seen her swallow one of the hideous albino worms and the cultist, in turn, had watched as Cassandra was dragged before the corpulent magus of the Disciples of Dionin. There had been recognition in that mad-eyed stare of hers, but there had been something else as well. There had been incredible, agonising pain.

Dumbfounded, and yet morbidly fascinated at the same time, their minds reeling from all they had experienced during this long, dark night of the soul, Cassandra and Dick were like observers during the last days of Rome, as madness consumed Lambton Hall and its guests.

The Disciples of Dionin – made up of the great and the good of British society – appeared to be fleeing, all of them clutching their heads and screaming in pain.

One of Captain Drysdale's soldiers ran past – his shirt and his fly unbuttoned – paused, realising that the redcoats' prisoner was loose within the house. Dick's uppercut sent the soldier spinning into unconsciousness as he collapsed against the wall.

Cassandra and Dick followed the fleeing cultists towards the main doors. Cassandra had not even realised that they were passing the alcove containing Sir John Lambton's armour, until she heard the voice, chiming like cut crystal inside her head.

She winced, in shock more than pain, and closed her eyes. But when she opened them again, she wasn't in Lambton Hall any more.

Out of the darkness stars appeared and for reasons that she couldn't begin to fathom, Cassandra knew that she wasn't on Earth anymore.

And the voice spoke again.

She could hear it quite clearly inside her head and although it sounded like no other language she had ever heard spoken before, at the same time she could understand every word. However, from the faltering way in which the voice spoke to her – in the same voice in which her own thoughts spoke to her – she felt that it was struggling to use concepts that she would understand.

The voice told her about the worms – creatures from another world, parasites – and more visions of the monstrous maggot-worms assailed her, causing her to recoil.

The images of the grotesquely writhing worms dissolved and swam, resolving into the rolling landscape of England, only an England pre-dating the world she knew at the end of the eighteenth century. This was England from long before the concept of an England had ever even existed, and the voice told her that centuries ago the worms had fallen to Earth trapped within their frozen meteorite cocoons.

Then she too was falling towards the Earth, granted an impossible vision of the planet as seen from beyond, the curve of the watery sphere disappearing as she fell at a terrifying velocity through the dense white clouds smothering the planet. The clouds parted and she was hurtling towards an arid, desert landscape. She was unable to tear her gaze away even as flames licked at her body. And then, ground-fall.

The voice told her that it too had come to Earth, centuries ago, to hunt the parasite down and eliminate it before it could cause significant harm, but the ship in which it had sailed across the heavens, had fallen from the sky, landing amid the trackless wastes of the continent that would one day be called Africa. It had been killed in the crash. The crystal skull was all that remained of this hunter.

And only then did Cassandra realise that it was the crystal skull – Lambton Hall's screaming skull – that was speaking to her.

Suddenly Cassandra was back in the long gallery, standing before the glass display case, staring into the voids of the orbits of the inhuman skull, the empty eye-sockets boring back into her.

As she watched, a scaly, crystalline hide began to cover the sparkling skull. Eyes like balls of marble swelled within the empty sockets and Cassandra could discern features rising from the blue-tinged mineral flesh. At the same time she saw a silver metal, that flowed as freely as mercury, fill the flaws within the crystal, running like blood in the needle-thin channels. The voice told her that in life it had been artificially joined with a symbiote, a creature of living metal, that provided it with weapons and other tactical abilities.

And suddenly her mind escaped the confines of her physical surroundings and she was no longer within Lambton Hall any more. She was...

... somewhere else, an arid wind, heavy with the scents of spices, tugging at his drifting body.

Cassandra's mind reeled as she listened to the voice. And it had so much to say, in words that she barely understood, and now using concepts that made even less sense.

Looking down, through the rising dust storm, she saw cloth-swathed figures digging in the shifting sands of the desert, and the voice told her that the sentient star-metal was recovered from the crash-site, along with the hunter's crystalline remains, both eventually coming into the possession of Sir John Lambton whilst he was crusading in the Holy Land, and so at last to England.

And when Sir John returned home, he found the locality of Lambton under attack from the alien worm. Under the influence of the skull – the fabled Head of Baphomet supposedly worshipped by the Templars, a heathen idol brought back from heathen lands – Sir John fashioned the star-metal weapons and armour to destroy the parasite.

The battle was fierce and went down in legend. Legend also remembered that the worm could regenerate itself. But what it forgot was that when Sir John recovered every part of the unnatural creature's body and subjected it to the star-metal's touch, a tiny piece that had been washed away by the Wear was not recovered.

Sir John scoured the countryside thereabouts, searching for the missing piece, but it was never found. And when he died he passed his miraculous suit of armour to his son, and to his descendants, along with the solemn obligation to watch for the worm's return and, if such a thing came to pass, to seek the monster out and destroy it again.

Little did Sir John know that the treacherous Wear had washed the last remaining piece of the worm's flesh into caves that lay beneath the grounds of his own ancestral lands. There in the darkness below the earth, the sliver of worm-flesh survived and slowly regenerated until it had grown into a whole new creature, feeding on the slugs and spiders that dwelt in those dark caverns.

And it was there that Sir William Lambton found it, whilst having the grounds of his ancestral home landscaped. The sacred duty that Sir John had placed upon his heirs, only half-remembered now in myth, its importance forgotten, Sir William had found the worm and become host to the first of a new spawning.

In her mind's eye, Cassandra saw the moment when Sir William had become host to the creature's young, intoxicated by its musky excretions, and felt sick all over again.

Questions filled Cassandra's mind as she tried to absorb all that the skull passed on to her. How could she even hear the voice, when before she had not? If the worm was nothing more than a parasite, how had it become the focus for a cult in this age of reason and enlightenment?

And the voice of Baphomet answered her, as if it could somehow hear her unspoken thoughts, as if they were somehow conversing, mind to mind.

The worm presented a dire threat to the future of her world, the voice told Cassandra. For, although it was only a parasite, driven by nothing more sinister than instinct and the need that exists in all living things to perpetuate the species, in taking a host the worm had also absorbed its intelligence.

Whereas on other worlds, it might penetrate colonies of more primitive species and live out its mundane existence causing little harm other than to its host, in a human body it would be subject to all the whims and conflicting emotions of a human being and that was what made it so dangerous.

And then Cassandra understood, at an almost instinctive level, how the voice could communicate with her, how there had been another presence there within her mind all the while it had imparted its vital information. Just as Sir William and the Disciples of Dionin had become bonded to the diabolic parasites, so Cassandra had become bonded with the same living metal entity that had travelled to Earth along with the hunter, all those centuries ago.

The shot that should have killed her had been fired from Sir William's gun, the gun that had been made from the worm slayer's sword, the sword that Sir John Lambton had fashioned from the star-metal.

The moment the tiny sphere of star-metal had entered her body, awoken from its dormant state by the heat of the pistol's discharge, it had liquefied and entered her bloodstream, the tiny component parts of it – like individual workers in an ant colony – set about repairing her wounds and healing her body.

Now she understood why her eyes had been able to register the body heat of the monstrous worm and the highwayman in the utter darkness of the cave. Now she understood how she had been able to extrude lethal silver claws from her fingertips and how that had been enough to put an end to the mother of all worms.

And now she understood the reason for the madness consuming Lambton Hall. What one knew, they all knew; the other worms inhabiting the bodies of the cultists had felt the agonised death-throes of their parent as keenly as they would have felt their own. Quite simply, the pain had driven them mad.

The worms had also drawn upon their hosts' natural drive to survive; if something had killed the immortal worm god, it could kill them too. They were in danger. They had to get away.

Cassandra opened her eyes.

"Are you all right? You're sweating."

It was Dick. His hands were clasping her shoulders.

"How long have I been like this?" she asked.

"No time at all. You just starting shaking."

Cassandra stared into the sparkling pits of the skull's eye-sockets; the scaled flesh was gone now.

"We have to stop them," Cassandra said.

"Stop them? Who? These maniacs? I'm getting out of here, and if you've any sense left in you you'll do the same."

But Cassandra wasn't listening to him; she was gazing at the ancient suit of armour, with its curious bladed plates, blades that she now knew had been fashioned from the very essence of the living liquid metal of the otherworldly war-symbiote.

She reached out to touch the suit but stopped, her fingertips barely an inch from the tarnished silver surface. As she watched, the silvery coating on the blades liquefied, what had one minute apparently been solid metal became a gelatinous fluid that ran from the blades onto the suit, in coursing rivulets. These then drew together into one homogenous mass and lifted free of the armour in one long strand, drawn towards her hand like iron fillings to a magnet.

She could feel goose pimples rising all over her body. The liquid metal tendril seemed to hesitate for a second and then crossed the divide, flowing over her hand and coating her fingers.

Her hand felt suddenly numb. Cassandra held it up, marvelling at the mirrored sheen of the substance now clinging to her flesh, seeing her own wondering expression reflected there. The liquid metal was quickly absorbed through the pin-hole wounds in the tips of her fingers.

And then she was looking at naked flesh again, the liquid metal running like silvery blood through her veins.

"In the Devil's name, what the hell was that?" the highwayman gasped, backing away in horror.

"Dick, it's all right," Cassandra said as calmly as she could manage. And she did feel calm, calmer than she had ever felt since embarking on her mission. "I understand what has to be done. I understand everything now.

"Well I'm glad you do, because I sure as hell don't! I've seen enough! I'm getting out of here!"

"Stay with me, Dick. Help me. I can't do this alone. They have to be stopped, you do understand that, don't you? I saved your life. You are in my debt."

"No! God's bones, no! I've seen enough madness this night to last me a lifetime. No." He backed away from her towards the open doors of the house. "I'll play no part in your crazed quest for revenge. I'm only interested in doing what I've always done – and that's to look after number one! Milady, it is time we went our separate ways. I bid you farewell. *Adieu!*"

Turning on his heels, he sprinted along the corridor, after the fleeing cultists and their panicking lackeys, and disappeared through the open doors.

So be it, Cassandra thought bitterly as she watched him depart.

With barely a moment's hesitation she too set off after the cultists, but with a wholly different purpose in mind.

Stumbling out of the house into the cold November morning she came upon a scene of utter chaos and confusion.

Coaches clattered from the stabling yard and through the main gate of Lambton Hall – horses whipped into a frenzy by desperate drivers – carrying away the worm-infested hosts as night itself took flight before the coming dawn.

She was too late; her quarry was getting away. She would have to act quickly.

From her vantage point at the top of the steps, she scanned the courtyard, searching for a suitable steed. Instead her eyes fell upon Captain Drysdale, Galloping Dick's former captor, and his troop of redcoats. The soldiers were milling around a black lacquered carriage bearing the crest of the Lambton family.

Long fingers twitched the corner of the black velvet curtain pulled across the window and Cassandra saw the Dragoon captain converse briefly with whoever was inside.

Cold dread suddenly knotted her stomach and, in that instant, Drysdale turned. His expression darkened as he pointed in her direction with his unsheathed rapier.

"Seize her!"

VIII

The Changeling

Before she could put up any kind of resistance, Cassandra was quickly and efficiently surrounded by the Dragoons. She twisted and kicked as two hefty soldiers seized her, but it was futile. In another minute someone had brought a length of hemp rope and bound her arms to her side, looping the rope tightly several times around her waist.

As the rest of Sir William Lambton's guests fled from the house, the door of the crested carriage was thrown open and Cassandra was bundled inside.

She half-fell onto the cracked leather seat, struggling to sit up, fully aware of the fact that there was already at least one other person already in there with her.

The door slammed shut again and, at a single command from Captain Drysdale, the carriage jolted off over the cobbles.

"What did you do?" a voice hissed from the other side of the carriage.

Cassandra peered into the gloom, the black velvet preventing most light from entering the carriage. A strange musky scent filled the air, a smell curiously familiar to her now.

"I said, what did you do!"

Cassandra blinked, and then suddenly she could see; a corpulent figure picked out in patches of heat and cold, the carriage seat creaking under his enormous weight. He was holding one hand to his head, the other clutching the goitre at his throat.

"I... I..."

"I know you're a spy, sent here to find out all you can about my Disciples of Dionin," Sir William Lambton snarled. "I know that our position here has been compromised. But what I don't understand is how you could survive both being shot and the fall? And how did you kill the Divinity?

"Oh yes, I know that you have committed deicide, that you have slain our Lord and Master. We were all forced to experience the agonies of our Lord's death, but I still don't understand how you did it! How could you slay the Godhead when my misguided ancestor could not? *Tell me!*"

Cassandra took a breath to speak.

"Oh, never mind!" Sir William said. "I see that I am just going to have to take you apart to find out for myself. And, I have to say, I shall take great pleasure in doing so."

The jolting carriage throwing its passengers from side to side, the bloated peer lunged at Cassandra, fingers knotted into claws, determined, it seemed, to take her apart with his bare hands.

He was still wearing his robe from the ceremony and this fell open now, exposing his rippling nakedness. Cassandra could feel his distended stomach rippling as he pressed his massive, trembling bulk against her, as something slithered and writhed beneath the pallid, blue-veined flesh.

Screaming and kicking at the wobbling mass of the Lord of Lambton, magus of the Disciples of Dionin, she knew that if she didn't somehow free herself, then Sir William would be able to keep his macabre promise. But the rope that pinned her arms to her side had been wrapped tight around her body. Even as she rubbed her wrists raw, she knew that she wasn't going to be able to free herself in time.

"Stop struggling!" the peer puffed as he pinned her beneath his obesity. "There's someone I want you to meet."

The curtain flapped open as the carriage jolted downhill and, as the first piercing rays of a new day broke over the wooded horizon to the east, Cassandra was granted a clear view of what was happening before her.

Sir William was making horrible gargling retching noises, as his head bobbed backwards and forwards, saliva drooling from his open mouth. His eyes rolled up into his head as he attempted to regurgitate his parasite.

An acrid smell of bile rose from the man's infested innards, mixed with the musky pheromone-scent exuded by the cult's worm god, and Cassandra could not help but stare into the dark pit of the peer's gaping gullet.

Then she saw it; a bulbous white head, slick with mucus, squeezing its way past the man's tonsils and then, with one last great gagging convulsion, the parasite pushed clear of the man's mouth. She saw the elastic jowls suddenly stretched taut as a drum-skin and heard the pop of the man's jaw dislocating, as the worm strained to reach for her, its leech-like mouthparts chomping hungrily.

It was getting hard to breathe now, and Cassandra's struggling was becoming more feeble by the second. Her vision began to grey at the edges and she knew that it would only be a matter of moments before she blacked out.

It suddenly felt like it would be the easiest thing in the world to give up so that the pain might go away, so that she might rest. And at that moment, something spoke to her through the still small voice of her subconscious, telling her that the only way out of this was to stop thinking like a normal human being, for she could consider herself a normal human being no longer. She must learn to embrace her new abilities, working in consort with the symbiotic entity that now lived again within her.

As the darkness threatened to overwhelm her, clarity of purpose returned and she focused on the liquid metal now coursing through her veins. In her mind's eye she saw the tiny component parts, like a swarm of ants racing through her body to where it was needed to defend the nest, and saw again the offensive armour of Sir John Lambton Knight of Rhodes, saw the light glinting off its razor-sharp blades.

There was a slick cutting sound and, in an instant, myriad blades burst from Cassandra's arms, slicing through the bonds that bound her, the hemp sizzling in places as if the blades were red hot.

With a high-pitched shriek, the pus-white parasite recoiled and the corpulent peer stumbled from her to collapse on the seat opposite, gurgling horribly, unable to articulate his own thoughts as the worm's body was still blocking his throat.

The severed ropes fell from Cassandra and she rose unsteadily, still reeling from the pain the emerging blades had inflicted, the metal withdrawing into her flesh, leaving a myriad puncture marks, and the shredded sleeves of her shirt spotted crimson with her own blood.

Forcing the pain to the back of her mind, she knew that she had to press home her advantage. Focusing her thoughts once more, she remembered the moment, not so long ago, down in the dark beneath the hill, when the parent organism had sought to make a meal of her and how, unconsciously, she had discovered the means to kill it.

Long metal claws, like white-hot skewers, burst from her fingertips and she slashed clumsily at the recoiling worm.

The worm shrieked as Sir William gurgled, expressing his own discomfort as the worm's experiences were relayed to its host's mind.

What one knew, all knew, the voice of Baphomet had told her. The worm knew the metal could harm it, kill it even. Trapped in the confines of the carriage, tied to its overweight human host, the instinct for survival overrode all others and the worm saw that there was only one way out.

With a horrible sucking noise, eight feet of segmented worm shot from the man's mouth. Sir William's body collapsed in on itself as the parasite pulled free.

With another peristaltic spasm the worm launched itself through the curtained window of the carriage, leaving the Lord of Lambton to tumble onto the floor between the seats, nothing more than an empty sack of sagging skin and clattering bones.

Barely giving Sir William a second look, Cassandra flung open the door. Marshalling her strength, giving the stony surface of the road hurtling by beneath her only a cursory glance, trusting to blind luck rather more than judgement, she threw herself out of the speeding coach, after the escaping worm.

Captain Drysdale watched incredulously as something like a snake – and yet, at the same time, looking like a pallid leech – escaped from the carriage and slithered away towards the river, quickly followed by the woman, whom only minutes before had been chucked into the back of the carriage, bound securely.

Urging his steed forward he drew parallel with the coach and peered in through the open, swinging door.

He had expected to see Sir William Lambton there, but the gaunt man lying in a gasping heap between the seats, his red robe speckled with what looked like blood or bile, looked practically nothing like him.

"Sir William?"

"Drysdale!" the cadaverous bag of bones wheezed, as he tried to push his dislocated jaw back into place. "Stop her."

IX

The Dandy Highwayman

The River Wear tumbled over water-smoothed boulders as it broiled downstream, the broken water of the rapids glittering like quicksilver in the first golden light of dawn.

The worm slipped through the long grass of the riverbank.

The morning was clear but cold, and Cassandra's breath steamed in the air before her as she bounded after the parasite, almost losing her footing more than once on the uneven terrain.

For something which had no real limbs to speak of, the thing was moving incredibly fast. But she was closing on it nonetheless. The only thing she wasn't certain of was whether she would to catch up with it before it made it to the river.

Despite being focused on the worm, over the sound of her own laboured breathing, she could hear the pounding of hooves on the turf behind her.

She dared a glance behind her and saw the redcoat captain galloping towards her, rapier in hand, ready to cut her down in an instant. Behind him, the rest of the troop stayed with the fleeing carriage.

Re-doubling her efforts she quickened her pace, as concerned now with escaping the Dragoon captain as she was with catching up with the parasite, already fearing that she didn't have a hope of evading the captain's ruthless blade. Her best bet was to see if she could make it to the river.

She was suddenly aware of another frantic drumming rhythm, as another horse charged towards them. Then she heard a shout of "Yaah!" and her heart leapt.

Sliding to a halt in the dew-wet grass, her feet slipping out from under her, coming down on her rump, Cassandra threw another glance behind her.

A figure of horseback, clad in a suit of spiked armour, was careering towards the Dragoon captain. The rider clasped his steed's reins in one hand whilst wielding a flintlock pistol in the other. Cassandra knew it could only be Galloping Dick Runyan.

Without giving a word of warning, her curious knight in shining armour took aim and fired. Drysdale's startled expression became one of utter disbelief as the shot punched him clean out of the saddle.

As the captain's mount galloped away in panic, back towards the road, those Dragoons accompanying Sir William's racing coach steered their horses off the road and after the highwayman, their own pistols raised. A series of sharp retorts broke the morning stillness.

The staccato cracks were followed by a series of deadened metal *pangs*, as Sir John Lambton's legendary armour stopped the shots dead.

Her heart leaping at the highwayman's gallant rescue, Cassandra had barely slid to a halt before she was up on her feet again in pursuit of the worm.

She heard the splash as the parasite dropped into the river. Four more strides took her to the water's edge. Swinging her arms out in front of her, Cassandra dived into the river.

It only took a moment for the tumbling torrent to eradicate all traces of her entry into its tumultuous depths. A second passed. Two. Three. Four.

In an eruption of dark water, Cassandra burst from the river, the monstrous worm-spawn clasped in her hands, the creature writhing in torment as her needle-claws burrowed deep inside its hateful flesh.

The worm screamed at the burning acid touch of the silvered talons and, in its agonised death-throes, it tried to trap Cassandra within its constricting coils. Worm and woman fell back into the water, but Cassandra clung on.

Where the living star-metal struck, the worm's flesh withered, blackened and liquefied.

Possessed of a fury the like of which she had never known, Cassandra fought on, even when the worm managed to twist itself around her neck and tore at the exposed flesh of her arms with its jaws.

But still she clung on and slowly, piece by piece, the flesh of the unnatural worm dissolved into a tarry slime. Then all that remained was its eyeless head, screaming silently at her as she held it in her hands, then that too shrivelled and the last piece of the parasite's vile body was washed away downstream by the treacherous waters of the Wear.

X

Silver Nemesis

As the sun continued to climb across the crisp blue sky, shining like a sovereign, chasing away the last of the rainclouds along with the night, it painted the landscape with its warm autumnal palette, limning the bodies of the fallen Dragoons in white gold. The others – Sir William and the rest of the Disciples of Dionin – had fled with the coming of the dawn.

Cassandra looked from the bodies of the fallen soldiers to where their killer stood, helmet in hand, patting the flanks of the horse he had ridden to her rescue, a horse with a white flash on its muzzle.

"You came back for me," Cassandra said. "Why?"

"Oh, you know how it is. You said it yourself. You saved my life, so I saved yours. I was in your debt."

"Oh, I see," Cassandra said, smiling coyly. "And that was the only reason was it?"

"Well, I never could resist a damsel in distress."

"Oh, so I'm a damsel in distress, am I?" Cassandra challenged, studying her hands again, seeing the molten silver coursing through her veins once more now that the claws had retracted back into her body.

"No, milady, you are... I don't rightly know what you are, but you're not that. You're something else entirely."

"They got away, Dick," Cassandra said, gazing down the road in the direction the cultists had fled. "Sir William, Sackville and the rest. Although, admittedly, Lord Lambton will be in a pretty poor state now."

An anxious expression clouded Dick's face. "But we're quits now, right? I am no longer in your debt."

"The cult was not the be all and end. Sir William was working to some greater plan, and that plan could still be put into action. It's my destiny to find them, hunt them down and stop them; I see that now.

"I could use a man like you, to help me in my quest, though." She smiled. "My very own knight in shining armour."

"God's bones, woman! I told you before, I'm only interested in looking after number one. Having a partner's not my scene."

"What about... Abershawe, wasn't it?"

"Yes, exactly; and look what happened to him. Look, like you said, the rest got away, and they'll be sending reinforcements back soon, you can count on it. And I don't plan on being here when they arrive. And if you've got any sense, milady, you'll do the same. So I bid you *adieu*!"

And with that, Galloping Dick Runyan put one foot in the stirrups, mounted his horse and with a shout of "Quicksilver, away!" he cantered along the road, leaving Cassandra alone with the bodies of the fallen.

Shaking, the King picked himself up off the floor of the audience chamber and collapsed back into his chair.

He stared in open-mouthed horror at the bloated body of the peer lying face-down on the tiled floor, and at the grotesque white worm-like creature projecting from the man's mouth. The thing was rapidly necrotising before his eyes, becoming nothing more than a bubbling black sludge.

He looked from the cooling corpse and the dissolving slug-worm to the woman standing between them, decked out in all the finery of the court, although her extravagant clothes were now spotted with blood – both hers and that of the traitor, lying dead at her feet. She had lost her pearl-bedecked wig in her tussle with the king's attacker also.

The king was aware of one more person present with them in the room, watching them from the shadows, a man dressed all in black, with a face like a knife.

He looked from her the steely expression on her face to the lethal silver claws that were withdrawing into the bunched fists of her hands.

"Wh-What are you?" he gasped.

"My name is Cassandra Tyrell, your majesty."

"*The* Tyrrells?"

"Yes, *those* Tyrrells. And have no fear, your majesty, I'm on your side, unlike our mutual acquaintance, Sir George Sackville."

"Astonishing. Then I owe you my heartfelt thanks. My life, in fact. I cannot thank you enough. There'll be a ladyship in this for you, at the very least," he said, unable to stop his gaze returning to her hands. "Lady…"

He broke off, struck dumb by what he was witnessing, as the silvered points of ten, wire-thin stiletto blades disappeared back into her hands, flowing like mercury into the pin-holes in her fingertips.

"My Lady Quicksilver."

LO! 'tis a gala night
Within the lonesome latter years!
An angel throng, bewinged, bedight
In veils, and drowned in tears,
Sit in a theatre, to see
A play of hopes and fears,
While the orchestra breathes fitfully
The music of the spheres.

Mimes, in the form of God on high,
Mutter and mumble low,
And hither and thither fly—
Mere puppets they, who come and go
At bidding of vast formless things
That shift the scenery to and fro,
Flapping from out their Condor wings
Invisible Woe!

That motley drama!—oh, be sure
It shall not be forgot!
With its Phantom chased for evermore,
By a crowd that seize it not,
Through a circle that ever returneth in
To the self-same spot,
And much of Madness, and more of Sin
And Horror the soul of the plot.

But see, amid the mimic rout,
A crawling shape intrude!
A blood-red thing that writhes from out
The scenic solitude!
It writhes!—it writhes!—with mortal pangs
The mimes become its food,
And the angels sob at vermin fangs
In human gore imbued.

Out—out are the lights—out all!
And over each quivering form,
The curtain, a funeral pall,
Comes down with the rush of a storm,

And the angels, all pallid and wan,
Uprising, unveiling, affirm
That the play is the tragedy "Man,"
And its hero the Conqueror Worm.

(from *Ligeia*, by Edgar Allen Poe)

THE END

PAX BRITANNIA

For more information on this
and other titles visit...

Abaddon
Books

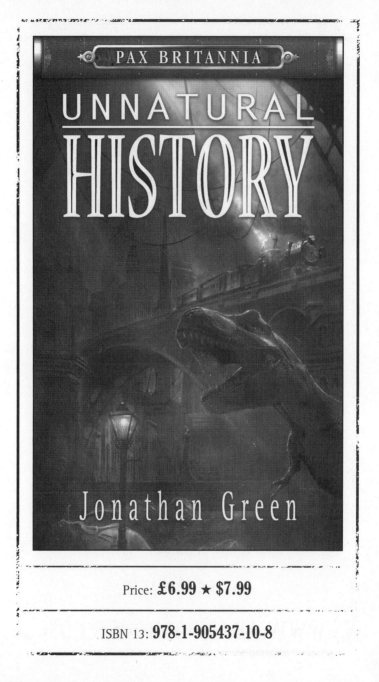

PAX BRITANNIA

UNNATURAL HISTORY

Jonathan Green

Price: **£6.99** ★ **$7.99**

ISBN 13: **978-1-905437-10-8**

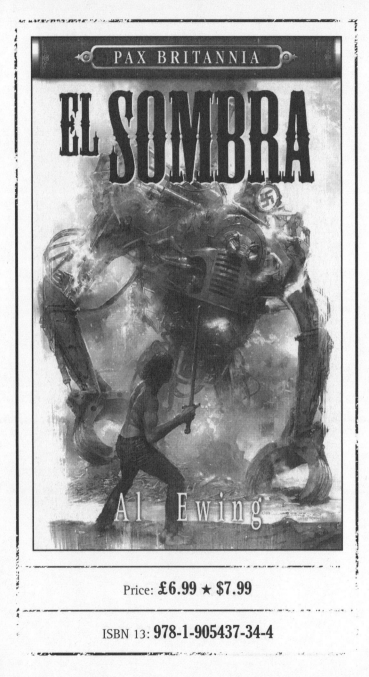

PAX BRITANNIA

EL SOMBRA

Al Ewing

Price: **£6.99** ★ **$7.99**

ISBN 13: **978-1-905437-34-4**

Price: **£6.99** ★ **$7.99**

ISBN 13: **978-1-905437-60-3**

PAX BRITANNIA

HUMAN NATURE

JONATHAN GREEN

Price: **£6.99 ★ $7.99**

ISBN 13: **978-1-905437-86-3**

December 2009 (UK) ★ January 2010 (US)

ISBN 13: **978-1-906735-30-2**

TWILIGHT of KERBEROS

SHADOW MAGE

MATTHEW SPRANGE

Price: **£6.99** ★ **$7.99**

ISBN 13: **978-1-905437-54-2**

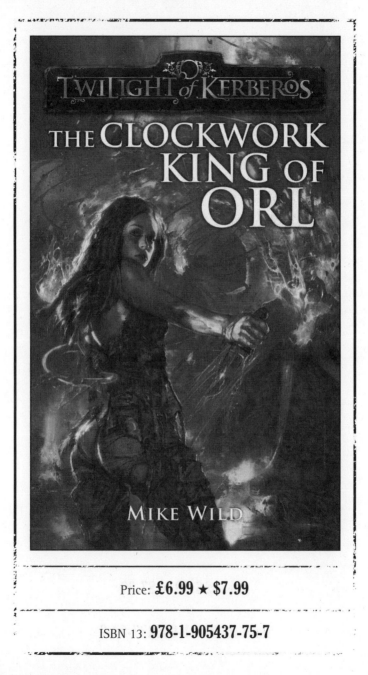

TWILIGHT of KERBEROS

THE LIGHT OF HEAVEN

DAVID A. MCINTEE

Price: **£6.99** ★ **$7.99**

ISBN 13: **978-1-905437-87-0**

Price: **£6.99** ★ **$7.99**

ISBN 13: **978-1-906735-13-5**

TWILIGHT *of* KERBEROS

The CALL *of* KERBEROS

JONATHAN OLIVER

Price: **£6.99** ★ **$7.99**

ISBN 13: **978-1-906735-28-9**